Etta Mae's Worst
Bad-Luck Day

Also by Ann B. Ross

Etta Mae's Worst
Bad-Luck Day

ANN B. ROSS

VIKING

VIKING
Published by the Penguin Group
Penguin Group (USA) LLC
375 Hudson Street
New York, New York 10014

USA | Canada | UK | Ireland | Australia | New Zealand | India | South Africa | China
penguin.com
A Penguin Random House Company

First published by Viking Penguin, a member of Penguin Group (USA) LLC, 2014

Library of Congress Cataloging-in-Publication Data

Ross, Ann B.
Etta Mae's worst bad-luck day : a Miss Julia novel / Ann B. Ross.
pages cm
ISBN 978-0-670-02437-7
1. Single women—Fiction.   2. Older men—Fiction.   3. May-December
romances—Fiction.   I. Title.
PS3568.O84198E88   2014
813'.54—dc23
2014004502

Printed in the United States of America
1   3   5   7   9   10   8   6   4   2

Set in Fairfield LT Std
Designed by Alissa Rose Theodor

This is for Deborah Schneider and Carolyn Carlson with
many thanks for believing in Etta Mae and her story.

Etta Mae's Worst Bad-Luck Day

From the Desk of Julia Springer Murdoch

I'll tell you right off that I'm not in the habit of talking about people, listening to gossip, or spreading rumors regardless of how tempting it is to pick up the telephone. Do unto others, I always say. I will admit, however, that occasionally I hear a tasty tidbit that just seems meant to be passed along. Yet I've learned that it's best to first go to the source and check my facts. What one may think is deliciously passable could turn out to be completely inaccurate, thus changing one's entire view of the subject in question.

That's what happened to me. I've known Etta Mae Wiggins for several years now, but I'd known of her for much longer. Everybody had.

Not, I assure you, that she was the talk of the town—she lived, after all, in Delmont some ten miles or so from Abbotsville, so she wasn't always the number one topic of conversation. In fact, most of us had never met her and wouldn't have known her if we'd passed her on the street.

But just let somebody mention a divorce or a remarriage, and someone else would pop up and ask, "Is Etta Mae Wiggins at it again?"

She was, I think, the epitome of what we thought of as a loose woman—smart, flashy, bold, and well endowed—not a young woman with whom a husband should be left alone. I know of which I speak, for the time that Sam was confined to his house with a broken leg, she was the Handy Home Helper who came twice a week to assist with his therapy and do minor chores for him. That's when I first met her, and I'll tell you the truth, she put my back up immediately. She was *much too helpful, standing too close, and petting and pampering him until I thought I'd throw up. That was long before Sam declared himself to me, and I was eaten up with jealousy even though I hadn't been able to put a name to it, having never felt that way about Wesley Lloyd Springer. More's the pity, but that's another story.*

Hazel Marie Pickens, née Puckett, had known Etta Mae since they were in county schools together, although because Hazel Marie was a few years older, they'd never been particularly close. I must mention, however, in spite of Etta Mae's checkered marital career and her spotty reputation, that Hazel Marie has never had an unkind word to say about Etta Mae, which I should've taken notice of early on, but didn't because Hazel Marie never has an unkind word about anyone. And let me say here that I never should have listened to the gossip about Etta Mae, considering what my own husband at the time—Wesley Lloyd Springer, now deceased—was up to. Be careful of what you laugh at. It could come back to haunt you.

But be that as it may, what I'd heard about Etta Mae Wiggins did not put me in mind to welcome a friendship with her, and I learned—incomprehensible as it seems—that she had pretty much felt the same way about me. But in spite of the great difference in our ages—no need to mention how great—we came to know each other through a series of incidences in which we were thrown together through no premeditation of either of us. I had reason to call on her for help, and each time she'd responded willingly and eagerly, although her enthusiasm could noticeably wane on certain occasions—like, for instance, when I had need to slip through a bamboo thicket in Florida, or to climb the Abbot County Courthouse dome, or to rescue Mr. Pickens from the clutches of a West Virginia sheriff. But waning enthusiasm never stopped her from following my lead, and, I'll tell you the truth, I would've never accomplished all I have without her right beside me. Or, more often, right behind me.

It was on a few of those trips together that I began to see beneath the surface of Etta Mae Wiggins, although that surface was noticeably attractive, especially to a particular type of the opposite gender, like a certain NASCAR driver, that sheriff I've already mentioned, and innumerable husbands afflicted with eyes they couldn't keep from sliding in her direction.

See, now, a lot of people would blame her for that, but I didn't and I don't. I put the blame right where it belongs—on grown men who can't keep their eyes or their hands to themselves.

So most of the gossip about her loose and easy ways came about because of what some people hoped to get, not because of what they'd actually gotten. And the biggest and most astounding bit of gossip made the rounds a few years ago, before Etta Mae and I knew any more about each other than that I owned the Hillandale Trailer Park and she was a resident in same who was forever calling me to complain about one thing or another.

I put a stop to that by hiring her to manage the place so she could take her complaints to herself. Unbeknownst to me, however, at the very same time she was up to her neck in what became the talk of the town for weeks. She told me about it later—much later—after we had warmed to each other and she knew I would not condemn her for it.

On the contrary, I admire her to this day. That is not to say that I would've done the same nor would I recommend what she did to anybody else. Still, given the same set of circumstances, who knows what one would do?

Now, in case anyone unfamiliar with Abbotsville, Delmont, and the residents thereof (including your humble correspondent) happens to come across this story, don't worry about it. All you need to know is contained herein, and you'll be the better for reading it. Etta Mae's story is a salutary one, wholesome and beneficial to anyone who is struggling to improve, to get ahead, and to win respect.

I would dearly love to tell you this story myself, but as I've mentioned, I don't carry tales. She, however, is now far enough from the experience to be able to talk about it, and once Etta Mae starts talking, she's hard to stop.

So this is Etta Mae's story—or one of them, at least—told in her own words just as it all happened a few years ago when she was alone in this world without the benefit of my watchful oversight and stabilizing influence. And when you know her story as I do—what she was up against and what she tried to do about it—who among us would throw the first stone?

Respectfully yours,

Miss Julia

Chapter 1

Just so you'll know, my name's Etta Mae, Etta Mae Wiggins. Granny always says it doesn't matter what your name happens to be, it's how you act that counts. But when I look around at some of my kin and their actions, I know what everybody thinks when they hear *Wiggins*. They think lazy, shiftless, no-account, backwoods trailer trash. But they'd be wrong about that last part, because none of us ever lived in a trailer. Except me, but only because Bernie Whitlow, my number two ex, bought me one when we got married. And that's where I still live, out off Springer Road in Hillandale Trailer Park a couple of miles from Delmont, and right by myself, too, ever since I kicked Bernie out.

Regardless of where you live—trailer or mansion or somewhere in between—and regardless of what Granny says, names do count. They tell who you are, where you've come from, and what you've made of yourself, all in one word. I could've called myself Etta Mae Taggert or Etta Mae Whitlow or Etta Mae Connard, since I've been, or intend to be, one or the other at various times of my life. In between, though, I've always gone back to Wiggins, and I don't know why unless it's because I figured I had to start at the bottom all over again each time.

At the bottom again was where I was after I got rid of Bernie, and good riddance. I'd learned my lesson by then, and it was about time since I'd made two bad choices in a row. Three, if you count Bobby Lee. Four, if you include Jerry Johnson, which I don't because he hadn't lasted long enough, having his heart set on running around NASCAR racetracks instead of running around with me.

I had my sights set on a higher prize this time, having figured out what it was I really wanted. And none too soon, since I was knocking at the door of thirty years of age. What it was that I deep-down wanted was a name that people would have to respect. Mrs. Howard Connard, Senior, is who I wanted to be.

And if I played my cards right, I'd get what I wanted. But I didn't intend to be another *first* Mrs. Howard Connard, Senior, in any way, shape, nor form. The first Mrs. Connard had been a dumpy little woman as near as I could tell from her picture in the newspaper that time years ago when her house had been on the garden tour, and I don't want to be unkind, but she could've lost a few pounds and it wouldn't have hurt her. Even so, every woman in town who had the means modeled themselves on her. She was the first woman every spring to put away her winter coat with the fur collar and show up at the First Methodist Church of Delmont in a mink stole with a Lady Hamilton camellia pinned on it. That was the signal to all the other ladies that winter was over. She was a fashion statement all by herself, in spite of the extra weight she carried. Some people can get away with it.

She might've been a hard act to follow in some people's eyes, but not in Mr. Howard's. You should've seen them light up in his head every time I came to check his blood pressure and give him his physical therapy. That was my job, to look in on the sick and elderly and incapacitated on a twice-weekly basis.

I was one of Lurline Corn's Handy Home Helpers, a Medicare-Approved Home Health Care Agency. There were five of us, and we were under contract to provide semiprofessional home nursing care to senior citizens in failing health. We provided a real service, because we'd give bed baths and back rubs, treat bedsores, and encourage exercise. We changed sheets, cleaned kitchens, wrote letters, and did all sorts of helpful, as well as some fairly nasty, things for people who couldn't do for themselves. None of us were registered nurses, nor even practical ones, although Lurline helped me get my certified nursing assistant degree so she'd have a CNA on her staff and qualify for Medicare reimbursements. Mostly, though, we were just hardworking people who didn't mind doing for our fellow man and getting paid for it.

Lurline had a nice little business going for her, and I wished I'd thought of it myself instead of wasting good years doing makeovers for Mary Kay, taking telephone orders for aluminum siding, and selling cleaning products for Amway.

You're probably getting an idea by now of what being the second Mrs. Howard Connard, Senior, meant to me, but you'd have the whole picture if you knew Mr. Howard, or even of him. He was a man to be reckoned with around Delmont in terms of respect and powers-that-be. He was *Mr. Connard, sir* to most everybody, but I called him Mr. Howard out of respect for his advanced age and our employer-employee relationship it all started out with.

The reason Mr. Howard occupied such a position in the minds of Delmontians, and of all Abbot Countians as well, was because he knew money—how to make it and how to use it. Take, for instance, how he'd seen the handwriting on the wall before the textile business even started its downhill slide. Everybody hated it when he closed the thread mill, sending jobs to China and Taiwan and the like, but we were proud that one of our own knew how to get ahead and stay there. Even if nobody else did.

I mean, it gave the rest of us hope, even though Tinch Moore knew in his heart that recapping tires wouldn't bring in a fortune.

And Harry Tinsley knew that his Ace Hardware Store wouldn't set the world on fire, and Bea Shelton knew that setting hair wasn't going to put her on easy street, even after she installed tanning beds. But Mr. Howard had made it big, and he belonged to Delmont.

And to me. If I could keep him healthy enough to get through all the prenuptial activities and up to the altar at the First Methodist, come December. That's when we wanted to have the wedding, when my bridesmaids could wear velvet. And also, I was hoping by that time he'd be speaking a little clearer and be able to stand without a walker and have a little more strength in his various appendages to manage a honeymoon. Stroke patients take a lot of rehabilitation, you know, which was part of my job, and we'd made our plans while I exercised him. We were keeping it a secret, just between the two of us, because we didn't want any interference from people who'd want to meddle in our May–December romance.

Mr. Howard, though, could hardly wait and he could hardly keep his good hand off me. I'd had to watch him like a hawk from the first day I'd shown up and introduced myself as his Handy Home Helper. But that's a man for you. Doesn't matter if they're old or young, weak or strong, men just have this grabbing instinct built inside that they can't, or won't, keep under control. At least that's been my experience with them, and I've known a few.

Thinking about men in general and Mr. Howard in particular, I had to smile as I drove to his house for another therapeutic session. Remembering how quick he was with that hand. And where he could get it to before I could catch it.

But I stopped smiling when I turned into my intended's long, tree-lined driveway in my '98 Camaro, with its faded gray body paint, rattling tailpipe, busted AC, duct-taped seat covers, and ninety-something-thousand miles. I knew, as soon as I pulled in

near the back entrance, that trouble was already parked and waiting for me. I didn't recognize the brushed gold Cadillac Seville
over by the garage, but I knew who had to be its owner. A visitor
would've parked in front.

I checked my makeup in the rearview mirror, especially my
eye shadow and liner. I just hate smudges. First impressions are
so important if you aim to get ahead. I wanted whoever it was,
though I knew it had to be Junior Connard, Mr. Howard's only
son, who should've been in Raleigh where he belonged, to see me
as the professional woman I was. I didn't want to come across as
some low-rate, scrub-the-floors kind of person with chewed-off
lipstick, nor some loose excuse of a woman with her makeup
caked on like a bar pickup, that he was probably expecting, either. Names are important, but the way you look can make up
for a lot.

You see how careful I was.

I sat there for a minute listening to the early morning quiet,
trying to gather my wits. I always liked to look out over the back
garden every time I came. So peaceful, all enclosed like it was
by shrubbery and flowering trees, with a big square of grass in
the middle. I'd read about it in *The Delmont Daily* that time it
was on the garden tour when Mr. Howard's first wife had her
picture made with her prized camellias blooming behind her. I
hadn't paid much attention to the article then, not having any
connection to Mr. Howard Connard, Senior, at the time, and not
being the type to tour any gardens, either. But the picture had
stuck in my mind all these years, and here lately, when I made
my regularly scheduled visits, I'd let myself imagine what I'd look
like posing in front of that same camellia bush.

Well, sitting around thinking about it wasn't getting it done.
So I got my black canvas bag and a grocery sack out of the backseat, took a deep breath, and headed for the door.

I knocked as usual but, not as usual, waited for Emmett to come to the door. He knew the days I came, so he was always in the kitchen waiting for me, and I'd give a courtesy knock and go on in. But with that brushed gold Seville sitting out there, I waited this time till he came to the door.

"Hi, Emmett," I said, bright and cheery, in spite of the agitation I felt.

He nodded, cut his eyes to the side like somebody was listening and taking notes, and said, "Mornin', Miss Etta."

Emmett had been with Mr. Howard for as long as anybody could remember, even before the first Mrs. Connard, Senior, passed. Black as a licorice stick and just as wiry, and as much of a gentleman as Mr. Howard himself. He wasn't much bigger than me, but he was strong enough to get Mr. Howard in and out of bed, and do for him whatever needed to be done, like dressing and shaving and the like. On top of that, Emmett kept the house up, vacuuming, dusting, and so forth, doing the things that a maid had done years ago. He'd been hired as the cook and general handyman when he first came, but now with no woman around and Mr. Howard practically on his last legs, he did it all. He lived in a couple of rooms over the garage, but here lately he'd been sleeping in the house in case Mr. Howard needed help during the night. Like with getting up to relieve himself, which he couldn't do by himself without the risk of falling and breaking a hip, which you always have to watch out for when it comes to senior citizens. He was weak on the left side, you know, from the strokes.

Since Mr. Howard had been laid up and needing the Handy Home Helpers, I'd offered to come over every now and again on my own time to give Emmett some time off, which, I liked to think, made him think kindly of me. I never pass up an opportunity to make a friend, since you never know when or where you might need one. Those were the times I'd bundle Mr. Howard up and take him for a drive for a change of scene. We'd drive around Delmont, then up on the Parkway, all the time talking about the views of the Smoky Mountains and the new people moving in who were bringing changes that neither of us liked. We'd almost always stop at the Dairy Queen and get a vanilla cone. It was the highlight of our time together.

That was when Mr. Howard and I got to know each other so well.

"How is he this morning?" I asked as usual, pretending I didn't suspect that Junior was lurking and listening to every word.

Emmett stood in the doorway, not exactly blocking it but not so that I could breeze in like I usually did.

"Uh, Miss Etta," he began, his old face lined with misery. "I hate to be the one to tell you this, but I got my 'structions. Mr. Junior, he say Mr. Howard don't need no more nursin', and I supposed to tell you don't come here no more."

Well, that just did it. Junior Connard didn't have the nerve to tell me to my face. And a good thing, too, because it flew all over me. I might've slapped him cross-eyed if he'd been standing there.

"Well," I said, trying hard to keep my professional aspect, in spite of the steam that was about to blow my top off. I knew Junior had to be nearby, listening to what he couldn't bring himself to do. Maybe hoping I'd pitch a fit so he'd feel justified in firing me.

And it was all I could do to keep from pitching one that would stunt his growth and curl his hair. If he had any left to curl.

I hadn't intended for Junior or anybody else to hear about our marital plans until they were a fate accomplished, but wouldn't you know somebody would let the cat out of the bag. I had a pretty good idea who it was, too. I'd only told one person, which I did before I could help myself. Lord knows poor Mr. Howard couldn't tell, since nobody but Emmett and me could understand him, the way his strokes had left him. But you can't keep a secret in this town. Somebody, and I knew who, had called Junior and told him he'd better get out of Raleigh and take a hand here before that Wiggins woman took his daddy for all he was worth.

So you might know Junior'd come running as soon as he heard the news. A loving son, you might say, worried about his daddy and wanting to save him from a gold digger. Ha, is all I have to say. That overgrown boy, pushing fifty and then some if he was a day, hadn't given one thought to his daddy for years. Sent him a crate of half-ripe pears at Christmas and a sorry-looking tie for his birthday. Didn't come see him, didn't write, didn't do anything but play golf and live off his trust fund. Not that I much blamed him, though, if what I'd heard was true. Everybody said that Mr. Howard had been a hard man in his prime, not caring who he stepped on or whose feelings he hurt. A lot of rich, powerful men are like that, you know, until old age or sickness lays them low; then their attitude changes in a hurry.

But I'd never seen the other side of Mr. Howard, because by the time I came to know him, he was just a shadow of his former self and as sweet as he could be. That's what a couple of strokes will do for you.

Now, what I thought Junior ought to've done was get on my good side. I'm not a greedy person nor a selfish one, and from all I'd heard, there was plenty to go around. He ought to've thanked his lucky stars that I'd come along—a trained and experienced home health care specialist to lighten his burden and make his daddy's old age a happier time than the old man'd ever had, bar none.

But none of this meant a thing under the present urgent circumstances, and I had to come up with something to keep our plans on track. I tapped my foot and looked off in the distance for a minute, trying to maintain my temper and handle the situation to my best advantage.

I mean, I was Mr. Howard's intended and that gave me a certain entry. On the other hand, I had a job to do and a contract that confirmed it.

So I smiled at Emmett, like it didn't matter to me one way or the other. It did, but one thing I'd learned was if you can't get what you want one way, there's always another. If you're smart enough to find it, and not let anybody know you're looking for it. So while my brain went into overdrive, figuring out what I could do next, I smiled some more.

"That's fine, Emmett," I said, just as businesslike and professional as I could be. Let Junior chew on that awhile. "I must've missed your message at the office, so I'll just go on to the next shut-in on my list. But I did pick up Mr. Howard's Metamucil and I brought him a bottle of prune juice. You might try him with a little of that and see what happens. Tell him I stopped by, and say hey to Junior for me. I heard he was trying to lose some of that weight, but the way I heard it, he's losing more hair than pounds."

And knowing that Junior was listening, I added, "Don't tell him I said that. See you later, Emmett, have a good one."

I went back to my car, fuming inside, but not giving away a thing to anybody who might've been watching. Needing time to get myself together before trying to drive, what with my trembling hands and boiling insides, I took out my record book and propped it on the steering wheel. I pretended to jot down notes of my visit, as Lurline makes us do, so Junior and Emmett wouldn't wonder why I was just sitting there.

What I wanted to do, though, was put my head back and howl. Every time, *every* time, I thought things were about to go my way, some awful thing rose up and put me back down. This time it was Junior trying to ruin the best chance I'd ever had.

But what he didn't know, I told myself as I scribbled *damn, damn, damn* on my record book, was that I was through being put down, shoved around, fired without cause, and treated like trash. What he didn't know was that he was tangling with a woman who wasn't going to be stopped this time.

Chapter 2

But first things first, and the first thing I was going to do was cook Lurline Corn's goose. So I put away my record book, cranked the car, and drove down the driveway, looking straight ahead with my nose in the air like I didn't have a worry in the world, in spite of the rumbling muffler and the cloud of black smoke trailing behind me.

Junior Connard might think he could get rid of me as easy as that, but he didn't know Etta Mae Wiggins.

As soon as I got to the end of the driveway, I turned up the country music station I kept my radio on, stomped the gas pedal, and shot out into the street—so mad I could've spit. Scraped the tailpipe on the curb, too. I didn't care. I hunched over the wheel, getting madder and madder. Lurline was going to regret the day she tried to cross me.

I'd thought she was my friend. I'd worked hard for her, always taking on the worst of our clients, the ones that the other girls couldn't or wouldn't handle. I'd increased her business and made money for her, and what did I get? A piddling twenty-five-cents-an-hour raise and a twenty-five-dollar bonus last Christmas. And she'd bought a new Mercury Cougar for herself, all the time moaning about the cost of overhead and how she didn't know how she was able to stay in business. Well, I could tell her that. She was able to stay in business because she had people like me doing the dirty work while she sat in an office making out deposit slips.

The thought of it made me grip the wheel harder and stomp on the gas, billboards and speed limit signs flashing by. All I could think of was Lurline's prissy self trying to run my personal business as well as her own.

And that *hair*! A woman in her fifties, which she'd never admit to being, just oughtn't use anything darker than Clairol number 120, Natural Dark Brown. But you couldn't tell her anything. Except, today, she was going to hear it from me.

I'd confided in her, thinking she'd wish me well. But no, she couldn't stand for anybody to better themselves. I should've had my head examined for telling her about me and Mr. Howard. I should've known she'd go behind my back and try to do me in. Why, I just bet she'd been on the phone to Junior as soon as I got out of her office, my heart singing with the joy of a future as the second Mrs. Howard Connard, Senior.

Oh, *dang and double-dang!*

Blue lights flashing in my rearview mirror. My foot came off the gas—instinct, you know—and I turned the radio down, hoping the cop car would swing past me on its way to somewhere else. But no, it slowed down with me and I saw an arm motioning out the window for me to pull over. This had to be my worst bad-luck day.

Slowing, I brought the car to rest on the shoulder. I held on to the steering wheel with both hands, my head hanging down between my arms. Other cars passed by, the drivers slowing down to crane their necks at my misfortune. I sat there avoiding their eyes and wondering what else could go wrong on this awful day. I couldn't afford a speeding ticket. I couldn't take time off from work to go to court, and it wouldn't do any good if I did. Lord, I was about to cry until I raised my head and looked in the side-view mirror.

He was climbing out of the patrol car, all six foot two inches and one hundred ninety pounds of him fitting into that dark blue deputy's uniform like it'd been handmade for him. I'd never been sure of what *sauntering* meant exactly, until I saw Bobby Lee Moser do some of it. I watched him fit his hat carefully on his head, worried about messing up that thick head of hair he was so proud of. Vain as a peacock. He reached back into his car and brought out a ticket book, then he sauntered over to my window, grinning like he was God's gift to every woman in the world.

Well, at one time I'd thought he was.

By the time he got to my car and leaned down to look in my window, the grin was gone. I couldn't see his eyes because of those black aviator shades that made him look hard as nails and just as cold.

"Ma'am," he said, just as serious and impersonal as he could get, overlooking the fact, I guess, that I knew how he looked with his pants off. "Do you know you were doing sixty in a forty-five zone? I could have your license for that. Now, where you going in such a hurry?"

"Bobby Lee," I said, "I don't have time to mess with you. Just give me a ticket and let me go. Or, better yet," I said, cocking my head and giving him a sweet smile, reminding him of times past, "why don't you just give me a warning? I promise to slow down, and besides, I've never gotten a speeding ticket before and you wouldn't want to ruin my record, would you?"

"Etta Mae," he said, dropping his voice in that bedroomy way he had, "I thought I'd already ruined your record, but seems to me you might need another session. I think we ought to get together sometime soon, don't you?"

"In your dreams, Bobby Lee," I snapped. "Now, I've got business to tend to, and I don't have time to fiddle with you. So just give me whatever kind of ticket you're going to give me and let me get on with it."

"Well," he said, squatting down beside my car so that his face was right next to mine. He rested one arm on the car door so that the short sleeve of his uniform hiked up enough for me to see part of the Airborne tattoo on his huge bicep. He knew that turned me on. "What I usually do in cases like this is take the suspect back to my car and give her a good talking-to. I don't know that I can just turn you loose so easy. Have to make sure you're not going to go off and be speeding again."

I could tell, in spite of not being able to see his eyes, that they were sparkling the way they used to do when he'd try to make me mad. He'd rather tease me than eat, and that was just one of the things that kept breaking us up over the years, the last and final time being just a few months back. I'm too serious a person to put up with that kind of foolishness for long. Having fun was all he could think about, and having fun was way down on my list of life's little necessities.

"Bobby Lee, I promise. I won't speed again, not even if you're lying somewhere bleeding to death and I'm the only one who can get to you. I'll observe the speed limit every step of the way. Now, please, I've got to go. My whole life depends on what I do today, and I've got to get on with it."

He ran his finger across my arm and frowned. "You in trouble, Etta Mae?"

"No, I'm not in trouble. I just have business to take care of. So just do what you have to, and let me go."

He took off his shades, giving me the full benefit of his dark eyes, and said, "Give me time. I'm thinking. So, tell me, how's Granny these days?"

"Granny's fine, thanks for asking, but she's not on my mind right this minute."

He grinned. "Want to know what's on my mind right this minute?"

"No, I do not, and don't tell me."

"Come on now, girl, I was just thinking about seeing Granny walking along the side of the road the other day. I offered her a ride, but she said she'd see me in hell first."

I had to laugh, though I hated giving in to it. "She's a pistol, all right."

"I ride by there a coupla times when I'm on night patrol in that sector. Watch out for her a little. She still keep that shotgun by her bed?"

"Oh, yeah, and I wouldn't shine the spotlight on her house, if I were you. She'll shoot it out for you." It made me weak to think of him taking special care of Granny. He used to do that for me, too, until I reported him. "Thanks for watching out for her."

"Glad to do it, but don't tell her it's me. She'd fill me with buckshot some night. That lady can sure carry a grudge." Then he leaned his head in close and said, "Just like you, darlin'. When're you gonna get over being mad at me?"

"Never, and I don't want to talk about it. Now, do what you have to do. I have to go."

He studied me for a long minute, while I pretended it didn't bother me. Him being so close, and all. Then he said, "Okay, it'll be a warning this time, but remember, I'm keeping my eye on you from here on out. Just think of me as Big Brother, watching over you all the time."

"Big boob is more like it."

"You always did have a mouth on you," he said, smiling with his eyes half closed as they traveled from my face to my waist. "Not that I'm complaining. I like a woman who can give as good as she takes."

"You just like a woman, period, Bobby Lee Moser." Darla

Davis came to mind, and it took an effort of will to keep my professional cool. "But I thank you for the warning. Now, if you'll
stop hanging on my car, I'll be on my way."

He stood up, tipped his hat at me, and said, "Give me a call
sometime. I been missing you."

I looked back in the rearview mirror as I pulled onto the road.
I saw him laugh and shake his head, then walk back to his car.
While I was still watching him, Trisha Yearwood came on the
radio singing "There Goes My Baby." I almost sprained my wrist
switching her off. That man could get to me like nobody else,
keeping me on edge and about half excited every time I was
around him. The problem was, he did it to every woman he met.
Bobby Lee and I had been off and on more times than I could
count, and it'd usually been his flirty ways that'd turned me off.
I'm the jealous type, and I couldn't put up with all the women he
drew like flies to honey. I swear, the man would hit on a holly
bush if he thought it was female.

Thank the Lord I wouldn't have to worry about Mr. Howard
in that regard. When you've got a man in a wheelchair or stumbling around on a walker, you pretty much know where he is and
what he's doing every minute of the day.

Chapter 3

I pulled into the back lot of the square white house that Lurline rented for her business. It was just a four-room, one-bath mill-town house like all the others on a side street in downtown Delmont.

A lot of small businesses and lawyers' offices had set up shop in the area after the thread mill closed some years ago. Lurline had fixed up the former living room as a waiting area for families who wanted to make arrangements for home care of their elderly loved ones. She had it decorated with a hooked rug, a deacon's bench, wingback chairs, and lots of doilies to keep the upholstery clean. Oh, and a brass eagle over the fireplace. Whatever her other faults, I had to give her credit for good taste when it came to home furnishings.

She'd made the former front bedroom into her office, and it was Early American too, but with a professional look from all the wood-grain file cabinets. Half of them were empty, I happened to know.

Entering through the back door, I marched through the kitchen, which was reserved for EMPLOYEES ONLY. That's where I'd spent hours and hours training Lurline's new girls in how to give bed baths and take care of bedsores and check urine for sugar and so forth and so on. And the thought of what I'd done for her made me even madder as I stormed through on my way to her office. She was lucky to have me since I was the only one of the

Handy Home Helpers with a degree in assistant nursing from the Abbot County Technical College, although, to be fair, she did help pay for my education. But I'd paid her back a thousand times over, according to my calculations. You'd think she'd show a little appreciation.

I poked my head into the waiting room to be sure no one was there, then walked right into her office. When she looked up and saw me, she closed her checkbook and frowned.

"Aren't you supposed to be seeing your patients?" She pulled the schedule in front of her, studied it, and said, "You've got Mrs. Evans and Mr. Hughes today. Surely you haven't finished already." I noticed she didn't mention Mr. Howard, so she'd known he was off the schedule.

I could've snatched her bald-headed for letting me go out there without a clue.

"Lurline," I said, surprised that steam didn't come out of my mouth at the same time. "What in the hell did you think you were doing? Did you think I wouldn't know it was you? *Why*, is what I want to know."

"I don't know what you're talking about." She was sulling up something awful. I could see it in her face, the way her prim little mouth tightened up, and hear it in her voice. She looked out the window, unable to face me. "And, besides," she said, swinging her head around and glaring at me, "what gives you the right to come in here and yell at me, cussing and carrying on like you don't need a job? You just better watch your step, young lady."

"I don't think you want to fire me, Lurline," I said, trying to hold back my temper. "You might have to go out and clean a few incontinent patients yourself." I took a deep breath and sat in one of the captain's chairs in front of her desk. I looked her over good, noting the white uniform she always wore so the families she interviewed would think she was a nurse and capable of doing what they paid her to do. Of course, the rhinestone-studded chain holding her glasses around her neck and the earrings dangling out from under that frizzy black hair put a damper on the effect. "Why did you have to call Junior Connard, Lurline? I trusted you, and wanted you to be happy for me."

She drew herself up and pursed her mouth, getting all huffy and self-righteous. "I'll have you know I'm not paying you to pursue your own interests. I have an obligation to the families not to let anyone take advantage of their loved ones. After all, they're the ones who foot the bills."

"Don't give me that!" I said, squinting up my eyes and giving it right back at her. "You just lost yourself a client, and that's the last thing you ever want to happen. Unless, of course, you're going to assign one of the other girls to Mr. Howard, but I warn you, he won't like it and might just cancel the contract himself. His mind is as clear as it ever was, you might be surprised to know. He won't take kindly to somebody he doesn't even know meddling in his business." I took a deep breath and went right on. "And if you think Junior Connard has any say in this, you are dead wrong. He doesn't pay one cent for his daddy's care. All expenses are paid by Mr. Howard's lawyer, Mr. Ernest Sitton, and you know it as well as I do. No," I said, shaking my head and clenching my fists, "obligation to the family wasn't the reason. The reason was, you just didn't want me to get ahead. You couldn't stand it that I had a chance to better myself. Just admit it, so I'll know what kind of friend you are."

"Now listen, Etta Mae." She leaned forward in her chair, arms crossed on the desk. She was switching into her I-know-what's-best-for-you way of talking to me. "I was thinking of you, too. You have a future here in this business and you don't want to go marrying that old wreck of a man. You're too young for that, and too pretty. Although, and I have been meaning to mention this, since it has to do with my business image, you need to touch up your roots a little more often. You have to watch these things when you go blond."

I jumped straight up out of my chair. "You've got a nerve! Before you start criticizing *my* hair, Lurline, why don't you take a look in the mirror? You're too old for that dark color, and I don't know why somebody hasn't told you before this!"

She jerked back in her chair like I'd slapped her. Which I wanted to do so bad I had to hold myself back. "There's no need to get personal," she said.

"What you mean is, there's no need for *me* to get personal." I leaned across her desk, so she'd see I meant business. "But it's all right for you to criticize me. Well, I'm going to tell you something, and it'll be the last thing I ever tell you. It's not over yet. Junior Connard has had his say, but his daddy hasn't had his. And his daddy's crazy about me, and he won't take this sitting down!"

Poor old Mr. Howard couldn't do anything but sit down, but I didn't bring that up.

I whirled around and headed for the door, intending to slam it on my way out.

"You going to Mrs. Evans first?" Lurline asked.

"Yes, then to Mr. Hughes. Then I'm going to straighten this mess out *on my own time,* and I'll thank you to keep your nose out of my business from now on."

And I did slam the door behind me, but not real hard.

It took most of the day to finish with the others on my list, and it was after six by the time I parked the Camaro by my single-wide. And sat there, stunned at the mess strewn around the door. Garbage cans overturned, with coffee grounds and newspapers and tomato cans and chicken bones and Hardee's wrappers all across the concrete slab that was my patio. Plus a chair on its side and my geranium uprooted. I leaned my head on the steering wheel, teary-eyed and sick at heart, until the thought of the whole awful day upset me so bad I didn't know whether to cuss or cry.

This was the absolute last straw. If people couldn't keep their dang dogs out of other people's garbage, then they needed to be penned up. Either the dogs or the people, didn't matter which.

I crawled out of the car and stood there with my hands on my hips, surveying the damage. My single-wide was the only asset I had from two marriages and two divorces, and I was grateful for it and proud of it. When Skip Taggert, my number one ex, hit the road, I'd been so far in the hole I thought I'd never get out. You wouldn't believe the debts he left me with. I'd had to move back in with Granny, and get one of those credit managers to negotiate with all the people he owed money to. Why, I couldn't even get a telephone in my own name. Took me six years to get out from under, and it was only with Bernie's help that I was able to then.

I'd played it cool with Bernie, not letting him get past first base until the ring was on my finger. He would've done anything for me, and just about did. He paid up the last of my debts, and I went into that marriage free and clear. He was the happiest man alive to do it for me, too. I made sure of that. We set up housekeeping in the pre-owned single-wide I'm still living in, and you couldn't have found a prouder woman, nor one so determined to express gratitude. Bernie got so much gratitude, in fact, that he could hardly drag into work every morning for a good six months.

Things went downhill, though, when I found out about his gambling habit. But I'd learned a few things from my past experience and made him put the trailer in my name so he couldn't lose it by drawing to a straight flush. Good thing, too, because he lost his position with A-One Quality New & Used Cars when he bet his Nissan demonstrator on the Carolina Panthers. Which shows you how much sense he had.

My single-wide was as nice as any in Hillandale Trailer Park, and I worked hard to keep it that way. I'd had a green-and-white-striped awning put over the slab in front of the door. It made a real pleasant entrance with the pot of geraniums by the steps, a short-legged grill for when I cooked out, and the two green plastic chairs from Walmart's. Whatever my other faults, I kept a neat, clean house and tried to improve my surroundings wherever I was.

Now the place looked like a pigpen. I could've cried and did, a little bit, while I picked up the mess and swept up the rest of it, straightening the chairs and repotting the geranium. One bloom had been broken off, but I tamped the soil around the plant, hoping what I was muttering under my breath wouldn't kill it for good.

Then I went inside and locked the door behind me—you can't be too careful when you live in a trailer park—turned on the AC, and went straight to the shower. No matter how clean you are in your personal habits, when you work around old and sick people, their odor gets all over you.

Wrapped in my old chenille robe, I went into the bedroom to look at my Barbie collection. That always calmed me down, seeing those pretty dolls lined up on the barewood bookcase I'd bought just for them. I loved to dream that I was like one of them, dressed in the proper attire and taking part in all the fun activities that I'd never had a chance to do. Well, and never would, either.

Sighing, I picked up the threadbare giraffe with the limp neck that Bobby Lee had won for me at the fair one year, and hugged it tight. Out of all the stuffed animals I had propped up on my pillows, that old giraffe was the one I loved the best.

Tucking it under my arm, I went to the kitchenette, where I popped a Bud Light, then went around the counter that divided the room in two. I flopped down in Bernie's leatherette recliner in the living area to rest from my labors and try to gather my wits. I swiveled the chair so I could admire the way my new floral-upholstered couch went with the burnt orange shag carpet on the floor. I was buying it on time from Braden's Furniture, but the monthly payments were worth it for the pleasure it gave me. Even the first Mrs. Connard, Senior, hadn't had anything near like it in her house.

Chapter 4

After a while I reached for the phone, feeling about half ready to tackle old lady Springer, who owned the Hillandale Trailer Park, and complain again about garbage pickup and dogs running loose to damage property and mess up a person's whole day and general outlook on life. I dialed her number, knowing it by heart since I'd had to call it so often.

"Mrs. Springer?" I asked as she answered her phone. "This is Etta Mae Wiggins, remember me? I'm a friend of Hazel Marie's and I spent the night at your house back in that late winter storm we had when I was Mr. Sam Murdoch's home health care nurse after he broke his leg? And I was at Binkie and Coleman's wedding? And I rent a space in the Hillandale Trailer Park that you own? And I always pay my rent on time?"

"I know who you are, Miss Wiggins." The woman could rub me raw just with the tone of her voice, but I didn't let on.

"Well, I'm sorry to be calling and complaining again, but it's been over a week and the garbageman hasn't been here, and on top of that, somebody's dogs have been. I came home to a mess today you wouldn't believe, and I knew you'd want to know about it."

"What do you want me to do about it, Miss Wiggins?"

Get another garbageman! Call the dog pound! Lock somebody up! Come over here and live with it and see how you like it, I wanted to say. Instead I bit my lip and said, "I'd appreciate it if you'd make the owners of the dogs keep them penned up. At least."

"Well," she said, with a long sigh. Like I was putting her out, but she was just too much of a lady to say so. It just burned me up. "I'll see what I can do, but if you don't know whose dogs they are, I don't know that anything can be done."

"Well, something better be," I said, trying my best to stay professional, but firm. "I work hard all day, cleaning up after other people, and I don't need to come home and have to clean up after a pack of dogs!" The whole day was catching up with me, and I was about to lose it. "And I know good and well, Mrs. Springer, that if I just left that mess out there, you'd be sending me an eviction notice."

"Your lease requires you to keep your space neat and clean," she said. I *knew* that. That's what I was trying to do. That's why I was calling her. Was everybody after me? Was every effort I made going to be shot down? Seemed like I couldn't get anywhere for trying.

"Yes, ma'am," I said, hoping she couldn't tell that I was about to cry. "I do try to keep my place neat and clean, but I need some help here."

She took another deep breath, and said, "I'll see what I can do."

Now, see? That's what I've been talking about. If Mrs. Howard Connard, Senior, had called with a complaint, that woman would've fallen all over herself to straighten it out. But let Etta Mae Wiggins complain and you see what happens.

With an ache in my heart at the unfairness of it all, I hung up. At least the inside of my trailer was neat and attractive, the floral sofa the stunning centerpiece of my home decor. Rubbing my face against Bobby Lee's giraffe and setting aside Mrs. Julia Springer, I turned my mind to some hard thinking and careful planning, now that a snag in the form of Junior Connard had popped up. Mr. Howard would be counting on me to figure something out, because he knew I wasn't the type to sit back and let Junior or anybody else mess up our plans.

Reaching for the remote, I turned on the TV, zipping through stations until I got to CMT, the country music station that I always listened to when I had hard thinking to do. Tracy Lawrence was singing about time marching on, and don't it ever. There's so much truth in country music, if people would only take it to heart. I sank back into the recliner and flipped it to maximum recline. I lay back and studied my bare feet with Roundup Red polish painted on my toes. Then I cocked my left leg up so I could admire the tiny butterfly tattooed in blue and green and rose on the inside of my ankle. Bobby Lee had gone crazy over it. He used to reach across the bed and grab me by the ankle so he could . . . But that was in some of our more intimate moments.

I didn't have the time nor the inclination to dwell on Bobby Lee Moser. Now was the time to think of the future. The *immediate* future, and what I could do to outmaneuver Junior Connard.

I knew Junior wouldn't stay around Delmont long. He'd made his life over in Raleigh, and in the year or so I'd been looking after Mr. Howard, Junior had never once come to see him. If I hadn't known so much about the Connard family already, due to the fact that everybody in Delmont kept up with everybody else, especially the most prominent family in town, I would've never known there was a Junior.

So it wasn't like I had to worry about Junior staying around and taking over Mr. Howard's care himself. And from what I'd heard, there was no danger of his current wife letting herself be saddled with a stroke-stricken father-in-law. She was a TV anchorperson on *Your Live Local Late-Breaking News at Six O'Clock* in Raleigh, and not about to interrupt her career to look after anybody twenty-four hours a day. I could just see her messing up that lacquered hair as she got Mr. Howard settled on the commode.

The one thing I did have to worry about was Junior putting Mr. Howard in a nursing home with a restriction on who visited him. There were three nursing homes in the area, two over in Abbotsville and one right outside Delmont. I didn't think much of any of them, though they all had state licenses. Last year I'd helped get old Mrs. Stanton moved into the Mountain Ridge Rest Home, and I wouldn't put my dog in there. If I had a dog. Poor old thing, she'd cried and held on to me that day till I thought I'd cry with her. Her daughter'd said she had Alzheimer's, but I think she was just old and confused. I mean, wouldn't you be confused if your daughter came into your house and cleaned and straightened and moved everything out of its place so you couldn't find your glasses or your pocketbook or your nightgown?

You have to realize that old people don't like change. And they don't like people, even if they are kin, coming in and taking over what's been theirs for seventy years, either.

I didn't think Junior would consider the Mountain Ridge Rest Home or the Bonny Acres, but he might the Aycock Center because it was private and expensive. I figured that he'd think the more expensive the better, especially since the payments wouldn't come out of his pocket. He could go back to Raleigh satisfied that his old daddy was getting the best of care and that somebody would always be around to keep me away from him.

So that was one possibility, one that I thought I could get around. There're ways to get around any restrictions Junior might set up in this town. It might take some time, though, and I didn't have time to waste.

Well, *I* had plenty, but Mr. Howard probably didn't. Not that he was dying or anything like that, but once a victim of stroke, always a candidate for another one. That's what his doctor'd said. Along with instructions for Mr. Howard to avoid high-salt, high-fat foods and mental or physical stress. And you couldn't tell me that throwing him in a nursing home wouldn't bring about plenty of mental stress. I knew he wouldn't want to be committed to an old folks' home, and I knew he'd be fit to be tied if he couldn't have me around.

Instead of upsetting or depressing him, as his son was likely to do, I was the only one who knew how to give him something to live for.

He'd come to depend on me, see, and he knew he could rely on me to know what he could stand and what he couldn't. He could get right sprightly if I'd let him, but I always called a halt before he went too far and got too excited. I just eased him along a little at a time, all the while watching his pulse rate and checking how flushed his face was while he got some pleasures he thought he'd lost forever. Now, I don't want you to get the wrong idea of what went on when Mr. Howard and I were alone together. I was a churchgoing woman, had been ever since I broke up with Bobby Lee. All I'd done with Mr. Howard was let him find out that life still had something to offer, that there were things to look forward to, and that there was a possibility of having those things every day. And every night.

I know for a fact that I helped him, because his doctor said so. He was amazed at Mr. Howard's rapid rehabilitation, not to the point of having full use of his left side, of course, but enough to compliment me on the physical therapy I was practicing on Mr. Howard.

It wasn't the same for me, of course, as it was for Mr. Howard. But I never expected it to be. After two husbands and Bobby Lee, oh, and Junior Johnson for a little while, I'd had about all the thrills, and the heartaches that went along with them, that I could stand.

I figure everything's a trade-off. I could give Mr. Howard what he wanted, and he could give me what I wanted. And if we didn't want the same things, why, who's to say one was getting the better of the deal? We could both be happy if people would just let us alone.

But that was the very thing Junior was hell-bent on not doing. It just worried me sick to think how mad Mr. Howard was going to be when Junior dumped him in an old folks' home, and how unglued he'd be when I wouldn't be allowed to visit. That was a blueprint for another stroke. And another stroke might wipe his memory clean of what I meant to him. It might even kill him. We're talking life or death here.

The worst possible case would be if Junior took his daddy to Raleigh and put him in a nursing home there. No way would I have the means to commute two hundred miles often enough to get on the good side of an aide or an orderly who'd let me sneak in to see him.

I got so agitated at the thought that I had to get up for another Bud. One nice thing about living in a single-wide, you don't have to walk far to get to the refrigerator.

I watched Patty Loveless for a minute—that woman can mortally *sing*—then got myself reclined again to think out what I needed to do. First, I had to find out what Junior's plans were. Regardless of what he did—closed up the house, pensioned Emmett off, committed Mr. Howard—I could get around them if he just didn't take Mr. Howard out of town.

As I lay there wiggling my toes and sipping on the Bud, I heard the uneven growl and pop of what sounded like a dirt bike or a motorcycle whose timing was off, puttering and popping along somewhere in the trailer park. I pictured Jennie's husband, Mack, coming home from the Kawasaki Cycle Center where he worked to their double-wide across the street from me. From the sound of it, though, what he was riding needed more work than it'd gotten.

Then I heard footsteps on the cement slab, and somebody banged on my door. I jumped up and tied my robe tighter, wondering who was visiting me at eight o'clock at night. I glanced in the mirror by the door and fluffed up my hair.

Lurline had been right; my roots could've used some help.

I put on the chain lock and cracked the door. Lord, my heart sank to my toes when I saw who it was.

Chapter 5

~

"What in the world are *you* doing here?"

"Lemme in, Etta Mae," he said, pushing against the door as he glanced over his shoulder. "I need help, and you're the only one I could think of. Come on, hon, lemme in." His hand, grease-stained knuckles and all, curled around the door.

"Oh, no, Skip Taggert, you're not getting in here. I had my fill of you a long time ago. Now, get on away from here."

He mashed his face right up in the crack between the door and the trailer so I could see the blond stubble around his mouth, and said real low and pleading, "Etta Mae, I ain't foolin'. I need help real bad. I'm in big trouble, and you just got to help me. I got nowhere else to go."

"I've already helped you to the tune of fifteen thousand dollars' worth of bills you ran out on. Who do you owe now?"

"It ain't like that, Etta Mae," he said, whispering across the chain so close that I could smell his breath. Onions and beer. "Please, I don't owe anybody anything. This is something different, and it's big. Lemme in so I can tell you about it. You won't be sorry, I promise."

"You think I'm a fool? Is that what you think? Well, let me tell you I'm not. I learned my lesson with you when you left me with enough debts to choke a horse, so you might as well get on away from here."

"Etta Mae," he whispered, letting his big, flabby body slump against the door like he'd just given up on everything. "Please, I really need some help. I'm in big trouble."

I'd never heard Skip ask for anything. Usually, he just took what he wanted with never a thought of what it might cost him. Or anybody else, for that matter. He did look pitiful, though, and my heart always goes out to the pitiful and the helpless. Even when it's their own fault.

"Get off the door, then," I said with a click of my tongue, "and let me get the chain off. But I want you to know right up front that I'm not giving you a nickel so you'd just better not even ask."

"You won't be sorry, I promise."

"Uh-huh, I hear you." I slipped off the chain and stepped back. "Come on in, then." He held the door so that it wouldn't fully open and sidled inside. Then he stuck his head through the opening and peered out, looking one way and then the other.

Apparently satisfied, he closed the door, turned the latch, and put the chain back on.

"Thanks, Etta Mae," he said. "Thank you from the bottom of my heart. I 'preciate this more'n you'll ever know."

"Oh, sit down and shut up about it," I said, waving toward the couch.

"I will in a minute, but right now I got to go real bad. Which way's your john?"

"Down the hall," I said, pointing. "First door on the right, and close it behind you."

Unzipping as he went, he said, "I ain't even had time to stop at a bush."

I shook my head, watching him hurry to the bathroom. There'd been some big changes in the way he looked from the last time I'd seen him. Back then, he'd been a hunk, the star that every girl in school wanted to date. I thought of how he used to be everybody's friend, a good ole boy who'd thrilled this town every Friday night on the football field. We all thought he'd go places, like to Chapel Hill or State. But I found out quick enough that gaining a hundred yards every game didn't prepare a man for anything but pumping gas and guzzling beer at the Broad River Fish Camp. As long as he had ten dollars in his pocket for a few beers and a pool game, he never gave a thought to the next day when the rent was due or his truck needed tires.

But when he came back from the bathroom, I could see there was something heavy on his mind this time. He looked lost and pitiful and, worst of all, he'd taken no pains with his personal appearance. That told me something was bad wrong. His blue plaid shirt was half out of his jeans, with a buttonhole gaping open. His jeans were smeared with grease and grass stains, and no telling when they'd been washed. The biggest change, though, was the fifty or so extra pounds on him, making him look as round and pudgy as a baby. He certainly wasn't the boy I'd married before I knew any better.

But I'm an easy touch when it comes to the downtrodden, so I said, "You had supper, Skip? I could heat up some pizza, if you want it."

"Naw, I don't want anything." He flopped down on my new couch and leaned his head back against the pretty floral pattern that I'd paid extra for. I wished for one of Lurline's doilies. "Maybe some brew or something stronger, if you got it."

"I don't have anything stronger than Bud Light," I said, opening the refrigerator door and looking around inside. "And only two of them."

"Well, shoot, Etta Mae," he said. "I know you wadn't ever much of a drinker, but looks like you'd be a little better stocked than that."

"I wasn't exactly expecting you, you know." He took the can I held out to him, glanced at the unopened top, then up at me with a hurt look. Maybe that was when it got through to him that I wasn't going to wait on him hand and foot like I'd once done.

I sat down in the recliner far enough away to cut down on the body aroma I'd been smelling ever since he came in. This was a small trailer that was pretty tight against the elements.

"So what do you want, Skip? What kind of trouble are you in now?"

"Etta Mae," he said, coming up for air after emptying the can. "My luck has turned. You're not gonna believe this, but I've hit it big. I won't ever have to work again."

"Big deal!" I said. "When've you ever?"

"Now, hon," he said, his mouth drooping down like I'd cut him to the quick. "You got to admit I used to take good care of you. You didn't want for a thing."

"I sure didn't, except the money to pay for it. But I don't want to talk about the past; that's over and done with. I want to know what kind of trouble you're in and why you're bringing it to my door."

"You're not gonna believe it," he said again, this big, goofy grin spreading across his face.

He sat forward on the edge of the couch, his hands dangling between his legs. His smile spread even wider, waiting to hit me with his news. "What would you think if I told you what I've got in my pocket?"

I jumped straight up out of my chair. "I don't want to hear that nasty talk!" I headed for the door, mad enough to jerk it off its hinges. "Just get on out of here. Right now!"

"Wait, wait, hold on a minute," he said, holding both hands up and patting the air, "that's not what I meant. Come on, Etta Mae, I didn't mean a thing by that. I just said it wrong. I'm not coming on to you or nothing. Not that I wouldn't if you gave me half a chance. You're lookin' real good, hon, but this is bigger than anything me and you ever had goin' for us."

"Well, get on with it," I said, standing there fuming with my arms crossed under my breasts, just waiting for him to cross the line again.

"What would you say if I told you I got two million dollars in my pocket?"

"*What?* Where would the likes of you get two million dollars?"

"Hold on, and I'll tell you. Let me catch my breath a minute. I been on the run for two days." He bowed his head and shook it, letting me see how beat he was. I just rolled my eyes.

"On the run from who? More creditors?" Then it hit me. "The *Law?* Skip, I swear, are you running from the Law? Did you steal that money?"

"No! Whatta you think I am, Etta Mae? I don't owe anybody anything. Well, maybe I left a bar tab, but I didn't steal anything. Give me a break, hon, I just need a place to lay low for a while. That's where you come in, and it's nothing illegal, so you don't have to worry. I got enough to make it worth your while."

"Huh, it'd take a lot more than you'd ever have. So, if you didn't steal it, how'd you get this so-called two million dollars? What is it, Confederate money?"

"Look here," he said, standing up and pulling a worn leather wallet from his hip pocket. It was curved from being sat on so much. He opened it, stuffing gas receipts and dog-eared business cards back into it, and pulled out what looked like a ticket. "Know what this is?"

I opened my mouth to say it looked like a pass to the Asheville Speedway, but three taps on the door stopped me.

Skip jumped a mile, almost knocking me over. "Oh, shoot, damn, and dang it all, they're here!" he croaked, his voice hoarse and scared. He grabbed my arm and gave it a shake. "Quick, Etta Mae, hide me someplace. Tell 'em I'm not here; tell 'em you ain't seen me."

Chapter 6

"*Hide* you! What's going on, Skip? What're you mixed up in?"

"Come on, Etta Mae," he whispered, breathing fast and clamping down harder on my arm. "They won't bother you, but they're evermore after me. Just get rid of 'em. Tell 'em I'm not here an' you don't know where I am. Okay?" he said, giving my arm a shake. "Okay?"

I'd never seen Skip scared, and it wasn't a pretty sight as he scrunched down behind me. He cringed again when we heard three more light taps on the door, none of which sounded very threatening to me.

"Go get in the closet, then. No, wait," I said, thinking of his dirty self smushed in with my clean clothes. "The bathroom. Get in the shower stall." I pried his hand off my arm and turned him toward the hall. There weren't too many places a man of his size could hide anywhere, much less in an eight-hundred-square-foot house trailer. "I'll get rid of whoever it is. And then, I'll tell you right now, you're gonna be outta here."

"Yeah, okay. Just get rid of 'em. Tell 'em I ain't been here."

"I know what to say. Now go on," I said, giving him a push. "And close the shower curtain." I swear, you had to tell him the simplest things.

I watched him tiptoe past the kitchen and down the little hall into the bathroom. Before going in, he turned and looked at me, putting a finger to his lips and saying, "Sh-h-h." The man could make a preacher cuss.

I went to the door and called out, "Who is it?"

"It's me, Etta Mae," Lurline answered. "What's taking you so long? You got company in there?"

"No, I don't have company," I yelled, unlocking the bolts and chain. Here, she'd started on me again, accusing me, an engaged woman, of entertaining somebody behind locked doors. I could've smacked her to kingdom come, if she hadn't been such a good friend.

She still had on her uniform, which she wore everywhere except to church. She thought of it as a killing-two-birds-with-one-stone outfit, something to wear when she ran errands and did her shopping while advertising her business at the same time. I teased her one time and told her she ought to have *Handy Home Helpers* embroidered on the back of her uniforms. She didn't do it, but she bought a red nylon Windbreaker and had it stitched on that. In white. And gave me five dollars for my Suggestion for Bettering Business.

"I need a cigarette," she said as she walked in, all on edge and jumpy. "Where's your ashtray?"

"I'll get it. You want a beer?"

"I sure do," she said, putting my giraffe on the floor and sitting in my recliner. She rummaged in her purse, pulling out a pack of Doral Menthols and a Bic, and lit up. "I declare, Etta Mae, I've just been all upset today. Couldn't get anything done for worrying about you."

"Me? Why're you worried about me? You've just about ruined my life, but I don't know why that should upset you." I handed her the ashtray and my last can of beer and sat down on the couch. It smelled of motor oil from the last occupant.

"Oh, Etta Mae, you know I love you like a daughter," she said, wiping one little tear from her cheek. "Although, as you know, there's not that much difference in our ages."

Ha, I thought, *only about twenty years!*

She sniffed and went on, "And maybe I did wrong calling Junior Connard, but you know I had your interests at heart. You'll thank me one of these days for doing it."

"Well, today's not one of them." I leaned back and studied her as she sipped daintily from the can. She preferred a glass and I knew it, but I wanted her to get a taste of my attitude for a change.

Lurline had been a good friend to me, but at the same time she'd decided to run my life, too. She thought she knew what was best for everybody, but since I was the only one obligated to her I had to put up with her advice and meddling. But that had just come to a screeching halt.

"Don't be mad at me, Etta Mae. I wouldn't hurt you for the world. You know I wouldn't." She was really beginning to tear up, and I was beginning to feel bad. I can't hurt a fly, much less another person. Even if that person is a busybody and a know-it-all.

"I tell you," she went on, carefully dabbing at her eyes with a lace-edged handkerchief, not wanting to smear her makeup. "I have just suffered all day long, worrying about you and so upset that you misunderstood what I was doing for you. I've come to apologize if I hurt you in any way. Please accept my apology, Etta Mae, I don't want there to be anything but good feelings between us."

Well, what can you do? All she'd tried to do was save me from an old, demanding man who'd keep me from enjoying life. As if that's what I was doing now.

"Oh, Lurline, for goodness' sake, of course I forgive you. On one condition," I said, making my voice firm so she'd get the message. "No more interference, okay? I mean it now, because I intend to marry Mr. Howard in spite of this setback you've inflicted on me."

"Thank you, honey, for accepting my apology. You won't be sorry," she said, quickly drying her tears. She took an Estée Lauder compact with her zodiac sign on it out of her purse and checked her mascara. Then she snapped it shut and said, "Now, Etta Mae, now that we've got that out of the way, you really need to think over the other options you have. Don't close the door on any of them just because that old man's there for the taking. I think . . . Etta Mae, is that grease on your lovely new couch?"

I sat up and looked at the back of the couch. Sure enough, there was a stain right where Skip had leaned his head.

"Oh, no!" I gasped. "It's ruined."

"No it's not. Go get some of that Grease Grabber I bought you and I'll get it out. I declare, Etta Mae, I told you to leave the plastic covers on. If you're going to have nice things and *keep* them nice, you have to take care of them."

I heaved a sigh, just done in by one more awful thing happening, and went to the kitchen for the grease cleaner.

"While you're looking for it," Lurline said, getting up from the recliner, "I'll just use the little girls' room."

And off she went to the bathroom while I stood there trying to say, "No, don't, it's broken, wait, I'll get you something . . ."

But I couldn't get a word out before she'd closed the door. I heard her put the seat down and I cringed. Dang that Skip, that's just the sort of thing Lurline would notice.

When she screamed, the sound of it bounced from one end of the trailer to the other. The bathroom door slammed open, banging against the wall, and she came running out, jerking and pulling at her Easy Curves girdle. It was halfway down her thighs, making her run with her knees clamped together.

"There's a man in your bathroom!" she gasped, her eyes about to pop out of her head. "Etta Mae, there's a man in there! Right in the shower stall, watching and *listening* to me use the bathroom!" She hopped and jittered around, rotating her hips back and forth as she struggled to get her girdle up. Then she threw her head back and screamed, "Help! A man's in here!"

"For God's sake, Lurline," I said, taking her by the shoulders and giving her a shake. "Stop that screeching! This is a trailer park, remember? Nobody'll pay any attention. Now, hush!"

She looked at me, wild-eyed and frantic, still tugging at her girdle. She had her uniform hiked up around her waist, with the skirttail partly stuffed into the girdle. "Get a knife!" she said, her voice hoarse with the effort to whisper. "Your butcher knife, where is it?"

I gave her another shake. "We don't need a butcher knife. Now, just calm down; nobody's going to hurt us."

"But . . . but, there's a man in the bathroom. We got to protect ourselves till we can get help."

"Oh, for goodness' sake, Lurline. It's just ole Skip. Remember? You used to love him to death and he just showed up right before you got here. Skip!" I called. "Come on out here and let Lurline see you."

He came sidling out, his head cocked down and grinning like a little boy caught doing something he shouldn't've been doing. Not an unusual situation for him. She took one look at him, jerked her uniform down in front, and threw her arms around him. "Skip! Oh, honey, where've you been, you bad boy? Oh, God, it's so good to see you. Let me look at you, honey. My goodness, but you look fine, all filled out and handsome as ever."

"Hey, Lurline," Skip said, beaming down at her.

She hugged him again. "Etta Mae, why didn't you tell me my favorite boy was back in town?"

"He didn't want anybody to know it," I said, leaning against the counter, disgusted with the welcome she was giving him. I didn't want Skip to be getting encouragement to stick around any longer than he had to.

She slapped him playfully on the chest and said, "You ole mean thing, you didn't want me to know? Why, Skip Taggert, I was always your biggest fan and your best buddy, and you know it."

That was a jab at me, because she'd never thought I'd treated him right. Lurline had had a soft spot for Skip ever since he was a tiny boy—he was a cousin or distant nephew, step- or half-something or another. She'd mothered and petted him all through school and our marriage, slipping him money, bailing him out of jail, and taking his side in spite of all evidence to the contrary. She'd been on cloud nine when I married Skip, figuring she'd arranged it all with a bit of help from heaven. Then she'd hardly spoken to me for a year after I kicked him out, giving in long enough, though, to tell me I was selfish and hateful for doing it. It was only after I'd given up on Bernie that she'd seen hope for me again. That's when she'd paid for my CNA course so I could help her with her business.

"I sure have missed you, Lurline," Skip said as he put an arm around her shoulders.

She stroked his chest, adoring him with her smile. "I knew you'd be back," she said, like he hadn't left with a string of creditors after him. "Now, you and Etta Mae kiss and make up, you hear? That's what I've been wanting."

"Me, too, Lurline," Skip said, like a little boy looking to his mother to make things right. "That's what I want, too."

Yeah, I thought as I watched her pet and croon over him with him loving every minute of it, *and people in hell want ice water, too.*

I reached over and jerked the back of her skirttail out of her girdle.

Chapter 7

"Okay, Skip," I said, pushing away from the counter. "Let's get on with it. What's your big news?"

"Well, I . . . ah, it's . . . ah." He glanced at me over Lurline's head. Then his eyes flicked up at the ceiling, searching for something to say. Then he brightened with a new thought. "I bought me a motorcycle!"

"Oh, honey," Lurline cooed. "That's wonderful. I hope you got a Harley."

"Yeah, a Low Rider. Used, but I got it runnin' pretty good."

Then Skip began to wink and blink at me like he was having a spell of the St. Vitus' dance. I shrugged. I didn't care whether he told Lurline his big news or not. It was his secret, and frankly I'd just as soon he kept it.

Actually, though, Skip was showing some sense for a change. After my recent experience with Lurline and secrets, I didn't trust her, either.

All of this went on over Lurline's head, in more ways than one.

"Now, Etta Mae," Lurline said, "do you have a place for this boy to sleep tonight?" She cut her eyes at me, her mouth curved in a knowing smirk.

"No, I do not. He'll have to fend for himself, because I don't take in boarders, company, guests, or ex-husbands."

"Oh, you bad girl, you. You can't just turn him out after his long trip. Where'd you come from, Skip?"

"Gastonia," he said. "And I am pretty tired."

I rolled my eyes. Gastonia, a two-hour trip. "Sorry," I said. "There's no room in this inn. Take him home with you, Lurline, if you're worried about him. You have more room than I do."

"Oh, I will. Come on with me, Skip, I'll take care of you."

"Well, dang, Lurline," he said. "Me and Etta Mae, we got lots to talk about."

"Tomorrow," I said, putting as much starch in the word as I could. "I'm tired. I worked all day, unlike some, and it's past my bedtime. I'm not about to stay up talking all night."

"It's settled then," Lurline said. She got her purse from beside the recliner. "We'll go to my house and let this party pooper get her beauty rest."

Skip looked from one to the other of us, clearly befuddled by the decision being made for him. Not an unusual case, by any means.

"Etta Mae . . ." he began, wanting me to let him stay.

"Tomorrow," I said again, unlocking the door and holding it open. "I'll see you when I get off work. You just stay at Lurline's until I call you."

I hoped he got the message I was sending: if you're scared, lay low, Lurline's place is as safe as here. But you never know what Skip gets.

I locked the door behind them. Then I went into the kitchen and put half a pizza, left over from the day before, into the oven. By that time I wasn't really hungry, but you have to keep your strength up. Especially if you have things to do. Which I did.

While it heated, I changed into jeans and a cropped tank top. I pulled on my boots, cowboy style that I just loved, and brushed my hair.

I ate standing at the counter, washing down the pizza with a glass of milk. Not the best taste combination, but I'm real careful about my nutrition. I grew up about half malnourished, so I take a vitamin every day even if they do cost an arm and a leg.

When I finished, I buckled a fanny pack around my waist, so I'd have my hands free. Cramming my driver's license, a twenty, and a tube of lip gloss into it, I turned off the lights, locked the door, and left.

The night air was still and muggy, even though it was September—the hottest and driest one on record—and late enough for the temperature to've dropped a few degrees, which it hadn't done. The car was stifling, but I rolled down the windows and started out, hoping to stir up a breeze.

There wasn't much traffic on the highway, and not much more in Delmont. The Porky Park Drive-Thru and the Dairy Queen were doing a good business, and the blocks around the Skyway movie theater were filled with parked cars. I drove slowly around the town square, not wanting to attract any police attention, especially Bobby Lee's, then turned onto Old Oak Avenue. Three blocks from Main Street, and the fine old houses of Delmont's rich families began to show up. Well, not exactly show up, because the larger the house the farther back from the street it was and the more trees blocked it from view. There were no cars parked at the curb, because these people had wide driveways and parking courts and garages. When you pulled into one of the long drives, drove under magnolia and maple trees, and around hemlock hedges, it was like closing off the rest of the world.

When I got to Mr. Howard's house, I slowed with one eye on the rearview mirror and the other trying to peer through the trees and shrubbery. There were a couple of lights on downstairs, but none outside, so I couldn't tell if Junior's car was still there or not. At the end of the street, I turned around and drove past again. From that angle, I saw lights on over the garage, which was what I was hoping for.

I picked up speed and drove back to the square, parking so that it would look like I was at the movie. Not that anyone would care where I was, but Bobby Lee knew my car and I didn't want him poking around in my business.

I walked quickly across the square and down Old Oak, keeping in the shadows as much as I could. When I got to Mr. Howard's house, I was grateful for the first Mrs. Connard, Senior's interest in gardening. It was easy enough to glide from one huge azalea bush to another, right up to the stairs on the far side of the garage.

I tiptoed up the stairs and tapped on the door. The low mumble of the television immediately went off, and so did the lights. I tapped again.

"Emmett," I whispered as loud as I dared. "It's me, Etta Mae Wiggins. I need to talk to you."

"What you doin' here? I don't need no trouble." He must have been standing right next to the door.

"Me either," I said. "But I'm worried about Mr. Howard. Please, open the door. I'll only stay a minute."

Nothing but silence while Emmett considered where his bread was best buttered. Not that I blamed him. We all do that when we have choices to make.

Then he unlocked the door and opened it halfway. His white shirt gleamed in the dark, but that was all of him I could make out.

"Miss Etta, I can't ax you in," he said. "You know that wouldn't be right."

"I know, Emmett, and I didn't come to visit or to get you in trouble. I just need to know what's going on. How's Mr. Howard?"

"Mr. Howard, he so mad he 'bout to blow up. He done cussed Mr. Junior up one side and down the other. 'Course, Mr. Junior don't know it 'cause he can't understand him. But I sure can, an' I ain't never heard such talk. Why, Miss Etta, he even tried to fight Mr. Junior. Give him a hard swat one time with his good arm."

"Oh, me," I said, agitated now that I couldn't go in and calm Mr. Howard down. "Emmett, that could lead to another stroke. What's Junior doing to make him so mad?"

"Tole him he wadn't bein' taken care of here an' he was takin' him to Raleigh soon as he could make 'rangements. Tole him peoples're taking advantage of him here, that peoples was stealin' from him. Miss Etta, you know I ain't never stole nothin' from nobody, specially from Mr. Howard."

"Well, that just makes me mad as fire. Of course you haven't stolen anything. He's just telling Mr. Howard that to turn him against you so he can get Mr. Howard away from me."

"It ain't right, Miss Etta," Emmett said, and I could hear the hurt in his voice. "It ain't right what he's doin' to Mr. Howard, and it ain't right to put the blame on me."

"I know it, but it's really me he's aiming at. Look, Emmett, we've got to do something."

"Ain't nothin' we can do," he said, with that hopeless tone that had come too many times from me. That was back before I decided to make some things go my way for a change. "Mr. Junior," Emmett went on, "he done tole me to pack up what Mr. Howard gonna need, an' then pack up myself an' be outta here day after tomorrow. Miss Etta, he firin' me an' ain't nothin' been said 'bout no pension what Mr. Howard been promisin' me when I retired. I don't know what I'm gonna do. I been livin' here come close to twenty year, an' countin' on that pension to take care of me when Mr. Howard pass on."

He was scared and I could see why. You work all your life for somebody, depend on their promises, and, right when you're too old to start over again, find out that the promises weren't worth the breath it took to make them.

Emmett was probably twice my age, but I already knew what it was like to be afraid of what was coming. Or not coming, as the case might be. My own middle age was getting too close for comfort, especially with no savings, no pension, and no prospects, except for Mr. Howard.

So right then I decided to make it worth Emmett's while to help us both out.

Well, and help Mr. Howard out, too.

Chapter 8

The back door of the house slammed and we both jumped a mile. Footsteps crunched on the gravel heading toward the garage.

"Oh, Lord, that's Junior," I whispered, frantic at the thought of being caught and put in jail for trespassing. Which Junior was just mean enough to do. "Let me in, Emmett. Please, if he catches me here, we're both in trouble."

Emmett hesitated a second, then opened the door wide enough for me to slip into the dark room. He closed the door softly, and we both stood trembling, listening to the footsteps coming closer and closer. I could hear Emmett's breath catch like mine was doing as we waited to hear Junior climb the stairs.

Instead, the footsteps stopped at the bottom of the stairs, and we heard Junior call, "Emmett, you awake? Emmett?"

I think Emmett stopped breathing then, and my heart skipped a beat as we stood beside each other in the dark, scared out of our wits.

"Emmett?" Junior called again. Then after a long minute or two, his footsteps scratched on the gravel again as he walked away.

We stayed still and quiet as we listened, both of us afraid to move. Then we heard a car door open and close, and the sound of a rich GM motor start up. We didn't move until the car turned around and moved down the driveway.

"You got to go, Miss Etta," Emmett whispered. "I can't take no more chances like that."

"Me either," I whispered back. "But where's he going this time of night, and why's he leaving Mr. Howard by himself?"

"No tellin' where he goin'," Emmett said. "Maybe to the Porky Park. That man like to eat, but never what I got in the kitchen for Mr. Howard's diet. I 'spect he callin' me to listen out for his daddy while he gone."

"Well, I'm getting out of here while the getting's good," I said, opening the door and listening to be sure no one was lingering at the foot of the stairs.

"Wait a minute," I said, turning back to Emmett. "Why don't you go with me, and let me sneak in to speak to Mr. Howard?"

"*Uh-uh,*" Emmett said, shaking his head. "Don' ax me to do such a thing, Miss Etta. He might come back an' catch us in there. Uh-uh, I can't do that. No, ma'am."

"I won't stay but a minute," I pleaded. "I just want to be sure Mr. Howard's all right."

"No'm, I can't go 'gainst Mr. Junior. No'm, I can't."

I knew there was no budging him, so I asked him to try to find out exactly where Junior planned to take Mr. Howard and let me know. Then I thanked him and tiptoed down the stairs.

Knowing now how loud footsteps were on the gravel and knowing also that Emmett would be listening, I hurried across the parking area, taking little care to be quiet. Then, halfway down the drive, I slipped between the azalea bushes that lined the edge of the grass of the front yard.

I squatted down beside a large tree and waited until I thought Emmett would be sure I was gone. Then, moving as quietly as I could, I crossed the yard in front of the house, where I would be out of Emmett's line of sight and hearing. My worst fear was that Junior would come driving in and I'd be caught in the headlights with my eyes shining like a possum cringing on the center line, but I didn't let it stop me. Crawling behind the boxwoods next to the house, I edged around the far corner where I was reasonably safe from Junior's headlights and Emmett's sharp eyes.

I eased up to Mr. Howard's window and poked at the screen. Just as I'd hoped, the window was wide open. Mr. Howard didn't like air-conditioning, since he suffered from the cold even on the hottest day of the hottest fall we'd ever had. He lived in flannel pajamas with a blanket wrapped around him most of the time.

I scratched at the screen of the window closest to the head of his bed. "Mr. Howard," I called softly. "Mr. Howard, it's me, Etta Mae."

I heard the rustle of bedclothes, and I called softly again, not wanting to scare him. "Mr. Howard, how you doing, honey?"

"Wha' . . . ?"

"It's Etta Mae, I just came by to see if you're all right."

I heard him groan and strain to sit up in bed, so I said, "Don't try to get up. Just lie still, 'cause I've got to go in a minute."

"Uh-uh, 'Unior," he croaked.

"Junior's gone out for a while, so I can't stay long. I just want you to know that me and Emmett, uh, I and Emmett, are trying to look after you. I don't want you going and getting upset, re-gardless of what Junior does. We'll find you, and I'll do my best to fix things like you want them."

"Ehra Mae, he . . . He'p me."

Lord, it nearly broke my heart to hear that fierce old man beg for help. "I'm going to. Don't you worry now, you just take care of yourself, and don't forget me."

He reached with his good right hand and pressed it against the screen. I put my hand over his thin, cold one, trying to warm both it and his old heart.

"Not 'orget, Ehra Mae. Ge' me 'way from here."

"I'm going to," I told him. "I'm going to do everything I can. I just want you to take care of yourself and give me time to see what I can do. I've got to go now, you ole sweet thing, before Junior gets back. If you need me, tell Emmett and he'll call me. I'm going now. You get some sleep, and dream about me."

I slipped down below the window, hearing him still calling my name. Oh, I hated to leave him, but I knew it wouldn't do anybody any good if Junior caught me.

I hurried across the yard and out onto the sidewalk, still fearing Junior's headlights. It was a relief to get to my car and just sit for a while to let my heart slow its pounding.

I opened the glove compartment and felt around till I found a Snickers bar. I sat there eating it, trying to figure out what I could do to outwit Junior. Or what anybody could do. As it was, he held all the cards, being the next of kin, and everybody assuming Mr. Howard had stroked out his mind, as well as his left side.

I took a big bite of candy and chewed it for a long time, wondering just how old it was. The thing that bothered me the most was why I hadn't gone ahead and married Mr. Howard when I had the chance. I could've brought in the Reverend Haliday from the Universal Harvest Church, which is where I went. He would've done it in a minute, but I'd held out for something better. Mr. Howard kept pleading for us just to go to the magistrate's office, where it could've been done before anybody knew of it. But I'd wanted it done right, so nobody could say I'd taken advantage. I'd wanted the preacher from Delmont's First Methodist, Mr. Howard's church. And I'd wanted his lawyer as a witness, which would've meant putting his stamp of approval on the match. Besides that, though, I'd wanted a real church wedding for a change, with newspaper announcements, a wedding portrait, and bridesmaids all in velvet walking down the aisle holding white floral sprays with gold glitter on them.

I hadn't wanted anything under the cover or suspicious in any way. The whole point, well, almost the whole point, of marrying Mr. Howard was to get up in the world. So I'd waited, hoping Mr. Howard's steady improvement would get him to the point of making the arrangements himself, which no one in the world would've questioned.

Well, I'd tried to do everything right, and look where it had gotten me. Out in the cold, is where.

I saw a cop car turn the corner heading down the street where I was parked. It probably wasn't Bobby Lee, but I didn't want any of the cops seeing me and telling him I'd been sitting by myself in a car at midnight. So I lay down on the seat, crumpling the candy wrapper under my shoulder. In that uncomfortable position, I had my first clear thought of the evening. I knew what had to be done.

The only reason I wasn't already Mrs. Howard Connard, Senior, was because I'd wanted the knot tied tight and right—holding out for a big church do with engraved invitations and wedding gifts and light blue tuxedos with ruffled shirts. And a honeymoon at Disney World.

But you don't have to have all the trimmings to make a marriage legal. Who'd know that better than me? So what I needed to do was forget about bridesmaids and floral sprays, and just go ahead and get the job done before Junior knew what'd hit him.

Chapter 9

The trailer park was quiet when I pulled the car into my slot, at least as quiet as it ever got. There were supposed to be pole lights that came on at dark along the central street, but most of them were out. A few lights were on in several of the mobile homes I'd passed on the way to mine, which was in one of the darker spots.

I made up my mind to call old lady Springer again—she owned half the county and had plenty of money for lightbulbs—the next morning and complain about the streetlights. I knew she didn't like me, hadn't had any use for me ever since that time I took care of Mr. Sam Murdoch when he broke his leg. I couldn't help it if men liked looking at me. It could be a burden sometimes, which I've had to learn to live with. And I didn't help matters by always calling and complaining to Mrs. Springer about the slack way she ran the trailer court. But, dang it, when you own something and rent it to people, you ought to keep up the maintenance. If it wasn't trash all over the place and hookups that wouldn't work, it was rowdy parties and loud neighbors. I sighed, thinking it was probably that way everywhere.

I parked by my trailer and sat in the car awhile, still strung out over leaving Mr. Howard. If Junior was planning to take him to Raleigh the day after tomorrow, I didn't have much time. But time for what, and in what order? There were a dozen different things to do, now that I'd made up my mind to do them, not the least of which was to clue Mr. Howard in to the change of plans. Then there was Skip with one of his get-rich-quick schemes, which I could surely do without at this point in time. And Lurline sticking her nose in where it didn't belong. I'd call her first thing in the morning, tell her I was sick and couldn't work. That would give me all day, and, one way or the other, I was going to have my way this time. In spite of Skip or Lurline or Junior. Especially Junior.

I heaved another sigh, tired to my bones after all I'd been through during the day. I got out of the car and walked to my front door, fussing to myself about another light being out. I always left the outside light on over my door even when I was home, but it'd blown out again.

I fumbled to get the key in the door, cussing softly under my breath because it was so blamed dark. As I tried to fit in the key, the door shifted and swung open an inch or two.

Lord, it scared me. I'd locked the door. I *always* lock my door. I know what kind of people live in a trailer park. Then it came to me. Skip Taggert, blame his hide. He was bound and determined to tell me his big secret tonight, and he wouldn't think a thing about breaking in to do it.

I was so mad I swung the door open, reached in, flipped on the living room light, and liked to died right that minute. There he was, lying on my couch sound asleep and snoring like a Poulan.

I headed toward him, furious enough to bash him good, and stopped dead in my tracks. The room was teetotally trashed. I couldn't believe it. The kitchen cabinets were hanging open, and all my plates, glasses, pots, and pans were on the floor. My canned goods were all over the place, my recliner and lamp table overturned, and the blamed refrigerator had been cleared out with the door left open. Using electricity I'd have to pay for.

I was mad enough to chew nails. That blasted Skip had wrecked my house, and there he lay drunk as a coot, stretched out on the couch with his face buried in a cushion.

"Skip, dad blame it!" I yelled, grabbing him by the shoulder. "Get your sorry self up and clean up this mess. You think you can just come in here and trash my trailer! Get yourself up from there!" I gave him a good, hard shake, holding myself back from giving him a swat over the head.

"Skip! Wake up, damn it, or you're gonna wake up in jail!" I pulled at him, straining to turn him over. God, he was heavy, crammed into the couch the way he was. And his shoes! He was lying on my couch with his shoes on! I took hold of his arm and shoulder with both hands, got some leverage with my foot, and jerked him over on his back.

I was so shocked, I turned loose and flopped hard to the floor on my bottom. I just sat there, staring at him. It wasn't Skip. Jesus Lord, it was Junior Connard. Junior Connard, with the whites of his eyes shining through half-closed lids. Junior Con-nard, with a bloody mess on the side of his head. That had bled all over my new floral-patterned living room couch.

I drew my knees up and put my head on them, trembling all over. What was he doing in my house? What was he doing, lying there bleeding on my couch? Who'd done this?

"Oh, God!" I said, what if he was dead? I jumped up and put my hand on his chest to see if he was breathing. My own breath was coming so hard and fast, and I was shaking so bad, I couldn't tell what he was doing.

They crowded into my trailer—deputies, EMS techs, and Jennie from next door. All I could do was sit in a corner and try to stop trembling at the thought of Mr. Howard's son being half or all the way killed in my trailer. It was not the preferred way to start a marriage.

The flash of blue lights from cop cars parked outside swirled through the window. People came and went through the open door, cutting their eyes at me as they passed. Finally, they got Junior out the door by strapping him to a stretcher and turning it sideways. I watched it all, my hands tucked between my knees, trying to get a grip.

"What happened here, Etta Mae?"

I looked up at Clyde Maybry in his dark blue uniform, standing over me with his fat face all stiff and closed off. Clyde had been a deputy for some twenty years, which was about twenty years too long.

"What?" My shoulders were shaking so bad I could hardly talk. Posttraumatic stress syndrome, I guessed, recalling my nursing handbook of common ailments.

"What happened here?"

"I don't know. I came home and . . . is he dead?"

"That ain't for you to worry about right now. I need for you to tell me how this happened."

"I don't know. I swear, I don't know. I just found him. Just found him, lying there."

"Now, Etta Mae, we all know how a little argument can get outta hand. Just make it easy on yourself and tell me what happened."

"You think . . . ? *I* didn't do this! Why, Clyde, I wasn't even here! I found him! I'm the one who called you!"

"You was somewhere else? With somebody who can back you up?"

"Well," I said, my brain running all over the place. Emmett could back me up, but would he? Mr. Howard could back me up, but could he? And I'd been so careful not to let anybody else see me.

"Maybe you better come on down to the station with me," Clyde said, touching my shoulder. "Come on now. Let's don't have no fussin' and fightin' about it."

"Fussin' and fightin'! Clyde Maybry, I'm just as upset about this as you are, and I want to know who did this as bad as you do, but you don't have to treat me like I'm gonna go crazy on you!"

"Well, but, Etta Mae, everybody knows you got a temper, and I expect that's what happened here. Come on now." He took my arm and pulled me to my feet. "We'll talk about this at the station where it's all nice and calm."

I let him lead me out to his cruiser, aware of my neighbors watching from the sidelines. If I hadn't been so scared, I'd've been embarrassed to death. Clyde pushed my head down, squashing my hair flat, as I climbed into the backseat.

There was no arguing with him. I did have a temper, and everybody knew what I'd done to Bobby Lee the time he danced twice in one night with Darla Davis out at the County Line Two-Step Tavern. And I mean on the same night he'd been in my bed all afternoon.

And, to make it worse, he'd been out there dancing with her to Garth Brooks singing "To Make You Love Me," and I'd thought that was *our* song.

I still wasn't sorry about the new windshield he'd had to put on his truck.

But that was all long gone and past. Right now, I was in the sweaty hands of Clyde Maybry, who'd love to lock me up and throw away the key. I scrunched down in the corner of the backseat, thinking about what Junior Connard could do to me, so scared now that I could hardly get my breath. I knew what happened to anybody who had run-ins with rich people in our neck of the woods.

But by the time we were halfway to the station, which was on a side street in downtown Delmont, I'd about gotten over being scared. Clyde didn't have a thing on me, and I'd be damned if he was going to treat me like a suspect or a perpetrator or whatever else he could think of.

"Clyde!" I yelled over the calls from his police band radio and the country music blaring from his car radio. I banged against the wire partition between us. "Clyde! Let me out of this cop car cage! I'm not under arrest and you don't have a right to put me back here. I ought to be riding up front with you, and besides it smells to high heaven back here."

"Can't do it, Etta Mae," he said, turning his head slightly toward me, his eyes still on the road. "Can't have a woman in the front seat. Too many opportunities for inappropriate behavior."

"On whose part, you big ox?" I was practically screaming at him. Clyde Maybry had hit on me one too many times with no success, and now he was getting back at me.

I flopped back against the seat and folded my arms, temporarily resigned to being treated like a criminal.

Then I popped back up again. "Well, tell me this. Is he dead?"

"No, he ain't dead. Just pret' near it. Man, Etta Mae, when you do a job, you evermore do it. Now, why don't you calm yourself down and get your story straight. I ain't supposed to tell you what to say, but I expect one thing just led to another and before you knew it he got conked on the head. That about the way it was?"

"No, and nowhere near it. What do you want me to do, Clyde, tell you how I tore up my trailer, too?"

"Well, I expect Junior had a part in that. Maybe that's what made you so mad. Now, you just tell it thataway, and we'll have this all wrapped up by morning."

"I'm not telling it any way except the way it was. Which is to say, I don't know anything about it. I wasn't there. You hear me, Clyde." I rattled the cage again. "I wasn't there!"

"Get a grip, Etta Mae. We're here." He turned off the radio

and nosed the car to the curb in front of the one-story brick sheriff's satellite office. The main one was in Abbotsville.

Clyde got out and unlocked my door, reached in, and helped me out, never turning loose of my arm. He marched me up the steps to the door and inside the station. The desk sergeant stared at me. A deputy named Wendell Something-or-Other held a cup of coffee halfway to his mouth as he stared at me. A teenager and his mother sitting on a bench stared at me, too.

My mouth got tight and my eyes turned into slits. Somebody was going to pay for the shame that had fallen on my head.

"Clyde, I'm going to say this in front of God and all these people, so hear me good. *I. Want. A. Lawyer.*"

He shrugged his fat-layered shoulders and said, "Okay, but I wouldn't think you'd need one. *If* what you told me is the truth."

"Well, *if* you believed what I told you, I wouldn't. So I'm not saying another word till my lawyer gets here." I planted my feet and glared at him. I knew my rights because I watched all the cop shows on television. And besides, Bobby Lee had once told me that all officers just hated it when suspects held out for a lawyer. I was in no mood to make Clyde Maybry happy.

"Okay, there's the phone," Clyde said, pointing at the desk. "Go call your lawyer."

That stopped me, because I hadn't thought that far ahead. I didn't have a lawyer, so who could I call? My first thought was to call Bobby Lee, but that wouldn't work. Bobby Lee would see that I was treated right, but he was a by-the-book deputy when it got down to the nitty-gritty. He'd hate like anything to put me in jail, but if he thought I was guilty he wouldn't cut me any slack at all.

"I need a phone book," I said, walking over to the desk and stalling for time. All I could think to do was look in the Yellow

Pages and hope a name would jump out at me. When the desk sergeant slid the book in front of me and I flipped to the Attorneys section, a name jumped.

As I ran my finger down the listings, my heart started pounding with the chance I was about to take. Mr. Ernest Sitton, Esquire, was Mr. Howard's lawyer and close friend. If I could get him to represent me in this mess, maybe he couldn't represent Junior against me and Mr. Howard, if Junior tried to put some legal blocks in our way down the aisle. Assuming, of course, that Junior came through healthy enough to need representing. But I was looking way ahead. If I played my cards right and got Lawyer Sitton tied up and on my side, maybe he'd stay there, if and when Junior got back to his mean self again.

Because even though Junior Connard had messed up mine and Mr. Howard's plans, I sure didn't want him to die. I still had pictures in my mind of a big, happy family with me and Mr. Howard having Junior and his wife for Christmas, and singing "Up on the House Top" together, with a big Christmas tree in the front window with blinking lights. Maybe all blue lights on a shiny aluminum tree. With snow coming down outside, and a fire blazing away in the fireplace, with Emmett in the kitchen cooking turkey and dressing, and everybody warm and happy like in a *Hallmark Hall of Fame Christmas Special*.

It could be that way, no reason why not, if Junior could just see his way to having me in the family.

"You gonna make that call?" Clyde picked up the receiver and handed it to me.

"Thank you very much." I snatched it from him and turned my back. "Now, if you'd just give me some privacy."

With trembling fingers, I dialed Mr. Ernest Sitton's home number, realizing that it was past midnight and he might get mad about being called so late and not even listen to me. Realizing, too, that if he turned me down, I'd probably spend the night in a cell, and maybe more than one. And realizing also that I was putting all my eggs in this one basket.

I couldn't believe it! Mr. Sitton was coming down to the station and sitting with me while Clyde asked his questions. And I didn't even have to mention Mr. Howard and our ongoing, but threatened, relationship. Which I wouldn't have done anyway, not wanting to have someone of Mr. Sitton's caliber lined up against me.

Still, I could hardly believe it. I'd just told him that I was being questioned about something I didn't know anything about, and he asked if I had two hundred dollars. When I said yes, with thanksgiving in my heart that his fee wouldn't be any more than that, he'd said, "I'll be there in twenty minutes. Meanwhile, keep your mouth shut."

Clyde put me in the interrogation room, which badly needed some helpful hints on decorating. There was a scarred wooden table, four metal chairs, one of them bent so bad it sat lopsided, and nothing else. A window faced the hall, but it was covered with blinds, so I couldn't see what was going on in the station.

After walking around and around that pitiful-looking table for ten minutes or so, I was ready to jump out of my skin. I'm the nervous type when I don't know what's going on.

Then the door opened and Wendell stuck his head in.

"Thought you might want some coffee," he said, holding out a Styrofoam cup. "Didn't know what you take, so I fixed it with cream and sugar."

"Thanks." I walked over and leaned against the door beside him, standing hip-shot to rest up from all the pacing I'd been doing. I took the cup, tilted my head, and gave him a mournful smile. It was all I could manage. "This is awful nice of you, Wendell. I sure won't forget it." I sipped at the hot, super-sweet stuff and looked up at him, wondering how he could help me. "This is just the worst night of my life, being dragged in here when I haven't done a thing. You don't know what it means to have someone as nice as you around."

He flushed red and said, "Well, ah, you know, not everybody that's brought in here has done anything wrong. So don't you worry. I'll, I mean, we'll look after you. I mean, well, Bobby Lee, he's my training officer, and I figure, well, you know."

"I do know, and he'll appreciate it, just like I do. Now, Wendell, I don't want to ask you to do anything illegal or anything like that, but if my lawyer can't get me out tonight, could you see your way to letting Bobby Lee know I'm here? He'll find out tomorrow anyway, when he comes on duty, but I thought maybe he'd like to know tonight."

"Why, sure, I could do that. I'll call him right now. Well, as soon as Clyde goes to the bathroom again. He's about ready to come out now, but he'll go again in a little while." His face turned even darker at the thought, I guess, of Clyde in the toilet. It wasn't a picture to thrill me, either.

"Whatever, but let's wait and see what my lawyer can do first. If he clears me, as he ought to do since I haven't done anything, then there's no need to bother Bobby Lee. But just knowing that you're out there, ready to help me out, makes hope spring eternal in my breast."

I smiled at him, sort of sad-like. "You like poetry, Wendell?"

"No'm, I mean, well, when you say it, it sounds real nice. I guess I better be going, Clyde'll be flushing any minute. Don't you worry now, me and Bobby Lee'll look after you."

"I feel so much better, knowing you're on my side." I smiled a real sad smile, looking up into his face. "You go on now, I don't want you to get in any trouble."

When he left, I sat at the table with the coffee and tried to drink it, not wanting to hurt Wendell's feelings. That's almost the worst thing you can do to a man. I won't mention the very worst. Drinking bad coffee was little enough to ask. I needed all the friends I could get.

Chapter 10

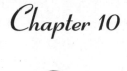

Hearing a commotion out in the hall, I stood up and faced the door. I'd never met Lawyer Sitton face-to-face, but I'd seen him around town, so when he flung open the door, I knew who he was. The way he banged into the room, slapping his briefcase on the table, with Clyde, Wendell, and the desk sergeant trailing behind him, showed me that he was a take-charge kind of person. And I was glad to have him take it.

Up close, he was a smaller man than I'd thought he was. Except for his midsection, which could've used some daily workouts. His gray hair was combed in strands over his nearly bald head, but he was as neat and well put together a paunchy, bald man as I'd ever seen. Everybody in Delmont admired and respected him because he could get anybody off on any charge. That was his reputation, and you didn't want to be up against him. I'd heard of people just dropping a lawsuit when they found out that Lawyer Sitton was on the other side. But here he was in the flesh, hardly as tall as Emmett, but with a lot less hair and a whole lot pinker. He had one of those fair complexions that couldn't take the sun. Washed-out-looking, if you know what I mean. To look at him, you'd never guess how big he was around town.

"Close that door, deputy," he said, as Clyde followed him in. "On your way out. Now, young lady, I have one question for you."

"Nossir," I answered. I looked straight over the glasses on his nose into his faded blue eyes, putting all the truth I had in my words. "I did not do it."

"That wasn't my question." He turned his briefcase toward him, jerked his vest straight—my Lord, a three-piece suit in the middle of the night—and posed his hands over the two clasps of his briefcase. But he didn't open them.

"My question is," he said, looking at me for the first time. "Do you have the two hundred dollars?"

"Oh. Nossir, not on me, I don't. But I've got twenty." I started digging in my fanny pack, pulling out the bill. "Will you take this as a down payment?"

"And the other one hundred and eighty?" He straightened up and moved one hand away from the briefcase.

"I've got it, I promise. It's in the bank and I'll get it first thing in the morning. I mean, if you can get me out of here, I will. Mr. Sitton, I promise you, I'm not a charity case. I own my own home and my car, and I have a job. I can pay you and I will."

"I'll trust you, then, but you don't know how many suspects have forgotten their debts once they're cleared." He took the twenty, folded it carefully, and put it in a money clip. When he slid the clip back into his pocket, he said, "I don't expect you to be one of them."

I'll tell you this, when he stared at me over those gold-framed glasses, I couldn't imagine being one of them.

"Now," he said, finally unsnapping the black leather briefcase. "Let's have it, then I'll call in that deputy who's so anxious to get in here."

So I did, but putting just a little spin on my story. I said that I *thought* the man on my couch was Junior Connard, but since I didn't really know him, I hadn't been sure.

"See," I said, hunching over the table, "I never ran with Junior's crowd, they were a little older than me and, you know, they didn't have to work after school, so I just know him from a distance. It could've been anybody of that build. Like I told you, I thought it was Skip Taggert at first."

"Your ex."

"Yessir, one of them."

"Could he have done it? Jealous ex-husband?"

"Oh, no. Skip's over at Lurline's. And he doesn't have anything to be jealous about. I hadn't seen him for years before yesterday evening."

"Hm-m-m. Seems like a lot of things happened to you yesterday evening."

"Yessir, you could say that."

"Come by my office right after the bank opens," Lawyer Sitton said, as we stood on the sidewalk in front of the station. It was almost four o'clock in the morning by my watch with the sweep second hand that I used to take pulses with.

"I will, yessir. You can count on it."

"I know I can," he said, turning toward his Lincoln Continental parked in the sheriff's reserved slot.

Clyde had done his questioning with Lawyer Sitton sitting right there listening to every word. When Clyde couldn't think of anything else to ask and still hadn't pinned anything on me, Mr. Sitton announced that I'd done my citizen's duty. It was time for the Delmont sheriff's office to release and thank me for my cooperation in investigating a crime against both a leading citizen and a solid citizen. It took me a minute to figure out that Junior Connard was the leading citizen, even though he lived in Raleigh, and I was the solid citizen, since I paid my bills. At least I was going to, come nine-fifteen in the A.M.

"You brought Ms. Wiggins down here, deputy," Mr. Sitton said as we'd left the interrogation room. "See that she gets home."

Now I waited in the cool early morning for Clyde to escort me home. He hadn't been too happy with the way his questioning had gone, being sure that I was lying. Of course I was, but not about Junior Connard and my trashed trailer. My story hadn't been the best, since I didn't have enough time to concoct a good one. I'd needed an alibi as to where I was while Junior was getting bashed on the head, and I couldn't use the real one until I'd had a chance to be sure Lawyer Sitton would stay on my side. For all I knew, he would've gotten up and walked out if I'd said I'd been in the bushes loving up Mr. Howard. Even if it was with a window screen between us.

So I'd said that I'd been with a certain person I couldn't name, and let them both think it was a married man. As I stood there waiting for Clyde, I felt tired and dirty as I thought how neither of them had found the lie hard to believe.

"Get in the car," Clyde said as he came out of the station and headed for his cruiser. "I ain't got all night."

I opened the front passenger door and got in, daring him to put me in the back.

He burned a little rubber as we left the station to let me know how he felt, but neither of us said a word. It was total silence until he pulled up in front of my trailer.

"Watch yourself, Etta Mae," he said as I opened the door.

I turned in the seat and looked at him. "Clyde," I said sweetly, "there's something I'd like to tell you to do, but I'm too much of a lady to say it. I expect you can figure it out yourself." And I slid out of the car and slammed the door.

I could've cried when I got in my trailer and turned on the lights. Things had been straightened up in the living room, but not the way I'd had them. I knew it'd been Jennie, bless her heart, who'd swept up the mess in the kitchen. But as I opened the cabinets, nothing was in the right place and not everything was there. Only one plate, three coffee mugs, and a jelly glass. Everything else had been broken. She'd put the furniture right side up, but my broken lamp was in the trash. When I walked back to the bedroom, I had to hang on to the door. My underclothes, T-shirts, and night things—everything from the dresser—were strewn all over the floor and the bed. Just thrown everywhere. And handled! Somebody's dirty hands had been all over my most intimate apparel. It made me sick. No way could I bring myself to just pick up and put them back in a drawer. I'd have to spray and wash every living thing in the place. I began to gather them in a pile, bringing panties out from under the bed and snatching a camisole off the lamp shade. I found my green mist Dream Angels bra, a sensual floral with exquisite scalloped edging from Victoria's Secret, over in the corner, still holding its shape as advertised. I snatched it up and saw greasy fingerprints inside the cups. It made my skin crawl.

I thought of turning it in to Clyde so he could run the prints and identify whoever'd fingered it, but thought better of it when I pictured Clyde handling it. Better to let the bastards, whoever they'd been, get away with it than have to put up with that.

Then, with another sudden bad thought, I started looking through the pile I'd made, slinging lingerie items every whichaway. I couldn't find them! My matching green mist lace bikini panties were gone! Stuffed in somebody's greasy pocket, I bet. Oh, God, think of somebody pulling it out for a few private moments he couldn't get any other way. I shivered at the thought.

After that, with fear of what I'd find, I looked over my Barbie dolls, picking them up and smoothing their outfits. The Skating Barbie had lost one of her skate blades, and, even worse, the Working-Out Barbie's limbs had popped loose. I could've cried.

One good thing, though, I'd never been able to get the Butterfly Art Barbie with the tattoo on her midriff before it was discontinued. It would've killed me to've lost that investment if she'd been manhandled like the others.

"Oh, no!" I stooped down and picked up the most valuable one with trembling hands. My NASCAR Barbie, number one in the series that celebrated the fiftieth anniversary of NASCAR racing that Junior Johnson had given me, had been slung or thrown against the dresser. I smoothed her blue driving suit and straightened her head, then got on my knees to look for her authentic racing helmet with the working visor. When I found it next to the closet, the visor was no longer working. A lost, lonely feeling swept over me, and I wanted to cry my eyes out at the unfairness that met me at every turn.

Instead, I stripped the bed and put on clean sheets, trying to occupy my mind with the practicalities. Then I scooped up my underclothes and threw them on the soiled sheets. I'd make the time to get to the Laundromat sometime during the day, so I'd have clean lingerie to start my new wedded life. By then it was close to five o'clock in the morning, and too late to get any sleep, not and get done what I had to get done. To say nothing of the fact that I was too scared to close my eyes, for fear of another visit from persons unknown. I didn't have a clue as to who'd done the damage to my trailer and to Junior.

Unless it'd been whoever was looking for Skip. I stood thinking about it for a minute, realizing that Junior had the same big, flabby build as Skip, and could've been mistaken for him. Especially in the dark. Just one more thing to lay at Skip's feet, along with the pile that was already there.

Trying to ignore the pounding in my head from all the worries in it, I took a shower and moisturized my face to keep it soft and dewy-fresh, as the label promised. Wrapped in my robe, I went to the kitchen and got a can of Coke from the refrigerator. I needed something better than coffee to settle my stomach and to fight a full-fledged headache. I poured a packet of Goody's Headache Powders, which Richard Petty swore by, into the Coke, and figured that would do the trick.

Before settling down in the recliner, I looked for my giraffe. There it was, limper than ever, draped over an arm of the couch. I picked it up and hugged it, then did what I'd been dreading and looked at my couch. Sure enough, there was Junior Connard's blood underneath the pillow that Jennie'd put over the stain. I did cry then, and cussed a little, too. I got an old towel, soaked it in cold water, and blotted up as much of it as I could. When I'd soaked the fabric as much as I dared, I gave up on it, hoping Lurline would know a better way to do it. She always did.

Chapter 11

~

I yawned, stretching in the recliner, as the soft gray light that brings on the best sleep filtered through the windows. The best sleep, that is, if you didn't have too much to do to crawl into bed and try to make up for a strung-out night during which I did not close my eyes, courtesy of the Delmont branch of the Abbot County Sheriff's Department.

I sat the Coke can on the little table that now wobbled, due to having been kicked across the room, and picked up a pad and pencil. I make a lot of notes, especially when I have a lot to do. That way, I'm sure I won't forget anything important. I'm the organized type.

And this was a day that needed organizing, for the idea that had been simmering in my mind ever since Emmett told me Junior intended to take Mr. Howard to Raleigh had come to full boil while I'd hunkered down on my car seat while parked at the Skyway movie theater. That idea now required some detailed thinking through.

Chewing on the eraser, I thought through all I would have to do in the coming day. Things would have to be planned out and done in the right order, too, because I'd be operating on no sleep and a lot of coffee, Coke, and Goody's Powders.

Here goes, I thought, and started my list.

1. Call Lurline and make sure Skip stayed in all night.
2. Check on Granny.

3. Talk to Skip. Make sure he hadn't been the one who brained Junior. If he had, why? What was Skip doing here, if he'd come back? Does he know who could've done it? Were they looking for him?
4. Call hospital. Find out Junior's condition.
5. Wash clothes (dang it).

I stopped at that point, trying to figure out if whoever had hit Junior had been after him, or had mistook him for Skip, who had been scared to death of somebody. That made the most sense. Junior could be mistaken for Skip from a distance, and whoever it'd been could've followed Skip to my trailer but not seen him leave. Then when they broke in, they found a man who looked like him. Sort of.

I went back to my list, crossed out part of it, and began to jot down the rest. I'd put them in order later.

6. Go to bank. Withdraw 180 dollars and some pocket money. Who knows? I might need it.
7. Take money to Mr. Sitton's office.
8. Go to hospital and try to see Junior. Find out what he was doing in my trailer. Did he break in?

I stopped again. If Junior was able to talk, could I threaten him with breaking and entering? Maybe, but only if he gave me a hard time about his daddy. He certainly had to answer for being in my trailer in the first place. The funny thing about it was, at the same time I was sneaking around his daddy's house, Junior was sneaking around mine. I had a good reason for being where I was, but did he? I smiled. Junior was going to find himself between a rock and a hard place.

If, that is, he wasn't unconscious or worse. That sobered me.

I didn't want him dead, or even hurt. I wanted him healthy, and happy for me and Mr. Howard. And for himself, too. I mean, you don't get a new stepmother every day.

Another thought struck me, and I put down my pencil. I leaned back in the recliner and stared at the ceiling. What if whoever it was had been looking for me? Or just breaking in to steal something? Maybe none of this had anything to do with either Skip or Junior.

But that didn't make sense. I had nothing worth stealing, except my Barbie doll collection, and none of them had been taken. Still, you'd be surprised at what people'll steal if they get half a chance. But nobody was that mad at me. Well, maybe Junior was. But he was the one on the receiving end, so that didn't work, either.

I went back to my list, adding Bea's Beauty Den. Then I crossed it out. There'd be no time for the tanning bed today. I tore off that sheet of paper and started again. Finally, I was finished. My final things-to-do list looked like this:

1. Call Lurline. Tell her I won't be in to work today. Ask if Skip went out last night.
2. Talk to Skip. Make sure he didn't slip out and come over here. Tell him I'll see him around noon at Lurline's.
3. Call hospital. See if Junior is dead.
4. Call Reverend Haliday.
5. Be at bank by 9:00. Withdraw money. Check balance, if any.
6. Take money to Mr. Sitton's office. Get receipt.
7. Go to hospital and see Junior. Tell him nicely that it's either approve of marriage or be arrested for breaking and entering.
8. Go see Skip. Find out exactly what his problem is and have nothing to do with it.

9. Go to Laundromat. (Put clothes in car before going to bank.)
10. Get Mr. Howard and license.
11. Get married today (if have time).
12. Tell Granny afterward.

I brought the phone from the kitchen counter and put it beside me on the little table. I sat for a minute, trying to get straight in my mind what to say to Lurline. The biggest problem would be keeping her from running over here to clean and straighten and worry me to death with her bossy ways.

I didn't have time for her today, but I couldn't just not show up for work. She would have to rearrange the schedule, giving my patients to one of the other girls. And I needed to know if Skip had been out and around during the night.

The thing was, I just couldn't imagine Skip doing what had been done to either Junior or my trailer. Unless, of course, Junior had already broken in and Skip found him inside, burglarizing my things. Skip wouldn't have stopped to ask questions. He'd've laid into him right and left. But if it'd happened like that, wouldn't Skip have waited for the police? That way, he'd be a hero again.

But, I thought, as I tapped the phone absently, Skip was running from somebody. Maybe he hadn't wanted to be in the newspaper, hero or not. And another thing, I hadn't seen or heard from Skip in a number of years. He could've done a lot more changing than just putting on weight.

I sighed, picked up the receiver, and dialed Lurline's home number, hoping she hadn't yet left for work. She started in right away with questions and instructions—I couldn't supply any answers before she was telling me what I ought to do.

"Lurline, I don't need any help." The woman was going to drive me crazy. I hadn't wanted to tell her the details of my night, but I also hadn't wanted to flat-out lie about why I couldn't go in to work. Nothing would do but she had to keep on until she'd wormed most of it out of me.

"Listen," I said, "Jennie's already done all the straightening I need right now. I appreciate your offer. You're a real good friend, but I've got to get out of here and go pay Mr. Sitton. That's why I can't come in today."

She rattled on about how blood would set in fabric and I'd never be able to get it out if I waited too much longer.

"Lurline," I interrupted. "Lurline, listen. I need to know if Skip stayed in all night."

"Of course he did," she said. Then there was dead silence on the line. "Etta Mae Wiggins," she finally said, and I could almost see her eyes squinch up, "you don't mean to tell me you suspect *Skip*? Why, he couldn't hurt a flea, and he was right here in my guest room bed all night long, and I'll swear to that on a stack of Bibles."

"Well, but I mean, could he've slipped out after you went to bed?"

"Absolutely not. I'm a light sleeper, you know that, Etta Mae. I hear everything that goes on around this house, and the slightest little noise wakes me up. Why, I haven't had a full night's sleep in I don't know how long, that's how light a sleeper I am. And another thing, I'm surprised at you for even thinking Skip would do such a thing. So, no, ma'am, he wasn't there, he didn't do it, and don't you go accusing him of it."

"Okay, Lurline. I had to ask. Now let me speak to him, please."

She didn't like it, but she gave Skip the phone. When he answered, I could hear the sleep still in his voice. Skip had never been an early riser, and I had to smile at the thought of Lurline rousting him out of bed to eat the heavy breakfast I knew she'd fixed for him.

"Hey, hon," he said, and yawned right over the phone lines. "I got to talk to you today. We got to make some plans and do it soon as we can."

"Skip, listen to me now and tell me the honest-to-God truth. Did you sneak out last night and come over here?"

"What?" Same ole Skip, couldn't answer a straight question.

"Just what I said. Did you come back to my trailer last night after you went to Lurline's? I need to know, Skip, it's important."

"Shoot, Etta Mae. I was so tired and worried, I didn't even turn over all night long. Why?"

"Because *somebody* was here last night. Broke in and everything. And another somebody's in the hospital because of it. All I'm saying is—and don't let on to Lurline—that whoever was here may have been looking for you. And I need to know who that is. I got taken down to the sheriff's and questioned half the night, and I don't want to be mixed up in any mess you've gotten yourself into. Now tell me what's going on."

"Well, dang, girl," he said. "I don't want you in any trouble." I rolled my eyes at that, because whose door had he come to with trouble on his heels? "Listen," he whispered, "I can't talk right now, but I'll come on over as soon as I eat breakfast and take care of everything for you."

"I won't be here. I've got things to do this morning, so you just stay right there. I'll come by Lurline's about noontime. She'll be at work, and I want the full story then. No holding back, Skip. I want to know everything you're into, because it looks like I'm into it, too. Up to my neck, in fact. And I especially want to know about that two million dollars you were talking about."

"Sh-h-h," he said, shushing me like Lurline could hear my

side of the conversation. I swear. "Don't say nothing about that, Etta Mae. Keep that under your hat, whatever you do. I'm gonna take care of everything, don't you worry."

When I got off the phone, I sat for a few minutes with one leg hiked up on the recliner, rubbing my foot. I didn't put much stock in Lurline's light sleeping. I'd heard her snore sitting straight up in her desk chair, but with all his faults, Skip had never out-and-out lied to me. So if he hadn't been here, who had?

I struck numbers 1 and 2 off my list, and dialed the hospital.

The county hospital was over in Abbotsville, and I didn't know a soul working in it well enough to expect any details on Junior's condition. So I asked for whatever floor he was on, and hoped the nurse who answered would at least tell me if he was alive or dead. One good thing, my call was transferred to a medical floor and not the intensive care unit, which meant Junior wasn't critical.

"We can't give out that information," the nurse told me with that snippy tone that three-year graduates use to us nurses with six-week degrees. "And, no, he can't have any visitors except family."

"Well, but," I said, trying to be pleasant but firm, "I'm calling for his father, who's not well. He asked me to get him an update on his son's condition. You know who his father is, don't you?"

There was silence on the line, as she thought about the Connard Extended Care Wing on the side of the hospital and the fact that Mr. Connard, Senior, had spent some time in it right after his last stroke. "All I can tell you," she finally said, "is that Mr. Junior Connard suffered a concussion and that he's getting along as well as can be expected."

I pushed a little. "Is he conscious?"

She hesitated again, then said, "More or less."

"His father will want to know if there's anything he needs, something I could bring to him?"

"He doesn't need anything but rest and what we're doing for him. Tell Mr. Connard, Senior, that we're taking good care of him, and if he continues to improve, he'll probably go home tomorrow."

That was exactly the information I wanted, but I needed to be sure. "No chance of him being discharged today? His daddy is real worried about him."

"Absolutely not today. I made rounds with Dr. Nuckolls just a little while ago, and he left orders for bed rest and more X-rays this afternoon. In fact, I wouldn't even count on him being discharged tomorrow. Could be the day after."

Well, that gave me some breathing room, and I hung up the phone with a lightening of my heart. I was also glad that Junior wasn't over there dying on us, too.

I struck number 3 off my list.

Chapter 12

~

Leaning my head back, I massaged the pressure points on my temples. Goody's Headache Powders weren't giving me the fast relief I was looking for, but it was sleep that I really needed. Lying back, I began to think of my next call and what I should say to the Reverend Buster Haliday. I wasn't what you might call an every-Sunday-churchgoing person, but I did show up now and again. Back at the beginnings of both my marriages, I'd been real faithful, singing in the choir and doing every-member canvasses with the best of them. I'd wanted to do my part as a respectable married woman, keeping house, going to church, and being a helpmate to whoever the husband of the moment happened to be. But as each of those marriages started on the downhill slide, I'd given up trying to be what it looked like I never would be. At least not without the help of whoever was supposed to be a helpmate to me.

But with Mr. Howard I could start over again, and maybe get it right this time.

I looked up the reverend's home number since it was still early, and felt a burden roll off my mind when he said he'd be happy to unite two Christian parties in holy matrimony to the everlasting glory of God. I didn't tell him exactly who the other party was going to be, but I assured him the other party had been a Methodist all his life, which seemed to me to be as much of a

Christian as anybody needed. The reverend hesitated over the Methodist part, saying that the Wesleyan belief in backsliding and falling from grace put them on questionable grounds. Theologically speaking. I told him, though, that the other party of whom I was speaking was a faithful Methodist, pledging annual tithes and donating an organ and a memorial garden to his first wife, and surely that proved he hadn't fallen too far, if at all.

Reverend Haliday agreed to marry us anytime we showed up, either late that afternoon or first thing the next morning. So much for my dream of being married in a big church on Main Street, with a photographer and rice and everything, but one preacher's as good as another when you're in a tight spot.

Close to seven-thirty and time to get dressed. I crossed through number 4 on my list, drained the last of my Coke, and headed for the bathroom. Looking in the mirror, I saw the effects of a sleepless night. Time for some intensive facial care. I smeared on Oil of Olay Foaming Face Wash with Aloe Vera to clean it good. After putting hot rollers in my hair, I started in with moisturizer and foundation, then some sparkly blue eye shadow, with a dark blue liner. Then I dabbed on two coats of Maybelline and brushed a nice peach blush on my cheekbones.

It was a shame I had to dress for my possible late afternoon wedding that early in the day, but there'd be no time to change later on. I didn't know what I'd wear if we had to wait till the next day, because I intended to go all out for the afternoon. Pushing aside hangers in the closet, I pulled out my newest and best dress that I'd worn to church on Easter and only a couple of times since then. I was real proud of it because it was a designer dress from the Kathie Lee Collection at Walmart's and looked like a million dollars on me. If I'd had the chance, I'd've bought something new for my wedding, but at least this was mostly white. A quality 100 percent rayon classic white dress with black polka dots. Signifying, I guess, my marital experiences of the past.

I slipped it on and ran my hands over it, admiring how it fit so close and smooth from my breasts to below my hips, then flared out at the bottom above my knees. My legs are one of my best features, if I do say so myself, so I don't go in for those long straight skirts that tangle around your legs and ride up on your knees every time you take a step. I straightened the V neckline, pleased that it ran deep enough to invite a glance but not a bug-eyed stare, and fastened the black patent leather belt tightly around my waist. Rummaging around on the closet floor, I found my high-heeled black patent leather sandals, frowning at the scuff marks on them. They could've used some help, but, pushed for time, I wiped them down with a wet washrag and buckled them on, glad that the Roundup Red polish on my toenails was holding up without a chip.

Out came the hot rollers, then a good brushing, a little back-combing for fullness, two tiny gold hoops on the rim of one ear, Diamonique studs and a pair of white hoop earrings in both, some lip gloss, and I was ready. I stood in front of the narrow full-length mirror on the back of the bedroom door, turning to get a side view, and smiled at the way the dress curved over my bottom and flounced out below.

After several hefty sprays—it had to last all day—of Elizabeth Taylor's Passion over and in the most effective places, I bundled up the dirty clothes, hating to touch them as I shoved them into pillowcases. Then I grabbed my black patent leather purse with the gold chain and slung it over my shoulder. Ready for the day and my new life.

On my way out, the phone rang, and I almost let it go. Instead, I snatched it up, thinking it would be Skip determined to come over. I wish it had been.

"Ms. Wiggins?" Miss Julia Springer's voice jolted me.

"Yes, ma'am." *What could she want with me?*

"I understand there was a disturbance at your trailer last night."

Oh, me, I moaned to myself. Then, "Uh, well, yes, ma'am, there was, but it was none of my doing." *Clyde,* I thought, *that sorry thing just had to tattle.*

"That's neither here nor there. According to your lease, that sort of carrying-on gives me cause to evict you, but Hazel Marie thinks you deserve another chance." She didn't even give me a chance to tell her I'd been an innocent bystander. I gripped the phone so tight that my hand was shaking, wanting to let her have it. But she went on without a thought to my feelings. "We've been talking this morning, and I've come up with a proposition for you. I'd like you to drop by my house sometime today so we can discuss it."

What kind of proposition could she propose? I didn't have time to find out, today of all days. On the other hand, I couldn't afford to antagonize the old biddy. I needed my trailer in her park until I was legal and safe as Mr. Howard's wife. My mind was going ninety miles an hour, recalling that she'd known Mr. Howard for years—people in their income bracket stick together—and I knew she wouldn't approve of our plans for a minute. I had to keep her thinking I'd be up a creek if she evicted me.

But what I wanted to do was tell her to take her trailer park and stick it where the sun didn't shine.

Instead, I said, "Why, yes, ma'am, I think I can make it. I have to be in Abbotsville this morning, anyway, so I'll swing by in a couple of hours."

I hung up the phone, wondering what in the world she could want. I'd just have to grit my teeth and go see. Looking around my trailer once more, I picked up my laundry and hiked the chain of my purse on my shoulder, mentally squeezing a stop at Mrs. Springer's house between numbers 7 and 8 on my long list of things to do. I hated to leave the trailer with a broken lock, which I'd forgotten to put on my list, but I had no choice.

After throwing the dirty clothes in the backseat of the car and checking the time, I walked across the crumbling asphalt that divided the two rows of trailers. Picking my way across the yard and stepping around plastic tricycles, rubber balls, an over-turned lawn chair, and an empty Pampers box, I knocked on the door of Jennie's double-wide.

"Come on in, whoever it is," she yelled.

I stuck my head in, saying, "It's just me. Are you up?"

"Lord, yes," Jennie said, walking out from a bedroom, a cig-arette and a coffee mug in one hand, and a *Cosmo* magazine in the other. She had on a seersucker robe that came to her knees over a long nightgown with the hem out.

Jennie was about my age, but after four kids she didn't look it. She'd put on weight with each baby before she'd had a chance to lose what she'd put on from the previous one. Her hair hadn't been combed, but from the state of her kitchen with dishes piled up and cereal spilled on the counter and the floor, I could see why. Two kids in underpants lay on the floor, glued to the televi-sion, and I could hear the other two somewhere in the back, jumping up and down on a bed.

"Come on in, hon, and have a seat." Jennie waved at a chair. "I swear, every morning about this time I'm about ready to beat the hell outta these young 'uns."

She flopped down on the daybed she used as a couch, reached over, turned off the television, and swatted the backside of a child who screamed that he was watching Nickelodeon. "Go get dressed," she screamed back. Then lifting her voice even more, she yelled at another child in the back of the trailer, "If I have to come in there, you'll be sorry." Then, smiling at me, she said, "Don't you look nice. Take a load off and tell me all about last night."

"I'll have to tell you later, Jennie," I said, perching on the edge of a chair. There was something that looked like jelly on the back of it. "I just wanted to thank you for all you did. I really appreciate how you straightened my trailer and everything. But listen, I wanted to ask you, did you hear anything over there last night? I mean, somebody broke in, and I can't figure out who or why."

"Honey, I didn't hear a thing. A deputy asked me that, too, but you know what it's like over here." An ear-piercing scream came from the bedroom, and she yelled, *"Cut it out, whatever you're doing!"*

She leaned toward me and said, "Was that really *the* Junior Connard in your trailer?"

"Yeah, it sure was, but I don't know what he was doing there."

"Oh, now, don't give me that." Her smile was almost a smirk, but a nice, teasing one. "Honey, if I had a thing going with Junior Connard, I'd be proud of it. He's loaded, you know, or at least his daddy is."

"Believe me, Jennie, I don't have anything going with Junior Connard. I haven't even seen him in years, and there he was coldcocked on my living room couch. I don't have a clue what he was doing there. Besides, he's married."

"When has that ever stopped anybody? Just ask that idiot I'm married to." She drank from her mug, then jumped up. "You want some coffee? God, I'm sorry, I should've offered you some before this. Where's my mind? *All right, you kids, I'm coming in there!*"

"No, no, I don't have time. I've got to get downtown and pay Mr. Sitton for keeping me out of jail last night. I swear, I ought to make Clyde Maybry pay that bill. There was no need to take me in for questioning, but you can't tell him a thing."

"Oh, yeah, tell me about it." She sat down again and pushed the hair off her face. "Clyde was dumb when we were in school and he hasn't improved any. Remember how he used to say, 'I don't get it' all the time? Well, he still don't, but it looks like you're okay now, all dolled up like that. Got a big day today?"

"Pretty big, I guess. Going to a lawyer's office and . . . lots of errands." I wanted to tell Jennie all my plans for the day—she'd've been thrilled for me—but I had to play my cards close to my chest until everything was said and done. Especially done.

"Well, I've got to get up from here and go," I said. "Mr. Sitton will be after me with more than Clyde Maybry if I don't get his bill paid by nine-fifteen on the dot. You know lawyers."

"Nope," she said, with a wide grin. "If I did I'd be a single woman again, and leave these kids with Mack. You take care now, hon, and I hope they catch whoever broke in on you."

"Thanks, Jennie, and if you can, will you keep an eye on things for me? The lock's still broken, not that it did much good when it wasn't. Still, I'd hate for anybody to just walk in."

"Sure, I'll send Mack over to look around. Now come gimme a hug before you go." She reached out with her heavy arms and pulled me close. I smelled cigarette smoke, baby powder, and peanut butter as I leaned against her shoulder. I blinked back tears so my mascara wouldn't run, thinking of how the only other hugs I'd had were from people who were on their way to something else.

She pushed me away, holding me at arm's length, smiling so the wrinkles at the corners of her eyes deepened. "Etta Mae, you're as pretty as a picture and always were. Every time I see you all dressed up like you are, I just get mad as fire all over again that you didn't get Homecoming Queen. Tara Jacobs ruined you with all those stories about you and Skip, and I could just smack her good every time I see her."

"Well, she was right about me and Skip, but that's water over the dam now. Too late to be queen of homecoming or anything else."

"Oh, I wouldn't be too sure about that," she said. "Way I hear it, Bobby Lee Moser would crown you any day of the week."

"Don't listen to everything you hear, especially about Bobby Lee. Got to go, Jennie. See you later, and thanks again."

I left then, going back across the asphalt to my car, my head swimming with all kinds of earlier and sadder pictures in my mind. Yes, I should've been Homecoming Queen, almost all the boys voted for me, but Tara Jacobs had most of the girls' votes, and the teachers' respect, too, and they were the ones who'd done the counting.

I liked Jennie, I really did, but I couldn't have much to do with her because she always brought up our high school days, and those old sad memories. You'd think anybody with four kids would get her mind out of high school and look to the future.

Like I was always trying to do, in spite of being reminded of Bobby Lee Moser every time I turned around and all the heart-stopping thrills I'd once had with him.

But it was my wedding day, and the time for thrills, heart-stopping or otherwise, was long past and gone.

Chapter 13

~

It was a few minutes before nine by the time I got to the Delmont branch of Wachovia Bank, and there wasn't a parking place left on Main Street. I drove past the nosed-in cars along the two blocks of downtown, hoping somebody would back out, all the time fuming about the Northern retirees who'd moved down here, crowding out the rest of us. Lurline says she always asks the Lord for a parking place and He finds one for her, but I don't have that kind of pull. Finally I found a space around the block on Rosewood, got out, and locked the car because of the pile of dirty clothes in the backseat. I didn't know who'd want them, but you never know.

I hurried down the sidewalk toward the bank, nervous now about being late with my payment. Lawyer Sitton was not a man to cross, or one to be late on when you've made a promise having to do with legal stuff. Paying no mind to the old men sitting on the sidewalk benches who followed me with their watery eyes, or to the lanky-haired, hairy-faced redneck who whistled and said "Babe" as I passed, I walked as fast as I could, my Kathie Lee dress swishing around my thighs.

Barreling through the heavy glass door of the bank, I ran right into Bobby Lee on his way out.

"Whoa," he said, those white teeth gleaming against his tanned face. "Etta Mae. Just the girl I always wanta see."

"Hey, Bobby Lee, how you doing?" I said, stepping around him. "Nice seeing you."

"Wait a minute. What's your hurry, sugar? Don't you have a little time for me?"

I stopped and looked up at him. He was out of uniform, in soft prewashed jeans that looked sprayed on, a white dress shirt with the sleeves rolled up, and his pointy-toed cowboy boots. A big square buckle on his belt. He looked good, but then, he always did.

"No, I don't have time for you, or for anybody else, either. I've got business to tend to."

"You always have business to tend to. You ought to slow down a little, darlin', not be in such a rush all the time."

Well, that pushed my button. "Bobby Lee," I said. "The reason I'm in such a rush is because of that idiot, Clyde Maybry, who took me in last night for something I did not do, and I had to get a lawyer to keep him from holding me all night long, and now I've got to get almost my last cent out of the bank and go pay for it, and do it within the next fifteen minutes. If you'd do something about the people you work with, I might have a little time to visit with you."

He reared back like he was dodging the words I threw at him. Then, hooking his thumbs in the waistband of his jeans, he said, "Well, my goodness," which sounded ridiculous coming from a man who could whisper the nastiest words you'd ever want to hear in the dark of the night.

Then he wiped the smile off his face and said, "Yeah, Wendell told me about that. Listen, Etta Mae, you should've called me. If I'd been on duty, none of that would've happened. You know I'd look after you."

"I don't know anything of the kind," I said, looking away from him so he wouldn't see the way I had to blink my eyes. "Clyde still doesn't believe me, so he's not going to be looking for who-ever really broke in and knocked Junior out. So what can you do about that?"

"I can fix Clyde, don't worry about him. Come on, Etta Mae, my truck's right down the street. Let's go sit down and talk about it."

"No," I said, squaring my shoulders. I reminded myself that I was through depending on the kind of men I'd always picked to take care of things, which none had ever done. What I wanted more than anything else was to *be* somebody. Somebody who was respected and listened to and treated in a nice way all the time. What I wanted was to be in a situation where nobody would ever again look at me and, without blinking an eye, think the worst. "I've got to cash a check and get to Mr. Sitton's office. Good to see you, Bobby Lee, but I have to go."

I went around him and over to a teller's window. I wrote a check to cash for two hundred and fifty dollars and slid it across to Mary Ann Dooley.

"I'd like my balance, too, please."

She smiled, hit some keys on her terminal, then counted out my money. She wrote a figure on a slip of paper and pushed it to me, along with the cash. I nearly folded at the knees when I saw my balance.

"Is this before or after the check I just cashed?"

"Oh, it's after. Not to worry, this check is covered," she said.

That helped. But the rent on my trailer space and hook-up would be due next week, then the light bill. Then the phone bill and cable TV. I might have to ask Lurline for a loan, which made my flesh crawl to think of.

Then I remembered that if everything went according to plan, I wouldn't have to worry about any of those bills or getting a loan or anything else. As Mrs. Howard Connard, Senior, I could write all the checks I wanted to and not give a thought to what the balance might be. Of course I wouldn't not give it a thought, since I planned to be just as careful with Mr. Howard's money as I was with my own. I'm the financially prudent type of person.

I turned and hurried out of the bank. Almost nine-fifteen, and I had two blocks to walk to Mr. Sitton's office above Eckerd's Drug Store. When I came out on the sidewalk, there was Bobby Lee leaning against the bank building.

He pushed off the wall and started walking with me. "I forgot to tell you," he said, "how tasty you're looking today." He side-stepped behind me, letting his hand brush my waist as he moved to my other side next to the traffic. He was always thoughtful that way, even though there were parked cars and a good twelve feet between us and the line of traffic.

"Don't give me a hard time, Bobby Lee. Can't you see I'm in the midst of conducting serious business here? I don't have time for you."

"Well, I'm trying to conduct some serious business, too. I want you to tell me all about last night, who was there, what happened, everything. I'm going to get to the bottom of this mess. Can't have my baby girl being accused of something she didn't do."

I stopped in the middle of the sidewalk, making a heavyset woman with a shopping bag swerve around me. "Two things, Bobby Lee. First, I've already been questioned on all that and I damn well don't appreciate being questioned again. And on a public sidewalk, at that. And number two, I am not your baby girl, and the sooner you get that through your thick head, the better off you'll be."

He stood smiling down at me, like he hadn't heard a word I'd said. Dense, is what he was. "Darlin'," he said in that soft voice that sends chills down your spine, "you know you been thinkin' about me, like I've been thinkin' about you, and dreamin' about us together. Sweetest thing in the world, you've got to admit.

Remember how we used to put a blanket in the back of my truck, and what about that motel out by the airport?"

I locked on his eyes, black as his cheating heart, and nearly got lost in them. "Bobby Lee," I whispered, leaning in close so he could get the full effect of Elizabeth Taylor's Passion rising up from the V neck of my dress. Right there in the middle of the sidewalk with people walking around both sides of us, I felt him begin to sway as his eyelids drooped halfway down. "Bobby Lee," I whispered again, "you can go straight to hell, and take Darla Davis with you."

And off I went, leaving him standing there. It took a minute, but then he began laughing, and the sound of it followed me all the way down the block.

I jerked open the door next to the drugstore and went up the stairs to Mr. Sitton's office. It was quiet up there and cool, with air conditioners running to block out the street sounds and everything else. Like people down there on the sidewalk laughing their heads off.

"I'm Etta Mae Wiggins and I want to pay my bill," I said to the receptionist, who was skinny as a rail, and not a bit improved by her dyed orange hair with her scalp shining through. Old as the hills and dried-up-looking, too.

She sniffed and took my money but not before looking me up and down. She reminded me of my civics teacher, who'd never liked me.

"I'll need a receipt," I said.

She pursed her mouth and said, "We always give receipts."

I let that pass because I wanted something else. "Is Mr. Sitton in? I'd really like to see him, if he's not too busy."

She didn't even look up from the receipt book she was writing in. "Mr. Sitton's always busy. You'll have to make an appointment." She tore out the receipt and held it straight up so I had to reach over for it. "But his appointment book is full for the next several weeks. There's a new lawyer in town who might be able to see you. I'd try him, if I were you."

I bit my lip to keep from telling her that she wasn't me, and a good thing, too, since she wouldn't be able to handle it. Instead, I took the receipt and thanked her as nicely as I could and left.

Just wait, I told myself as I went down the stairs. *One of these days when I'm Mrs. Howard Connard, Senior, I'll snatch that stuck-up witch bald-headed.*

At the bottom of the stairs, I looked out to see if Bobby Lee was waiting. I didn't see him anywhere, so I took the notepad out of my purse and struck off numbers 5 and 6 from my list.

Chapter 14

Before going back to the car, I swung into Eckerd's Drugs and started down the aisles. I wanted to have something to take to Junior when I went to the hospital. Maybe he would be more willing to talk to me when he saw that I knew it was the proper thing to take a gift when you made a hospital visit.

I couldn't decide what to get him, not knowing the name brands he liked or what he might need. Pajamas came to mind, but that was too personal. He might not appreciate me giving him something that close to the skin. Besides, I didn't think Eckerd's carried them. I looked at some shaving cream and men's cologne, but they didn't seem right, either. Finally I decided to go with something safe, something that everybody liked.

I carried the Whitman's Sampler to the counter, paid for it, and waited while the girl wrapped it for me.

Back in the car, I looked over my list again and tried to collect my thoughts before facing Junior. If I could even get in to see him.

Driving out of town, I passed the VFW clubhouse with its huge flag flapping lazily in the breeze. The public swimming pool next door was still and empty with kids back in school, but it sure looked inviting to me. My car was hot, even though I'd been lucky to've parked it in the shade. One of these days, I'd get the AC fixed. Maybe about the time the first snow fell.

Then I smiled, reminding myself again that after this day was over, I wouldn't have to worry about cracked compressors or dragging mufflers or ripped seat covers.

That's what I needed to keep in mind. Every time I had a sinking feeling about what the day would bring, I needed to remind myself to think of all the worries this day was also going to relieve me of.

Driving to Abbotsville didn't take long, even though the ten miles was on a curving mountain road. The new Walmart Super Store was over there, so I'd made the trip often enough to know the county seat fairly well.

After checking at the desk in the lobby of the hospital, I rode up in the elevator to the second-floor medical wing, clutching the Whitman's Sampler to my breast. With my other hand, I searched for a Kleenex in my purse, and used it to mop up the perspiration on my face. The hospital was cool, almost too much so, and a real shock after coming in from the heat. Still, I was sweating. Nerves, I guess. Since no one else was on the elevator, I held my arms out to the side to get some drying benefit underneath.

Turning right out of the elevator, I walked down the hall toward the nurses' desk. Holding my breath so my luck would hold, I was relieved to see that no one was there. Slipping behind the desk where I wasn't supposed to be, I quickly scanned the rows of charts and found Junior's room number. I headed toward Room 216 on tiptoes to keep my high heels from clacking on the tile floor. So far, so good, I thought, and hurried around the corner. There was a NO VISITORS sign on the door, which I knew did not apply to family or to professional staff. I qualified on both counts, but I didn't want to have to defend either one.

I tapped lightly and pushed open the door. Junior was lying on a slightly elevated bed, and the first thing I noticed was the bandage wrapped around his head. His eyes were closed and he looked awfully pale. I took in the sizable mound his body made under the covers, and could see how somebody might mistake him in the dark for Skip. It stretched my imagination to see how the first Mrs. Connard, Senior, managed to produce such a large figure of a man. It probably stretched hers, too. Recessive genes, I guessed.

I tiptoed to the side of the bed and whispered, "Junior? Mr. Connard? Are you awake?"

He opened one eye, then the other. "Blood pressure again?" he asked.

"No, I'm not a nurse. I mean, I am, but not a hospital nurse. I just came to see how you're doing."

He frowned and blinked like he couldn't focus his eyes. And he probably couldn't with his head busted open like it was. "Okay, I guess," he mumbled. "Helluva headache."

"I don't doubt it. What happened, you remember?"

"Don't know," he said, and brought a hand with a heavy gold ring on his finger out from under the covers and ran it over his face. "Minding my own business, and wake up in the hospital." He cut his eyes back to me, and winced with the movement. "You from the police?"

"No." I took a deep breath and plunged in. "I'm Etta Mae Wiggins."

"Who?"

"Etta Mae Wiggins. You know, I'm your daddy's home nurse and . . . friend."

"Oh. How is he?"

"He's fine, but we're all worried about you. He wants to know what you were doing when you got hurt."

"Just . . . I don't know. Went somewhere." He stopped and frowned again like the events of the night were all jumbled up in his brain. "Woke up here. Where's my wife?"

I'd forgotten about her. What if she came in while I was here? I looked over my shoulder at the door, which was still closed.

"I'll try to find her for you," I told him. "But don't you remember going to my trailer? That's where I—they—found you."

"Trailer?" He screwed up his mouth, thinking hard, and frowned at me again with an addled look on his face. "Who are you?"

"Etta Mae Wiggins," I said, loud and clear so I'd shake a memory or two loose. Then, deciding to risk it all, I said, "I'm your daddy's fiancée. Remember how happy you were when you heard about it?" Well, I had to try it.

"I was?"

"Oh, yes. It took a burden off your mind to have someone in the family taking care of him."

"Daddy's married?"

"*Getting* married," I said, and added, "real soon."

A tiny smile flicked at the corner of his mouth, and he said, "Why, that ole goat."

"I'm going over there in a little while. Is that all right with you?"

He blinked his eyes several times, mumbled something that sounded like "Okay," and before I knew it, he'd dropped off to sleep.

"I brought you some candy," I whispered, and put the Whitman's Sampler on the bedside table.

In an even lower whisper, I said, "Thank you for your blessing." And under my breath, I added, "Son." Then, relieved that Junior'd never be able to say I'd married his daddy behind his back, I turned to get out while the getting was good.

She opened the door just as I reached for it, and we stood face-to-face, both of us too shocked to speak. Mrs. Howard Connard, Junior, known as Valerie McLean, of the Raleigh and Pinehurst McLeans, anchor of *Your Live Local Late-Breaking News* on the Raleigh CBS affliate, drew back like she'd almost stepped in something.

She got herself together first, and demanded, "What are you doing in here?"

"I, ah, I just brought him some candy," I mumbled, feeling hot and sweaty, and short and frumpy, standing in front of the cool, thin-faced woman looking down on me. Danielle Steel, my favorite writer, would've called her a Nordic beauty. Everything about her, from the emerald green silk suit to the icy green eyes, was perfect. I'd never seen a TV personality up close before, especially one who glared at me like I was a waitress who'd gotten her order wrong. I wished I'd worn panty hose.

"From his daddy," I added, hoping she'd get out of the doorway so I could leave.

"He's not supposed to have visitors," she said, her voice as hard and cold as her face. "Can't you read? And just who do you think you are?"

"I am Etta Mae Wiggins," I said, my head coming up to face her. "And you don't have to speak to me like I'm a dog."

"I'll speak to you any way I please. You're not supposed to be in my husband's room, and I'm calling security right now." She moved toward the telephone by the bed.

I'd had enough by then. "Why don't you call the Delmont sheriff's office instead? They're dying to talk to him, and so am I. For instance, I want to know what he was doing in my trailer last night."

She put the phone down carefully and turned toward me. "*Your* trailer?" She looked me up and down and said, "Well, this isn't the first time he's been attracted to trash. Trailer or otherwise."

She could've slapped me in the face and I wouldn't have been more shocked. It takes more than a silk suit and a perfect complexion to make a lady, and this woman, TV personality or not, certainly wasn't one. A dozen things flashed through my mind to throw back at her, but I remembered that we were all going to be part of the same family. And families are supposed to get along and be happy. I swallowed hard.

Even so, I could feel my face getting hot as I tried my best to restrain the red haze that rose up so fast I could hardly see through it. Mr. Howard would want me to conduct myself like a lady, even if his daughter-in-law didn't, so I clenched my fists and said, "Well, he's *your* husband, so no wonder."

Then, turning on my heel, I left the room, clacking down the hall on my high heels and muttering, "Bitch, bitch, bitch" to myself all the way to the elevator.

Chapter 15

I threw my bag into the car and flopped in after it. When my bottom and the back of my legs hit the hot plastic seat covers, I almost went through the roof. I jumped back out and went through my dirty clothes until I found a towel. After spreading it on the driver's seat, I gingerly crawled back under the wheel.

I didn't start the car. I couldn't. I just sat there in the hospital visitors' parking lot, steaming over Valerie McLean Connard's contempt for me, which she'd made no effort to hide. And I didn't even think she'd recognized me as the one Junior had come to get his daddy away from. She'd taken one look at me and figured I wasn't worth the time of day. Just like Mr. Sitton's receptionist had, only taken to the nth degree. What was it that made people treat me like that? I was clean. I was neat and hardworking. And I had good manners and never went out of my way to hurt anybody. I couldn't understand it. But what I did understand was that when I had Mr. Howard's name tacked onto mine, they'd change their tune. Giving care and kindness to Mr. Howard for the rest of his pitiful life was no sacrifice in comparison to what he'd do for me. In spite of what Lurline thought.

I pulled down the visor and checked my mascara in the mirror, then got out my list and, with a shaking hand, checked off number 7.

Driving away from the hospital, I decided I deserved a treat for lunch after all I'd been through. I drove up to the drive-through window at McDonald's and ordered a Big Mac, small fries, and a large Coke. Parked under a tree in the lot, I ate my lunch while trying to put Valerie Connard out of my mind. Sufficient unto the morning were the evils thereof. Or something like that. I needed to concentrate on the afternoon to come, and let the evils of the morning go. At least until I was in a position to do something about them.

After wadding up the greasy wrappers and putting them in the trash, I got back into my car and tried to set my mind on facing Mrs. Julia Springer. I swear, I was in no shape to tackle her, but I didn't see that I had a choice. I had to play it out and pretend that my life wasn't about to change so that I'd never have to be at her beck and call again. After today, if everything went right, my rented space in her trailer park could be plowed over and left to go to seed, for all I'd care.

But first I had to make sure everything went right, and that meant not letting anyone know what I was planning to do. If I'd read Mrs. Springer right, and I was pretty sure I had, she'd be outraged at the thought of me marrying Mr. Howard. I just knew she'd do whatever she could to put a stumbling block in my way. Why, she might even join forces with Valerie, for all I knew. It was a wonder to me how people who'd already reached a level of success just hated to see anybody else rise up to join them.

So what I had to do was go see the woman, listen to what she had to say, and hold on to my temper. The proposition she'd mentioned had to mean some kind of deal she wanted me to agree to. Maybe the deal was that I either put a stop to visits by the sheriff to my trailer or she'd throw me out. But then again . . .

Maybe it was something good, and it could be, since she'd said it was Hazel Marie's idea. Hazel Marie, I thought, and smiled. She'd be happy for me, if I dared tell her who I'd be in a few hours. She knew what it was like to struggle for every little thing, and have people judge you regardless of what you did. Whatever Mrs. Springer had to propose to me, if it was any good, it would've come from Hazel Marie, who wasn't the kind to turn her back on those she'd left behind in the same mess she'd come from.

So, blowing out my breath, I started the car and drove to Polk Street, pulling up by the curb in front of the Springer house. I recalled how the last time I'd been there, on the occasion of Binkie and Coleman's June wedding, the yard had been filled with people milling around, along with balloons, rice, and birds swooping everywhere. And I thought back to the previous March, when the street and yards had been covered with ice and the power'd been off and Junior Johnson's big NASCAR hauler'd been parked across the street and old lady Springer'd been so jealous of Mr. Sam Murdoch that she couldn't see straight.

What a difference a few months and sixty-something degrees made.

Slinging my purse on my shoulder as I got out of the car, I smoothed out my dress and marched up the front walk. Mrs. Julia Springer didn't know it, but I was soon going to be on her financial level. When I was Mrs. Howard Connard, Senior, I'd be her equal in society, and she'd never be able to look down her nose at me again. In fact, I thought, as I walked onto her porch, the next time I came it would be as an invited guest to her famous Spring Tea.

At the same time that pleasant thought was running through my mind, my stomach was giving me a bad case of the jitters. What if she told me to vacate the premises, and do it today? That would put a crimp in any bride's wedding day, and mine more than most, because by the time I found another place to live and somebody to move me, Junior and Valerie would have Mr. Howard packed up and moved out of Delmont, and my life, as well.

I thought I might throw up at the thought, but I got a grip and rang the doorbell, as ready as I was going to be for whatever the old bat intended to throw at me.

"Come in, Miss Wiggins." Mrs. Springer held the door for me and I walked into her cool living room. "You know Hazel Marie, of course."

Hazel Marie gave me a hug, and I thought again how good she looked. So good, in fact, that you'd never know that she was a Puckett. It's amazing how three meals a day, prepared by someone else, and no worries about what bills you can afford to pay can smooth away wrinkles and put a glow in your complexion. A few trips to the Lancôme counter at Belk's help some, too.

"It's so good to see you, Etta Mae," Hazel Marie said. "My, you look nice. Come on in."

"Have a seat, Miss Wiggins," Mrs. Springer said, motioning to her hard-as-a-rock sofa with the claw feet that I'd have thrown out in a minute.

I sat gingerly as she and Hazel Marie took the matching chairs on each side of the fireplace. I took note of the glycerinized magnolia leaves between the andirons for the months when a fire wasn't needed, and thought I'd do the same in Mr. Howard's living room fireplace.

Rich people knew so many helpful household hints like that, and I determined to make a list of as many as I noticed, so that when Mr. Howard and I entertained, everybody would know I fit in with their way of doing things. I'm the quick-learning type.

"Now," Mrs. Springer said, like she was calling a meeting to order. "As I told you, Hazel Marie and I have been discussing how we could solve all these problems you've brought to my attention, and—"

"'Scuse me, Mrs. Springer," I said, leaning forward. "But I didn't cause that problem last night. Somebody I don't even know broke into my trailer and somebody else did the damage. Why, if I hadn't come home when I did, there's no telling what would've happened."

Hazel Marie frowned. "Somebody broke in? Are you all right, Etta Mae?"

Before I could do more than nod my head, Mrs. Springer breezed right on. "That's not exactly the way the sheriff's department tells it. But let's not get bogged down with the details." She waved her hand, like my version was a fly buzzing around. "Now, Miss Wiggins, far be it from me to meddle in your personal affairs, but since you are my tenant, I must caution you about mixing with the kind of people who create, um, difficulties with the Law." She stopped to be sure I was following her meaning. I was, and I wanted so bad to tell her that it'd been Junior Connard who was not only one of the kind of people she was talking about, but one of her own kind, as well.

With a little sniff, she went on, "You need to choose your associates with a little more discretion, and I hope you understand that I'm telling you this for your own good. I thought after I had the street paved and a fence put up that the complaints would stop. That hasn't happened, but Hazel Marie thinks a lot of you, and after talking it over, we've decided that more supervision is needed over there."

I looked from one to the other, fuming inside because Clyde Maybry had been on the phone, carrying tales and besmirching my reputation. I felt the skin on my face tighten, as I thought of what I'd like to do to him. And to old lady Springer, too, who had a nerve telling me how I ought to conduct myself. Holding myself in, though, I sat back and waited to hear the rest of it.

"Ms. Wiggins," Mrs. Springer went on, folding her hands in her lap and acting like the chairman of the board. "There are twenty-two renters in that park, and of all of them, you are the only one who makes calls of complaint—"

I scooted up onto the edge of the sofa. "Ma'am. Excuse me, ma'am, but I don't think I make trivial complaints. I mean, burnt-out lights, overturned garbage, broken asphalt, packs of dogs roaming around, and weeds growing everywhere, well, they're things I'd think you'd want to know about."

Hazel Marie looked at Mrs. Springer with this little smile on her face. She nodded at her, like she was saying, *See?* Then she turned to me and winked.

"That's exactly what I mean." Mrs. Springer nodded back at Hazel Marie, then said to me, "Here lately, every time the phone rings, I figure it's you bringing up another problem over there. So I agree with Hazel Marie that you do notice things and that you care about the condition of the park. But the call I got this morning," she went on, straightening that back another notch, like she had to get said everything she'd been stewing about, "was not about the park, but about you. Miss Wiggins, I just cannot have public disturbances, with the sheriff being called out and people injured on my property."

"Mrs. Springer," I said, clenching my hands in my lap and feeling a trickle of sweat down my back. "I swear on a stack of Bibles, that was not my doing." I turned to Hazel Marie, looking for help as the thought of being thrown out of the park right when I didn't have time for one other roadblock on my way to the altar raced through my mind. "Hazel Marie, you have to believe me, I had nothing to do with that. Clyde Maybry jumped to conclusions. He doesn't like me, and wouldn't listen to a word I said. But Mr. Ernest Sitton did," I said, playing my trump card.

"And Mr. Ernest Sitton said that I was an innocent bystander. He's my lawyer now."

I sat back, fighting tears and anger at the injustice of it all. I wanted so bad to tell them I was about to marry Mr. Howard Connard, Senior. I just wanted to throw it in Mrs. Julia Springer's face, and see how quick she changed her tune. I had to bite my lip, because so many unexpected things had happened in my life that I'd learned not to burn any bridges until I was safely on the other side. So I had to suck it up and take whatever she dished out.

"Etta Mae," Hazel Marie said, reaching over and patting my arm, "I know what Clyde Maybry's like, and we know you've had a hard time. But listen to what Miss Julia has to say. She's about to get to it, and it might solve a lot of problems for you."

Mrs. Springer had the nerve to sniff, like she didn't entirely agree. But she went on, "Yes, we are sympathetic, but you have to realize that any rowdy behavior on my property reflects badly on me. There is, however," she said, like it hurt her to admit it, "such a thing as Christian charity and making use of the particular qualities that people have. Hazel Marie has brought to my attention that you're doing me a service by looking after things. So what I've decided to do is offer you the position of manager of the park. I would expect you to take care of these problems, see that repairs are made, and take responsibility, in general, for keeping the property in good condition. In return, I will let you have your space for free. That would be your fee for service."

"Well," I said, flabbergasted by the offer, especially after mentally picturing my new floral-covered sofa being dumped on the side of the road because I didn't have a place to move it to. But instead of being evicted, I was being offered a position of authority. I took a deep breath and tried to look thoughtful as I considered her offer.

A little hard to do, as thoughts of that extra money in my

pocket flashed in my mind. What an opportunity! I could straighten out that place for her and make it a decent place to live. And save myself some money, too.

Then I thought of my plans to make an end run around Junior and Valerie and get myself married to Mr. Howard. If I managed to do that, I could flip off Mrs. Julia Springer and her Christian charity, which, let's face it, would benefit her more than me.

Still, I couldn't let on that, if everything went as planned, I wouldn't need either a job, even if it was a managerial one, or her free trailer space much longer.

Trying to show the proper respect and appreciation, which I knew she'd expect, I said, "Thank you, Mrs. Springer, ma'am. I accept your offer, and I'll do a good job for you, too. And, Hazel Marie, I really do thank you for thinking of it."

That was about all I could manage in the way of gratitude. Although I really did appreciate Hazel Marie's efforts on my behalf. I had a sneaking feeling that if it'd been up to Mrs. Springer, her charitable proposition would've been in the form of an eviction notice.

I took my leave then, as Mrs. Springer stood to indicate the business meeting was over. Hazel Marie hugged me again, saying, "Let's get together for lunch real soon."

She meant well, I knew, but when did I have time for lunch with my schedule of bedridden, crippled, arthritic, and needy patients filling my days? Which, as far as Hazel Marie knew, was what I'd be keeping on at, day in and day out, without the free time that she now enjoyed.

How soon they forget.

As I drove away, I couldn't decide whether I was mad at being treated like a charity case or secretly tickled at how Julia Springer was going to feel when she learned she'd thrown a bone to the newest Abbot County society lady.

On the other hand, I had to admit that if Mr. Howard hadn't been in my immediate future and I'd had to keep struggling on the pitiful salary Lurline paid me, I'd've been on cloud nine at the thought of freeing up that rent money. I could've had the AC in the car fixed or Bernie's recliner upholstered to match my new couch. Or maybe both, over time.

But that was neither here nor there now. The rest of the day and all I had to get done loomed in my mind, and my pulse rate jumped at the thought.

At the first red light, I checked Julia Springer off my list and hoped to my soul that she stayed checked.

Chapter 16

By the time I got back to Delmont, I'd set my mind to concentrating on Skip. I swear, I didn't need him showing up right at the most complicated time of my life. But he had, and I had to deal with him.

I skirted Main Street, going out Dell Street and turning onto Springer Road to the far side of town where Lurline lived. Her house was on the opposite side of the highway from the trailer park on a nice lot that had once been part of a farm, but had been built up considerably in the last few years. It was a small house compared to its new neighbors, but she kept it and the yard neat as a pin. The one-story redbrick house, with its white metal railings around the front porch, sat back from the road under an old oak. I pulled into the drive, then drove on to park in the shade of the metal carport next to the house.

Lurline's yard was freshly mown, without a weed in it and not a sprig of grass cuttings on the driveway or the porch steps. I walked onto the porch, crowded with an umbrella stand, three side tables, two rocking chairs, and a swing that hadn't been used since Raymond passed. Lurline couldn't stand to sit out front where people driving by could look at her, but Raymond had enjoyed waving at cars as they went by.

Before I could knock, Skip opened the door with a rush of cold air from the window air conditioners.

"I thought you'd never get here," he said. "Where you been, Etta Mae? We got to plan this thing out."

I stepped into Lurline's living room while he closed and locked the door. A large brown sofa with a multicolored crocheted afghan over the back took up one whole wall, with two beige recliners facing it in front of the picture window. A lamp on a table stood between them, which was supposed to look pretty from the street, but Lurline kept her lace curtains closed against the sun and prying eyes. A twenty-four-inch color television on a rollaround stand took up most of the far wall, placed as it was in front of a never-used fireplace.

I put my purse on the coffee table, careful not to get the blue plastic flower arrangement, *The Living Bible*, the *TV Guide*, and the colonial girl figurine out of line. Lurline was real touchy about keeping her decor just so, and I wondered how long she'd be able to put up with Skip and his messy ways.

"All right, Skip," I said, sitting down on the sofa. "Let's hear it, and I mean everything."

"You're gonna love it," he said, grinning as he sat in one of the recliners. "And you're not gonna believe it."

"I'll believe it, all right. After what happened at my trailer last night, I'm ready to believe anything. Now get to it, and don't leave anything out."

"Okay," he said, hitching himself up in the chair. "Here's how it was. I've been working at a Texaco station in Gastonia right off the interstate, a big one, lots of business. And doin' good, too, Etta Mae. You'd of been proud of me. Okay, okay," he said, seeing me roll my eyes, "I'm getting to it. Anyway, there was these two other ole boys, mechanics, friends of mine, who I knew from when we all used to live here in Delmont, that worked there, too. And we decided that we ought to go in together and go down to Georgia where big money's piled up and buy us some lottery tickets."

That sounded like Skip. Always looking for the easy money, convinced that with just one little piece of luck, he'd have it all. Myself now, I never believed in luck. Just hard work, and taking opportunities as they happened to come along.

"So?"

"So we pooled our money and drew straws to see who'd drive down and buy the tickets, and if any of them won, we'd split it three ways. And I won. I mean, I drew the short straw and I took all our money—five hundred dollars between us—and went down across the state line and bought our tickets."

I just stared at him. Five hundred dollars those idiots had thrown away, and I'd bet that ordinarily the three of them didn't have two nickels to rub together. But Skip was proud of what they'd done, sitting over there with his eyes lit up.

"I can't wait to hear the rest of this," I said.

"Well, the way it happened was like this. I bought the tickets, then as I was going out the store down there, I looked through my billfold and I had one five-dollar bill left. It was either use it for a Taco Bell dinner or another lottery ticket. You know, just for luck. So I bought one for myself and put it away, separate from the others.

"And, Etta Mae," he said, his face shining and his voice gasping with excitement, "my ticket won. That little ole last-minute, spur-of-the-minute ticket won two million dollars!"

"Get real, Skip. What're you doing hiding out in Delmont if you'd won that kind of money?"

"Well, see, that's the problem. We put the five hundred dollars' worth of tickets that belonged to the three of us in the safe at the Texaco station, so nobody could cheat on us, see? But I didn't say nothing about my extra ticket. I mean, I didn't have to tell about that one. I was the one had to take off from work and go down there and get 'em. And anybody else'd do the same thing, buy an extra one with his own money. Which is what I did. I didn't use our pool money for that one. Didn't even buy it in the same batch."

"You're saying that extra ticket won?"

"Yeah! Can you believe it? It was a winner! Man, I still can't believe it, but it's right here in my pocket just waitin' to be changed into two million dollars!" He flopped back against the chair, letting his arms dangle over the sides.

"And you told them?"

"Huh? Oh, well, yeah, Etta Mae, I couldn't keep it to myself, now could I? I mean, when I looked at the numbers on the TV and saw the very same ones on my ticket, well, what would *you* do?"

"You don't want to know."

"Yeah I do. Come on, Etta Mae, just tell me what you'd do if you'd won that kind of money."

"I'd pack my things and slip out of town without telling a soul. Skip, I swear, didn't you know those two would figure you owed them something?"

"Well, no. I mean, it was my own money, not any of theirs, that I bought it with. But I guess you're right. After I let out a whoop you could hear a mile around and showed everybody the winning ticket, I guess maybe I should've known not everybody'd be happy for me. But I don't know why they wouldn't. I bought it fair and square."

"It's a wonder somebody didn't knock you over the head and steal it from you. Which I think somebody tried to do in my trailer last night."

"Well, but I wasn't there."

"That's not the point, Skip," I pointed out to him, so exasperated with him I could've knocked him out myself. "The point is, if we're guessing right on what happened to Junior Connard, somebody followed you to Delmont, and since they didn't find the ticket on Junior or in my trailer, which they tore apart, they're still here looking for you."

His eyes got wide, as his brain worked through what I'd said. "That's right! Shoot fire, I bet they're lookin' all over for me right now." He leaned over to look toward the door.

"What're we gonna do, Etta Mae?"

"We?"

"Why, sure. I'm gonna share this with you, hon, you know that. I mean, you took me in when I didn't know where else to go, and what am I gonna do with two million, when one's aplenty for me?"

"If you feel that way, why don't you just share it with those friends of yours, and get them off your back?"

"They ain't gonna be satisfied with that. They want it all. Said I'd cheated them. And you know I never cheated in my life, Etta Mae. This was fair and square, and on the up and up all the way down the line. Now, hon, I want you to think about this, 'cause I feel like I kinda owe you a little. You know, for all the good times we had and for helping me out now. I'll do it either way, but if you'll help me get the money safe in a bank somewheres, and help me stay hid while we're doin' it, we'll share and share alike. Or, and this is what I'm hoping for, let's us get married again and we'll have all of it together."

"No, no, and no," I said, holding up both hands and shaking my head. "Don't even think it. We've tried that, and I'm not getting into it with you again. So you can just forget about getting married again."

"Well, I wouldn't mind it, Etta Mae."

"But I would. No offense, Skip, but we just weren't made for each other."

"Okay, then, but if you change your mind . . ."

"I won't. Now, let's figure out what you have to do. Where do you have to go to pick up that money? Atlanta?"

"Yeah, I guess."

"Then call the Asheville Airport and see when you can get a plane out. Then call whoever is supposed to give you the money and tell them what time you'll be landing so they'll have somebody waiting for you there."

"They'll do that?"

"I expect they'll know you have to be careful with that ticket. Whoever presents it to them is the winner, you know, and it might not have to be the one who actually bought it."

"A limo," he said. "Reckon they'll send a limo?"

"I don't know, Skip. More likely a cop car, but you have more things to worry about than a set of wheels. Now, what you ought to do is stay right here in Lurline's house and not go out at all. Don't answer the phone or the door, because I'm betting it was your buddies in my trailer last night, looking for you, and I'll bet they're still looking."

"How'm I gonna get to the airport?"

"Let me think a minute." I leaned an elbow on my knee and rested my chin in my hand, thinking. "You could get Lurline to drive you, but if I were you, I'd not tell her anything that's going on. She can't help it, but she can't keep a secret to save her life. So," I said with a sigh, "I guess I'll have to take you, but I can't do it until tomorrow at the earliest."

"You're not gonna regret this, hon, I promise. I'll be the happiest man in the world when I hand you a million dollars."

"Oh, Skip, I don't want your money. You just worry about staying out of sight. Now, I've got to go, so let me get up from here."

He frowned, hanging his head to one side. "I kinda thought we'd spend some time thinkin' up ways to spend all that money. You know, new cars—you sure do need one—maybe a trip. I was thinkin' about going over to Cherokee to that new casino they got over there."

"Skip, honey, you've won on a gamble, now don't go losing it on more gambling. You put that money in the bank and live on the interest, like rich folks do. I'm going now," I said, standing up and tearing a sheet off my notepad. "Here's where you can reach me if there's more trouble. It's Mr. Connard's house. I have to go by and see about him since his son's in the hospital."

He looked so down in the mouth about me leaving that I stopped beside his chair and kissed the top of his head. Just a big ole baby was all he was, and he needed somebody to take care of him. Only it wasn't going to be me.

"Stay locked in, now," I told him at the door. "Delmont's not that big, and if they're still looking for you, they'll find you. What do they look like, in case I see them?"

"You know 'em. It's Harley and Roy."

I turned around and stared at him. "Harley and . . . ? *Puckett?* You mean Harley and Roy *Puckett?* My God, Skip, a Puckett'd as soon kill you as look at you. I didn't know you were mixed up with that trash."

He shrugged. "They're all right. Roy got me my job at the Texaco station, after I ran into 'em at a Strong Man contest. They been in Gastonia for a while, workin' and makin' good money. It's just when they get mad that you have to stay outta their way."

"Well, see that you do," I told him, leaving the house and hoping he'd stay there. That Puckett riffraff was Delmont's claim to fame in the jail-time category, and had been for generation after generation for as long as anybody could remember. Well, except for Hazel Marie.

I got in the car and sat for a minute, wondering if I'd been too hasty. Skip was as honest as the day is long, and if he'd promised to give me half of his winnings, he'd do it. So there it was, all the money I'd ever need. All I had to do was throw in with him and I'd be set for life. All my bills paid, no more worries, and he wouldn't expect a thing out of me. No marriage, no fooling around if I put my foot down hard enough. He'd be as good as his word. I could have what I needed with no strings attached.

I opened the car door to go back inside, then thought about it some more. Was money what I wanted? *All* I wanted? I rubbed the back of my neck where an ache was starting up again, and thought of Valerie Connard and that receptionist and Clyde Maybry and Mrs. Julia Springer, and a dozen others who'd treated me like dirt. What I wanted, Skip couldn't give me and neither could a million dollars. Only Mr. Howard's name could do for me what I wanted. Although it didn't hurt that he had enough money to back up his name.

I crossed out number 8 on my list, swung my legs back into the car, and turned on the ignition.

Chapter 17

Checking my watch as I headed back toward downtown Delmont, I worried about getting everything on my list done. Time was the problem. I had to have Mr. Howard at the Abbot County Courthouse to get our license before the Register of Deeds office closed at five o'clock, and I personally wanted to be there early enough to get the entire deed done today. Both license and ceremony, considering that Junior might be home tomorrow with a clear head and a change of heart.

I wasn't worried about finding either the Register of Deeds office or the magistrate's office if we didn't have time to get to the Reverend Haliday's church. I'd made that civil circuit twice before on my marital rounds. It seemed to me, though, that it was time for me to have a church wedding, even if nobody attended but the immediate wedding party, and it was held in a country church instead of the First Methodist.

I could just picture Mr. Howard waiting in his wheelchair—I didn't want to put a strain on him by making him stand at the altar—and me walking down the aisle toward him.

Flowers! I'd forgotten about flowers. Every bride ought to have flowers, even if it was only a white orchid corsage on her shoulder or, even better, strapped on her wrist. What I'd really like, though, was a nice spray of baby's breath and white roses. Well, maybe pink ones would be more proper. Whatever, I wanted one with a handle underneath that I could hold at my waist as I walked down the aisle. Sadie's Floral Shop could make one up, that was no problem. The problem was time. And heat. Even if everything went according to plan, my wedding bouquet would be a wilted mess by the time the knot was ready to be tied.

So, glancing at my watch again, I decided to forget about florist flowers. I could pick something from Mrs. Howard Connard, Senior's garden, if it came to that. And if anything was blooming.

I slowed as I entered Main Street and drove toward the center of town, watching the street signs. The Laundromat I was looking for was on Maple, just a few doors off Main. There was good parking beside it, and it was the cleanest and quietest one in town.

As I parked, fuming over having to wash clothes on my special day, I had to calm myself down with the reminder that you have to take things as they come. You just have to deal with the unexpected, even if it tears your plans all to hell and back.

Thinking of whoever'd trashed my trailer the night before—and it had to've been those filthy Pucketts—made me mad all over again. I didn't need to be washing and drying clothes on my wedding day. Whoever heard of such a thing? Yet I couldn't bring myself to go into married life with dirty clothes, especially underclothes, considering the way they'd gotten that way with you-know-whose nasty hands all over them. I could've asked Emmett to run them through at Mr. Howard's house while we went to get the license. That would've relieved my anxiety about time, but I just couldn't ask Emmett to deal with my lingerie. It's so personal, you know. As the second Mrs. Howard Connard, Senior, I needed to be aware of such niceties.

So, bundling up my clothes from the backseat, I went into the moist heat of the Laundromat. Thank goodness, it wasn't crowded, but it was hot as hell. I began to perspire again as I loaded a washing machine, purchased a package of Tide and one of fabric softener, and pushed quarters into the slot.

When the machine started filling, I left to find a cool place to wait. I could feel my hair frizzing, but thanks to Kathie Lee, my dress was still wrinkle-free.

As I started down the sidewalk toward Freeman's Soda Shop for an icy cherry Coke, I found myself walking side by side with Mr. Ernest Sitton, Esquire.

"Mr. Sitton," I said, startled at finding him so available, even though it was on a public sidewalk. "I want to thank you again for rescuing me last night. I appreciate it more than I can say. And I paid my bill right on time this morning, like I said I would, although I have to tell you that your receptionist isn't the friendliest person in the world, if you don't mind me saying so."

He kept walking as he looked at me over the gold-rimmed glasses on his nose, frowning as if I'd interrupted some serious concentration. "Do I know you, young lady?"

"Yessir, you do. You kept me from being arrested last night, remember? I called you in the middle of the night, and you came right over to the jail and you put Deputy Maybry in his place, with no two ways about it. It was a pleasure to see you work, Mr. Sitton, sir."

"Ah, yes. Got me out of bed, too, didn't you?" He stepped around the roots where one of the trees that lined Main Street had lifted the sidewalk. I glanced at him and saw just the hint of a smile at the corner of his mouth, and I knew I'd found his weak spot. Every man has one, and it's usually the same one with all of them.

"Yessir, and I'm sorry about that, but when you said you'd be right down, well, I just can't tell you how my heart lifted up.

Everybody in town, and I wouldn't be surprised if everybody in the state, knows that you're the best lawyer anywhere."

"Do they now?" Another twitch of his mouth. Could've been a tic that I hadn't noticed the night before, but I was betting on a response to flattery. It works most every time.

"Yessir, and I can't tell you how many times I've heard people say, 'If you're ever in trouble, call Mr. Ernest Sitton. He's the one you want.' Why, you're known far and wide as the man to have, especially if you're guilty. But I wasn't and I'm not. Guilty, that is. But when I felt the long arm of the law after me, you were the first and only lawyer I thought of."

He gave me a quick glance, frowning now with no hint of a smile. "Tell me again who you are."

"Etta Mae Wiggins."

"Wiggins," he said. "Hm-m-m, Wiggins. Daddy, name of Rufe?"

"Well, I am guilty of that, but I hope you won't hold it against me. He passed away some years ago. And I'm doing real good. Good enough, in fact, to be able to afford the best lawyer in town."

He frowned at me again, and I gave him my best, admiring smile. And that twitch of his mouth wasn't a tic at all, for he smiled back. He had to wet his lips first, though, since it didn't look as if he'd had much practice at it.

As we neared Freeman's, I said, mentally counting the change in my purse, "Mr. Sitton, it'd be a real honor if you'd care to join me in a cherry Coke. Or whatever you'd like as a refreshment. I'd like to show my appreciation for being my lawyer, and maybe discuss some future dealings we might have."

He stopped walking, seeming confused and at a loss for words. Maybe nobody'd ever offered to treat him before and he didn't know how to act. "Ms. Wiggins," he said, "the only appreciation I want from you or anybody is the timely payment of my bill."

"Done!" I said, giving him the benefit of another dazzling smile. "At nine-fifteen this morning, just like I said I would."

"And," he said, as if the payment of my bill was an accepted fact, "as far as future dealings between you and me are concerned, all I can do is recommend that you stay out of trouble. Recidivists are not my favorite clients, and I very quickly refuse their business."

I didn't know what he was talking about, so I figured it didn't apply to me. It did bother me, though, that a man as smart as Lawyer Sitton used bad grammar. You'd think anybody with his education would know that *between you and I* is a more refined way of speaking than *between you and me*. But his mind was taken up with more important things.

"I'm sorry. I didn't make myself clear," I said. "I didn't mean future dealings with the sheriff, especially Clyde Maybry, or any other kind of trouble. It's just, well, I'll soon be in a position to, ah, work closely with you, and I just wanted to be on good terms with you. And, also, to kind of prepare you for some, maybe, necessary changes in the matter of, well, a longtime client, which you already have."

"Well, I must say you've piqued my interest, young lady. However, I'm on a tight schedule, so I'm going to have to delay any discussion about this intriguing matter. I'm certainly interested in anything that concerns a client of mine. Make an appointment with Miss Willet and we'll discuss it in the privacy of my office."

"Oh, thank you. I'll be happy to, in fact, I'd prefer to do it in your office. But, Mr. Sitton, you need to speak to that redheaded witch you have out front and tell her you want me to have an appointment. She's losing business for you. She told me to go to some other lawyer, that you couldn't see me. She's not good for your business, Mr. Sitton, and I'm just telling you this as a favor. You ought to have somebody in there who'd reflect the kind of man, and the kind of excellent lawyer, you are. Not some dried-up old prune who's not doing you a bit of good."

He nodded, looked down the street, and twitched his mouth again. "Miss Willet has been with me a long time, and she knows where the bodies are buried," he said, which didn't make a whole lot of sense to me. "But I'll tell her to give you an appointment whenever you call."

"It may take me a week or so," I said, beaming at him. I'd always gotten along with men better than women, and this was just another for instance. "I'm going to be awful busy in the next few days, but I need to see you, and you're going to be real surprised. And pleased, I hope."

"I look forward to it," he said, with a nod of his head almost like the bow of a gentleman.

Feeling like I'd done a good thing, I watched as he walked away, then I went into the soda shop.

After going back to the Laundromat and putting my clothes in a dryer, I waited on a hard plastic chair and skimmed through a six-month-old *People* magazine. I hadn't felt so good since before Lurline let the cat out of the bag to Junior. Things were looking up, even though time was running out. At least, to get everything on my list done in one day.

See, even when you have to do something like a load of dirty clothes on your wedding day, it can all work for the best. If I hadn't been at the Laundromat, I'd've never met Mr. Sitton on the street, and never known how nice a man he was. Much less have gotten past Miss High-and-Mighty Willet to make an appointment that he was looking forward to.

I had even peaked his interest, and all because I'd been at the right place at the right time, even though the hours of the day were ticking away.

Chapter 18

By the time I got my clothes folded and stacked on the backseat, it was past time to get to Mr. Howard's house. Even though striking off number 9 on my list gave me a sense of accomplishment, I was way off schedule, timewise. The three most important things were yet to do, with not much of the day left to do them in. I got so nervous just thinking about it that my hands were shaking.

Pulling into Mr. Howard's drive, I parked under the trees next to Emmett's staircase on the side of the garage. Junior's Cadillac Seville was nowhere to be seen, and for the first time, I wondered where it could be. He'd left in it while I was talking with Emmett the night before, and ended up unconscious on my couch, so where had he left it? I hoped the deputies had thought about his means of transportation before this and were looking for it, but it might not've entered Clyde's head.

Maybe I should call Bobby Lee.

Maybe I shouldn't. He'd want to know how I knew when and by what means Junior had left his daddy's house last night.

I walked to the side door of the house, tapped as I usually did, and went into the kitchen.

"Hi, Emmett."

He looked up from the sink where he was rinsing dishes before stacking them in the dishwasher. "Miss Etta Mae," he said, putting a salad plate carefully on the counter. "Miss Etta, what you doin' here? I don't need no trouble."

"I don't either, Emmett. But don't worry, I've been to see Junior over at the hospital and he knows I'm here."

He turned back to the sink and picked up the plate, relieved that he didn't have to throw me out. "Mr. Junior doin' all right?"

"Seemed to be. He was talking, but I doubt he's ready for a ten-mile race. Listen, Emmett, have any deputies questioned you about last night?"

"They sho' have. Two of 'em this morning, askin' when Mr. Junior left, where he goin', when I 'spectin' him back, an' I don't know what all."

I drew in a breath between my teeth. "Did you tell them I was here when he left?"

"They didn't ax me nothin' like that, an' I didn't offer nothin' but coffee and sweet rolls."

"Good," I said. "You and me both know I had nothing to do with Junior getting hurt." He cut his eyes over at me like he wasn't sure what he knew. "So," I hurried on, "how's Mr. Howard today?"

"He settin' in there waitin' on you, an' mad as a wet hen 'bout Mr. Junior takin' him to Raleigh. Miss Etta Mae, I had to tell him why them deputies was here, but I didn't tell him Mr. Junior be over to your trailer."

"I'm glad you didn't, because the fact of the matter is I didn't know he was over there till I got home and found him knocked out cold on my new couch."

Emmett kept his eyes on the dishes, not saying anything for several seconds, while I stood there knowing he still wasn't happy about something.

Finally, without looking up, he said, "You left here right after Mr. Junior pulled out. Some people might figure you followed him, an' some people might figure you got in a fight with him 'bout Mr. Howard."

"Some people would be wrong, too. I'd parked my car down by the Skyway, so I had several blocks to walk to get back to it. And after that, I got something to eat, so I didn't get home till around midnight.

"Emmett, listen, I didn't see Junior last night. I didn't talk to him, and I certainly didn't have a fight with him. Besides, he'd make about three of me, so no way could I've done anything to him. And another thing, since everybody's doubting my story, the big question is what was Junior doing there in the first place? Do you realize he had to *break the lock* to get in? I mean, that's a criminal offense! I'm not the one who ought to be worried around here."

"Mr. Junior did that?"

"Well, *I* certainly didn't break into my own trailer. I'll tell you, Emmett, Junior doesn't have a leg to stand on when it comes to me and Mr. Howard. Not now, he doesn't. I could sue him from here to kingdom come, and ruin his reputation, too. And make that skinny witch he's married to wish she'd never heard of me."

Emmett started smiling. He raised his head and looked out the window across the yard, and smiled some more. "Mr. Junior over the barrel now," he said.

"You got it. So some things are going to be changing around here, Emmett. And the first one is this: you're not going any- where and neither is Mr. Howard. Are you with me on this?"

"Yessum, I sho' is." He let the water drain out of the sink, then said, "How you gonna manage all that?"

"The same way the first Mrs. Howard Connard, Senior, did."

His eyes got big as he stared at me. "You mean . . . ?"

"I sure do. Me and Mr. Howard have been talking about it for a long time, but I didn't want anybody thinking I was taking advantage. But now, now with this threat to Mr. Howard's well-being, I think it's time I took a hand in what happens to him. Don't you?"

He stepped back from the sink, picked up a dishrag, and started drying his hands. "That need some thinkin' about," he said, carefully folding the dishrag and draping it over the faucet. "An' I b'lieve I just done all the thinkin' needin' to be done. It'll take some gettin' used to, but seem to me it be good, 'cause Mr. Junior, he can't do no more mischief 'round here."

Then a sudden thought stopped him. "When the happy day? You better move fast, Miss Etta, 'cause Junior be outta the hospital pretty soon, an' even though he not able to make trouble, that Miss Valerie, she somethin' else."

"Is she ever! I had the pleasure of meeting her at the hospital and, frankly, she's the one I'm worried about now. She's so cold, I don't think it'd bother her if I had Junior arrested and locked up."

"She cold, all right. She done called to tell me to fix up one of the bedrooms upstairs. She gon' spend the night here."

"Oh, Lord," I said, my heart skipping a beat. "When's she coming?"

"She just say tonight, an' to not fix no supper for her, she make a salat when she come in."

"Whew," I said, fanning my face with my hand. "That'll be enough time. I hope."

"Time for what? What you plannin' for?"

"A wedding, Emmett. I'm planning for a wedding in"—I looked at my watch—"about an hour and a half. If I can get everything done."

His eyes bugged out, and he said, "Do Mr. Howard know 'bout this?"

"Not yet," I said, laughing, "but he will in just a few minutes."

Chapter 19

⟋⟍

Leaving Emmett in the kitchen, I walked through the dining room, across the wide hall, and into the living room. It all looked like a picture in a magazine—damask sofas, cream-colored flocked wallpaper, silk drapes with fringe on them at the windows, dark oil paintings on the walls, Persian rugs on the hardwood floors, real flowers in Chinese-looking vases—it was enough to take your breath away, like it wasn't meant to be lived in. Mr. Howard had told me about the furnishings, as he called all the pretty things in his house, and I'd tried to learn about them.

I'd made him laugh when I'd said it didn't look like a place to curl up in your jammies with a bowl of popcorn and a cold one.

I thought the rooms were pretty, don't get me wrong, but I'll have to say, if I'd had the money the first Mrs. Howard Connard, Senior'd had, I'd've put more comfort and color into what I bought. I mean, there wasn't even a TV in the living room. What she'd done was real elegant, and lots of her things were cute as they could be, but it wasn't to my taste and I wasn't sure I'd ever be able to feel at home with them. They just weren't me.

But I wouldn't change a thing. Mr. Howard liked the decor the way it was, and I wouldn't do anything to upset him. Maybe he'd let me do up our bedroom in my own style, you know, with a pretty white-and-gold French Provincial suite. Maybe with lavender drapes and bedspread. My stuffed animals would look so pretty against a pile of satin pillows, with maybe a glass-fronted whatnot for my Barbie collection. As I pictured it in my mind, I remembered the hospital bed Mr. Howard slept in, and wondered how that would blend in. I wasn't sure that even I could make that work.

I wandered through those front rooms, not touching anything until I got to the long dining room table. I couldn't help but run my hand over its smooth, shiny top that Emmett kept polished to within an inch of its life. I jerked my hand back when I saw I'd made a handprint on it. Oh, Lord, reckon I'd ruined it? I took my dress tail and smoothed it back the way it was. Time for me to get out of there before I messed something up good.

I went down the hall and turned toward the downstairs bedroom that'd been fixed up for Mr. Howard after he could no longer manage the stairs. Tapping on the door, I stuck my head in. "Mr. Howard? Hey, you ole honey, it's me."

He was sitting in a chair, all dressed and neat and clean, wearing a white shirt and tie and a cashmere sweater. His half-dead left hand lay in his lap, and a cotton blanket was over his knees. Old people have poor circulation, you know, and Mr. Howard suffered from it as much as anybody I'd ever seen.

He turned his head, and his bleary old eyes lit up when he saw me. To see that made everything I was planning worthwhile. I'd never had anybody depend on me, and *appreciate* me, like Mr. Howard did. He'd told me one time that just knowing I was somewhere in this world made his heart lift up and fly. A man who'd say a thing like that, and mean it, was worth taking care of. At least, that was my thinking.

I rolled a footstool beside his chair and sat down. Taking his good right hand in mine, I said, "You sure look handsome today, sweetie. Got some big plans?"

He shook his head, that lopsided smile which was all he could manage on his face. "Yoo-o," he said. When he said, or tried to say, "You," I knew he meant he was looking good for me, and that his big plans for the day included a visit with me. When people have strong feelings for each other, they can say a lot in a few words. And a good thing, too, because the first thing a stroke does to you is affect the way you talk, and the last thing you recover as you get well, if you do get well, is control of your mouth and your tongue. I learned that at the Abbot County Technical College, along with a lot of other useful bits of information that I used in my everyday work with senior citizens.

So Mr. Howard and I, we communicated just fine, understanding each other in shorthand, so to speak. I also depended a lot on his facial expressions. Well, half facial expressions, because the strokes had left their mark mostly on his left side from the top of his head to the bottom of his feet. Otherwise, he was in real good health.

"I went to see Junior over at the hospital," I told him. Then at his frown, I hurried on. "He looks okay and the nurse said he'd be home tomorrow or the day after. I talked to him a little, and I hope you don't mind, but I told him what you and me've been talking about. And, Mr. Howard, honey, he didn't seem to mind! In fact, he smiled! What do you think of that!"

He growled deep in his throat, frowning and squeezing my hand.

"Now, don't get yourself upset," I said, stroking his thin arm through the layer of cashmere. "You haven't heard it all. I know all about how Junior's planning to move you to a Raleigh nursing home, but we can nip that in the bud. Junior was just worried about you, wanting you to have the care you need. That's why he was going to do that, so you mustn't be mad at him. He cares about you, and so do I."

I put his hand beside my face and rubbed it against my cheek as I went on. "You know how you've been talking about me and you, you and I, getting married, and I was afraid you didn't really mean it and that other people would think I was taking advantage? Well, I don't think that way anymore.

"Mr. Howard, honey, if you still want to, I'll marry you and take care of you till death do us part and I'll never put you in a nursing home or let anybody hurt you or upset you again. If you still want to."

"Ehra Mae, Ehra Mae." He cupped his good hand around my face, and his old eyes filled up, the good one overflowing with tears.

"Don't cry, honey," I said, grabbing a Kleenex and wiping his wrinkled face. "I hope that means you're happy." I laughed a little, about to tear up myself. "'Cause I sure am.

"Now, listen," I went on, "I told Junior we were getting married and he didn't have a thing to say against it. So I don't want you to think I'm trying to put something over on him. I don't want to cause any problems between you and your son. But I do think we ought to go ahead with it before that wife of his changes his mind."

He nodded his head and squeezed my hand as tight as he could manage.

"Here's my plan," I said, scooting closer to his chair. "In just a few minutes we'll get you in my car, 'cause we have to be at the courthouse in Abbotsville before five o'clock to get the marriage license. Both of us have to be there and sign for it, and isn't it lucky that you're right-handed and won't have any trouble signing your name? See, you can always find the bright side if you just look. Anyway, once we get the license, we can get married either at the magistrate's office, though it might be too late for that today, or we can go to Reverend Haliday's church and he'll marry us this afternoon, or first thing in the morning if that's the way it works out. Does that make you happy?"

He smiled so wide, he almost got it over to the left side of his face. He was so overcome that all he could do was nod his head up and down.

"It makes me happy, too," I said. That's one of the reasons I liked my job so much, making old, sad people happy. Though I'd never made one this happy before. "Now, I'm going to call Emmett to help me get you to the car. Is that all right? You feel like doing all that today?"

He tried again to speak, but the excitement made it hard for even me to understand him. He waved his good hand, still holding mine, pointing toward the closet.

"Oh, bless your sweet heart," I said, realizing what he wanted. "You want your suit coat, don't you? Let me get Emmett and we'll get you fixed up for your wedding day."

I could've cried with the classiness of it. Mr. Howard knew the right thing to do, and of course, he wouldn't want to get married in a sweater. He thought too much of me not to be dressed right and proper. I couldn't help but remember how Skip wore his letter jacket, purple and gold satin, at our ceremony, and how Bernie had worn a plaid sports jacket and tan polyester Sansabelts at the next one I went through. But Mr. Howard knew how a gentleman ought to dress.

When I called Emmett to come help us, Mr. Howard made it clear that he wanted to walk to the car. We got him up in the walker, which worried me no end because his left arm didn't have the strength he needed to manage it very well. But with Emmett there to steady him and Mr. Howard's determination, I figured I wasn't going to start our marriage by telling him he couldn't do something he wanted to do. Besides, the doctor'd said he needed excercise.

I folded the wheelchair and carried it out to the car, thinking he might be glad to have it before we got everything done. I pulled the car right up close to the kitchen door, and was waiting with the door open when Emmett and Mr. Howard got there.

While the two of us were trying to get Mr. Howard turned around so he could sit down on the front seat, I heard a motorcycle misfire out on the street. Just as Emmett swung Mr. Howard's legs inside the car, the familiar sound of a motor with fewer cylinders working than it ought to have came from the driveway.

I looked up to see the black Low Rider barrel into the yard from the driveway, skidding to a stop in the loose gravel beside my car. *Oh, God,* I thought as the driver took off his helmet, *what have I done to deserve this aggravation right when I didn't need any more?*

"Hey, Etta Mae," Skip said, swinging his leg off and kicking down the kickstand. "Y'all goin' somewhere?"

Chapter 20

I marched over and grabbed Skip's arm, turning him away from the car. Emmett, waiting beside it, watched this new development with a frown on his face.

"What are you doing here?" I demanded, so put out with him that it was all I could do to maintain. "Skip, I swear, didn't I tell you to stay at Lurline's?"

"Well, dang, Etta Mae . . ." He scratched his head, his hair damp and matted from sweating under his helmet.

"You just listen to me. You know Roy and Harley're looking for you and you know you ought to stay out of sight. Do you want to end up in the hospital like Junior Connard? Or worse? Dad blame it, where's your brain?"

"I couldn't help it, Etta Mae. I saw 'em. They drove up and parked across the street from Lurline's. They knew I was there. What was I supposed to do, stay there till they came in and got me?"

I drew in a long breath, thinking it would've served him right. "And just how'd they know you were there? Come on, Skip, how'd they find you? They couldn't've known where Lurline lived, so how'd they pick her house?"

"Well." He scuffed the toe of his boot in the gravel, unable to meet my eyes. "Well, maybe I got a cravin' for barbecue. You know, for lunch?" I propped my hands on my hips and glared at him. "I was careful, Etta Mae, I really was. I snuck around on back streets till I got to the Porky Park and ordered at the window. I was real careful, I promise."

I took a deep breath. What do you do with a fool?

"Well, you weren't careful enough. Obviously. It's plain as day they saw you and followed you back to Lurline's. What did you expect, Skip? It's broad daylight and they've been here almost twenty-four hours. I could find anybody in Delmont in twenty minutes in the dead of the night. All you had to do was stay inside." I could've shaken him, I was so put out. "Now what you've probably done is lead them over here."

"Well, dang it all, I had to find you. Lurline called and said Granny's looking for you. She'd called the office, wanting you to come see her as quick as you could, so I thought I better let you know."

That stopped me. Granny didn't usually call me at work, so when she did, I dropped everything and went to see about her. She'd had her phone taken out, because too many times its ringing had interrupted her stories on TV and the pro wrestling she loved. When she needed me, she'd go next door and use Boyce and Betty Sue's, not telling them what she wanted. Boyce was her third son who looked after her, which he did fairly well when she'd let him. Nine times out of ten when she called me, it was for something like finding her glasses or helping her turn a mattress.

I always worried, though, about that one time when something might be wrong. Granny had raised me when nobody else could or would, and I thought the world of her. When she called, I went.

Going by her house, plus doing something with Skip, was going to put a crimp in the day's activities. Well, it couldn't be helped. I took out my list of things to do, wadded it up, and crammed it back into my purse. I'd just have to do the best I could, even if everything didn't get done in one day.

While all this was going through my mind, Skip was standing there waiting to be told what to do next. Whirling around on him, with my hands on my hips, I said, "So what're we gonna do if they followed you here?"

"I don't think they did. I snuck out the back and come straight over here, hopin' to catch you before you left." He gave me that big, goofy grin that used to take me in every time. "An' I did, didn't I? Looks like just in time, too."

I just shook my head. "Let me think a minute," I said, biting my thumb and wondering how to get everything done in a day that was fast running out of hours. "I can take my patient out to Granny's with me. It'll be a nice ride for him. But you, I don't know what to do with you. You can't go to my trailer, and you sure can't go back to Lurline's. I've run out of hiding places. Did you call Atlanta and the airlines?"

"Not yet. I thought I'd get me something to eat first."

"I hope you enjoyed it," I muttered, knowing sarcasm was lost on him. Then, "How long do you have to turn that ticket in?"

"Thirty days, I think it is, so I got plenty of time to claim my winnings."

"That's good, I guess, but you don't have plenty of time when Pucketts're after you. And speaking of Pucketts, we better get moving. I swear to God, Skip, if they followed you here, I'm going to wring your neck."

I turned to look at Mr. Howard, waiting patiently in the car. I had a quick picture of what would happen if those two maniacs came speeding up the driveway, blocking us in and doing I-didn't-know-what to all of us, including Mr. Howard. It didn't bear thinking about. We had to get out of there.

"Get this thing out of sight," I said, kicking the motorcycle.

"Huh? Where? What you want me to do with it?"

"I want you to put it, let me see, behind the garage. Yes, get it around behind the garage, in the bushes, where nobody coming in can see it."

"Okay," he said, swinging a leg over the Low Rider. He stood, putting a foot on the starter. As he started to give it a mighty shove, I nearly swatted him off the thing.

"Dang it, Skip, *roll* the thing back there!"

"Roll it? You mean, walk it back there?"

"Yes! If the Pucketts're out on the street looking for you, they'll hear you start up. Use your head!" Then, at the hurt look on his face, I said, "I'm sorry, Skip, but I'm scared, too, and I have my patient to think of. Hurry up now, and get back here."

"You got a plan, Etta Mae?" He kicked up the kickstand and aimed the bike toward the garage.

"Yeah." I sighed. "I've got a plan."

While he headed toward the garage, I went back to the car. "Emmett," I said, "that's a near relation of mine who's not too bright. We all have to look after him. You know how it is with family. If anybody comes looking for him, just say you don't know him. Which you don't."

He nodded, watching Skip as he went behind the garage. "No'm," he said. "I don't."

"In fact," I went on, "why don't you take some time off and just not answer the door if anybody comes? Unless it's Junior's wife, of course."

"Yessum," he said, still unsure about what was going on and what it had to do with him.

"We're leaving now," I said, opening the car door and sliding inside. "Don't worry about Mr. Howard. You know I'll look after him, and we'll be back in an hour or two."

"What I gonna tell Miss Valerie if she ax where he at?"

I switched on the ignition as I thought for a minute. "Reckon he could be asleep and not want to be disturbed?" At the look he gave me, I said, "Guess not. Well, if she asks, just say somebody's taken him for a ride. On doctor's orders. If she doesn't ask, don't say anything. How's that?"

He nodded. "I do that. Mr. Howard," he said, leaning in the window, "you have a good time, hear?"

I reached over and patted Mr. Howard's half-dead hand. "I'm sorry about this, honey, but we're going to have to help somebody in need, and go by to see my granny for a little while. We won't stay long, and we'll be at the courthouse by five, just like we planned."

Skip came running up to the car. He leaned in my window, panting. "You ain't leavin', are you, Etta Mae? What you want me to do?"

"Get in the car, Skip," I said, leaning over the steering wheel and pulling the back of my seat up. "Get in the back on the floor. And don't mess with my clean clothes."

"On the floor?"

"*On the floor,* damn it! Excuse me, Mr. Howard, I'm a little flustered."

"Okay, okay," Skip said, as he pushed and shoved to get in, nearly squeezing me to death against the steering wheel. Finally, he got in and tried to curl up on the floorboard. "There's not much room down here, Etta Mae."

"I know it. It's a Camaro. But it's all you've got, so stay down, and I mean it. Mr. Howard, that big ole boy back there is Skip Taggert, and we're going to have to take him with us, much to my regret."

Mr. Howard tried to turn around to see Skip, but then he shrugged his right shoulder, gave me a half smile, and said, "Frien'?"

"Yeah, an old friend I can't seem to get rid of."

I headed the car down the driveway and out onto the street, turning toward Abbotsville and the courthouse, by way of a Granny detour, my soon-to-be husband in the front seat and one of my exes in the back.

Chapter 21

~

Granny's house was a short way off Mill Run Road, which veered north off the Abbotsville Highway, so it didn't take us too far out of the way. By the time we turned off the gravel road and onto the narrow dirt one that took us to Granny's, it was getting on past three-thirty and I was getting worried. I'd wanted to be Mrs. Howard Connard, Senior, by nightfall, and it didn't look like I was going to make it.

As I passed Boyce and Betty Sue's brick house with the wide, newly mown lawn and the new aboveground swimming pool shimmering in the heat, I reminded myself that they were doing the best they could with Granny, and I had no need to be mad at them. All her other sons and the two daughters had moved as far away as they could get, some to Charlotte, a couple to Georgia, and a few to the grave, so Boyce and Betty Sue and me were all she had.

"Can I get up now?" Skip asked, as I turned into Granny's drive and parked in the shade.

"Okay, get on up. Nobody's been behind us for three miles, and we're here," I said. As I opened the car door, I turned to Mr. Howard. "Just look at Granny's flowers up there on the porch. Aren't they a picture? Now, you just rest here while I see about her. I won't be but a minute."

"She sure needs a coat of paint," Skip said as he climbed out of the car behind me and eyed the peeling farmhouse. He put his hand on the middle of his back and leaned back, stretching out the kinks. "I could do it for her, if you want me to."

"She wouldn't let you. She likes things the way they are, unless she decides to do something herself."

As I headed toward the steps, Granny came barreling out on the porch, all sixty-seven years and ninety-two pounds of her, the screen door slamming behind her. She had on a faded pink housedress with tiny white stars all over it, a big white apron that almost swallowed her, and Reeboks at the end of her skinny legs.

"Etta Mae," she called, her white hair streaming behind her where strands of it had come loose from the bun. "Etta Mae, I'm gonna bust somebody to kingdom come. I'm glad you got here, sugar, 'cause I'm not gonna take any more of it."

"What's wrong, Granny?" I asked, relieved to see that no bones were broken, her glasses were on her nose, and the house was still standing. I figured I could handle most anything else.

"I'm gonna flail the daylights outta that woman, see if I don't."

"What's Betty Sue done now?"

"Took my canning jars, that's what. And won't give 'em back, says I give 'em to her last year. Now, Etta Mae, who'd believe a whopper like that? You ever known me to give away a Mason jar I know I'm gonna need when my pole beans come in?"

"Now, Granny, maybe she misunderstood. I tell you what, I'll get you some new ones. In fact, this weekend, I'll come get you and we'll go to Walmart's. You can get whatever you want then. You probably need some new rubber rings, anyway, don't you?"

"Well, I could use some, I guess. Besides, I always like a trip to Walmart's. They got everything you could want, and if they don't have it, you don't need it." She'd calmed down by then, her eyes moving back and forth with curiosity at my unlikely passengers. "Don't I know this big 'un, here?" she asked, peering up at Skip.

"Hey, Granny," Skip said. "I'm Skip, used to be your grandson-in-law, 'member?"

She snorted. "I've not lost my mind yet. You're the one broke my swing, sittin' on it, and the one left my girl with all them bills you owed. Pull that stunt again, buster, and I'll slap the doo-doo outta you."

Skip grinned. "Yeah, well."

Granny leaned over and craned her neck to look in the car. "Who's that ole fool? Looks half dead to me."

"Now, Granny, that's one of my patients, so leave him alone. He's resting." Mr. Howard had his head back on the car seat, taking a little nap.

"Do I know him?"

"I don't think so." I knew she knew of him, like everybody else, but I didn't want to get into what I was doing with him until I'd gotten it done.

"Well, you folks come on in the house. I got a ham in the stove, so there's plenty."

"We can't, Granny," I said, though I hated to come and go so fast. She got lonesome without somebody to talk to, though Betty Sue visited almost every day. Which didn't really count, because Granny was too mad to talk to her half the time.

"I'll be back Saturday," I told her, "and we'll spend the whole afternoon at Walmart's."

"Lord, child, I don't have that much to buy, nor that much to spend. Social Security don't cover that kinda spree. Well, I know you got to go, so come give me a hug, and be sure you tell Betty Sue I've had a bellyful of her sneaky ways."

"I will, Granny," I said, as I hugged her and patted her back. "I'll talk to her, but you ought not get so mad at her. It's not good for you, and it worries me when you get so upset."

"I'm through gettin' upset. If she ever puts her sticky hands on them new jars, I'm gonna smack her face." She cackled at the thought of it.

"Betty Sue's good to you, Granny. You shouldn't hurt her feelings." Turning to Skip, I said, "Crawl on in and let's get on the road."

"Couldn't I just stay out here with Granny? Nobody'd find me this far outta town."

"No, you cannot. I'm not putting Granny in danger, and you're not, either. Besides, don't you still owe Boyce for that Scag mower you bought on time? He lives right next door."

"Oh, yeah. I forgot."

I didn't tell him I'd paid it off to keep peace in the family. Let him stew for the two minutes he'd worry about it.

"Hurry up, then," I said, as he began wedging himself behind the front seat, "and watch my clothes back there.

"Granny, honey, I'm sorry I can't stay longer, but you can see I've got my hands full."

"You're a good girl, Etta Mae, but come over here outta earshot. I wanna ask you something."

We walked a few steps away, and she pulled me down to whisper in my ear, "Honey, what're you doing with that old man settin' there in your front seat with his mouth hanging open? He looks like he's on his last legs, but take my word for it, old men can surprise you. They'll jump you in a minute, an' I know what I'm talkin' about. He's after something, I can tell. So I don't want you to turn your back on him. It's a good thing you got that young 'un in there with you. You tell him to watch that ole fool."

"Oh, Granny," I said, laughing and hugging her again. "I don't think I have to worry about him. That old man can hardly do a thing for himself, and I'm just getting him out and around for a while."

I wanted to tell her where I was getting him out and around to, but Granny was about as bad with secrets as Lurline. She wouldn't tell on purpose. She'd just forget she wasn't supposed to tell it. I was too close to the prize to risk sharing it with her at that point.

I turned the car around and, waving to Granny through the dust stirred up behind us, headed back toward the Abbotsville Highway.

As I turned east on the highway, I said, "Get down on the floor, Skip. There's a lot of traffic this time of day, and it'll be hard to watch for the Pucketts. They could come up behind us before we know it."

"Do I have to?"

"Yes. I can't take any chances with my patient. So just do it."

He grumbled and mumbled as he got on the floorboard again, knocking against the seats and complaining about the cramped space. "It's hard to breathe down here," he said. "And I can't stretch out and I don't like being all scrunched up like this."

"Get over it," I said, and pulled out into the traffic on the Abbotsville Highway.

Chapter 22

"Etta Mae?" Skip's voice sounded hollow, echoing up from under Mr. Howard's bucket seat.

"What?"

"Can I get up now? This driveshaft's killin' me."

"I don't care if it is," I said. "We're hardly two miles out of Delmont, so you stay right where you are."

"My back's gonna be broke in two. An' it sure is hot down here."

"Well, just think what you're missing, Skip. You could be stretched out in one of Lurline's recliners watching *Roseanne* reruns, with a breeze from the air conditioner blowing right on you. On the other hand, you could also be in the hands of those real good friends of yours, getting your ticket punched in more ways than one. Now don't that driveshaft feel better?"

"I guess," he mumbled.

I kept watching the rearview mirror, checking to see if we were being followed. Then it struck me that I didn't know what I was looking for. Duh. That's what happens when you have too much on your mind.

"Skip, what kind of car do they drive?"

"Who?"

"Who do you think!"

"Oh. They got a '95 Ford Windstar GL."

"What kind of car is that?"

"It's a van."

"Okay."

I glanced again in the mirror, quickly counting two cars and a pickup behind us, but no van.

"Blue and white," Skip said.

"Okay."

"CB antenna."

"Okay."

We were well outside of Delmont on our way to Abbotsville by then, and I was able to speed up a little.

"Teeny little Rebel flag on it."

"Okay."

"Rusted-out fender on the driver's side."

"*Okay!*"

"Piece a junk's all it is."

"*Skip!*" Thinking, *Oh, God*.

He mumbled something, and I felt him move around back there, trying to get comfortable. A knee bumped the back of my seat, and he groaned.

"Can you maybe move your seat up a little, Etta Mae? And the old man's, too?"

"No, I cannot. My seat's as close as it'll get, and we're not going to move Mr. Howard. And don't call him an old man."

"Well, who is he, anyway?"

"He's Mr. Howard Connard, Senior, and don't you forget it."

Dead silence from the back, and I could almost hear the wheels go round in Skip's brain.

"That's ole man *Connard*?" he whispered. Like I said, everybody in Delmont knew Mr. Howard Connard, Senior. Or knew of him.

"Skip!" I yelled. "Show some respect!" Then, reaching over and patting Mr. Howard's leg, I said, "Don't mind him, Mr. Howard, honey. He has a good heart, in spite of the way he acts sometimes."

We were well on our way to Abbotsville by this time, which was too far past four o'clock. I was beginning to get anxious again, worrying about the time. You know how county offices are. They'll close their windows right on the dot of five, no matter how many are waiting in line. All I could do was hope that going-home traffic in Abbotsville wouldn't slow us down. I swear it got worse every year, what with tourists and Northern summer visitors. And Floridians! You wouldn't believe the way they drove. They were about to push us natives out and take over the whole county, something nobody liked unless they ran a business.

My mind was in a whirl and seemed like it was doing everything but keeping itself centered on the matters at hand. Too much could go wrong that didn't bear thinking about, I guess. Besides traffic, I had to worry about finding a parking place at the courthouse and how long it was going to take to get Mr. Howard out of the car and into his wheelchair. Oh, Lord, that walker! If he wanted to use the walker, it'd take us thirty minutes to get inside. And what if there was a line?

I should've picked Mr. Howard up early that morning and gotten the license. I shouldn't have waited till the end of the day.

But that's what I'd done and, as I'd had to do so many other times, I'd just have to make the best of it.

When we got into Abbotsville, I inched along the narrow streets, getting more and more anxious as I tried to watch the traffic, my watch, and the rearview mirror for a blue-and-white van. Finally, I turned into the parking lot by the courthouse, and was relieved to see several slots at the far edge of the lot. Dodging outgoing cars, I headed for a space and pulled in. Lord, it was hot, even with the windows down.

I pulled the rearview mirror over to check my makeup, which felt like it was running down my face. My hair looked awful—frizzy, sweaty, and windblown. Oh well, one good thing about marrying a senior citizen. They couldn't see so good.

I took Mr. Howard's hand and checked his pulse, looking also to see how pale he was and how he was holding up. "You doin' all right, honey?"

He smiled and nodded, and from the back floorboard, Skip said, "Not too good, Etta Mae. I might not never straighten up again."

I leaned my head down, wanting to bang it on the steering wheel. What else could you do?

I opened the door and got out. Pulling up the back of my seat, I said, "Okay, come on out, Skip. Since you're here, you might as well make yourself useful."

He crawled out of the car, crouching over and holding his back with one hand and hanging on to the car door with the other. "Golly, Miss Molly," he moaned, "I'm inna awful fix here. My leg's gone to sleep, an' my back's give out on me."

Pitiful, that's what he was, standing there on one leg, pawing the ground with the other foot, trying to make it take his weight, and bent all the way over from the waist. Pitiful, if I'd had any pity to give him. But he could've been over at Lurline's and out of my hair if he'd used his head instead of filling his stomach with Porky Park barbecue.

"Get with it, Skip. I don't have time to fiddle with you. I need you to get that wheelchair out of the trunk and open it up for Mr. Howard. Come on, now."

I unlocked the trunk, and waited while he hobbled over, lifting one leg up high and nearly falling every time it came down again. He held on to the side of the car with one hand, while catching himself on the ground with the other each time his numb leg gave out on him.

Which was every other step. He was still bent over during all these contortions, moaning about his back, and any other time, I'd've laughed my head off at the sight of him. But not this time. I stood there, tapping my foot and checking my watch, wanting to smack him to kingdom come for delaying us.

When he finally got to the trunk, panting and hopping on one foot, he stared at the folded wheelchair, which was at about his eye level the way he was bent over. Then he cocked his head up at me and said, "I don't know if I can do this."

"You better do it."

I went on around the car and opened Mr. Howard's door, reached in, and swung his legs out. "We're going in now and get our license. I think we've got plenty of time, so don't you worry." I leaned over and smiled real big for him. "Any second thoughts? Speak now or forever hold your peace."

"Na-uh," he said, reaching out for my hand.

"I got it, Etta Mae," Skip said as he rolled the wheelchair to us. I squatted down to be sure everything was locked in place, so there wouldn't be any more accidents than there'd already been. Skip, still in a bent position, watched me, then said, "What you want me to do now?"

"Take that side," I said, pointing to Mr. Howard, "and help me get him in it."

"Oh, lemme do it," Skip said, and picked Mr. Howard up like he was a baby and sat him down, nice and easy, in the chair. "There you go, Mr. Connard. What next, Etta Mae?"

"Nothing. You can stay in the car till we get back."

Skip looked around the parking lot. "Well, where y'all goin'?"

"In the courthouse. You just stay here."

Mr. Howard reached for Skip's hand with his good one and said, "Go, too." Which was as clear as anything he'd said in over a year.

"Mr. Howard, honey, we don't need him. Remember what me and you—I mean, I and you—came for?"

Mr. Howard pulled at Skip's hand and pointed with it to the courthouse. The only reason I could come up with was that he liked Skip's strong arms and back, though that wasn't in the best of shape at the moment. Mr. Howard had been used to Emmett and me tugging and lugging him around, and neither of us much bigger than he was, so I could see where he'd feel safer with Skip.

I didn't like it much, but if I could get that license with mine and Mr. Howard's names on it, I decided it didn't matter which ex-husband came with us. Though I'd've preferred none.

Chapter 23

I let Skip push the wheelchair, even though he looked as weak and crippled as Mr. Howard actually was. We went across the hot pavement toward the entrance to the basement of the court-house, where a lot of the county offices were located for easy access of just the kind of handicapped individuals I was in the present company of.

"Hold on a minute, Skip," I said, as we got into the hall. It was a relief to feel the air-conditioned air after what we'd been en-during. I stooped over and straightened Mr. Howard's tie and buttoned his suit coat. I knew he wanted to look presentable, and he did after I smoothed his hair down and gave him a smile.

"It might be a good idea," I said to him, "if you let me handle everything and not strain yourself trying to talk, okay? Let's go, Skip. The office is down this hall and around the corner."

Skip kept pushing, following me, and I noticed that both his back and his leg were the better for the exercise. Though neither was completely back to normal working condition.

"Where we goin', Etta Mae?" Skip whispered loudly. He'd been in enough courthouses, or rather court*rooms*, not to want to draw attention to himself.

"Me and—I mean, Mr. Howard and me—have some busi-ness to take care of," I told him. "And I don't want to hear any-thing from you while we're doing it. You ought to've stayed in the car, so you just act like you're not even here and don't know what's going on."

"Well, I don't."

"That's the way I want it. Here we are." I opened the door next to a sign that read REGISTER OF DEEDS.

Holding the door for Skip to push Mr. Howard through, I was relieved to see the waiting area empty. Not that it would've held many people, for almost immediately in front of us was a counter that came almost to my shoulders, and ran the width of the room.

"Push him on up here," I said to Skip. "Then you just stay back out of the way till we're through."

Skip pushed the wheelchair up against the counter, so that Mr. Howard had nothing to look at but the wood paneling on the front of it. I would've rearranged him if there'd been anything else for him to look at, but there wasn't. Not even a wanted poster to read.

Willing to please as he always was, Skip took a couple of limping steps back and leaned against the wall, propping his tingling leg against it. He looked around with interest, checking out the light fixtures in the ceiling and the tile on the floor, but even at his height there was little enough to see.

Leaning against the counter, I waited to be waited on. The room on the other side was large and spacious, but filled with desks and file cabinets and wastepaper cans. There was a white-haired woman banging away at a typewriter over in the far corner. She didn't look up.

Another woman, chewing gum like a cow with a cud, ambled across the room with an armload of papers. She was in a world of her own, and didn't turn her head. Closer to the counter, there was about the fattest woman I'd ever seen, and I've seen some. She was sitting at a desk in a little secretary's chair that, I swear, underneath her overlapping bottom, looked like one of those banana seats on a racing bicycle. She didn't pay any attention to me, either, as she shuffled papers from one pile to another.

I picked up a ballpoint pen laying there, and tapped it on the counter, polite-like. "Excuse me?" I said, trying to attract the fat woman's attention since she was the closest. "Excuse me, but can we get some help?"

She turned my way but didn't say anything, so I said, "We'd like to take out a marriage license, please."

She heaved a sigh and pointed to a big round clock on the wall. "I don't know why," she said to the air in front of her, "people can't come in during the eight business hours we keep every day. But here they come at fourteen minutes till five, knowing we close at five."

"Well, but we write real fast, and we've both done it before and know what to do. Please, we've come from Delmont and it'll be awful hard to get back over here. I promise we won't keep you late, if you'll just give us the forms."

I don't know how I could've been any nicer, but she sat where she was while the big hand jerked off another minute. My hands were trembling by then, as I thought of all I'd been through that day, to say nothing of the night before, and there I had to stand, watching this fat woman let my time run out. It was getting close to being all I could take.

Just as I was about to crawl over the counter and slap her silly, she moved, sighing loudly as she leaned on the desk to heft herself out of the chair. She waddled over, and I saw she was shorter even than me. We both glanced up at the clock, then looked at each other, almost eye to eye, over that shoulder-high counter.

"Fill this out, then," she said, sliding a form over to me. With an exasperated glance, she gave Skip a quick once-over, as if that was all he deserved. Then she leaned against her side of the counter, waiting for us and, I expect, counting off the minutes.

I quickly filled in the bride's part—my maiden name, where I lived, my parents' names, my age, how far I'd gone in school, and how many marriages this one would make for me. Then I squatted down beside Mr. Howard's chair and filled in his part, which he gave me the information for. I had a jolt when he told me his birth date and age, for my guess of his age had been off by a number of years because of his recent friskiness.

"I'm going to turn this in now," I whispered, beginning to rise from my squat. "Unless you've changed your mind. I don't want to rush you if you need to think about it some more, but if you do, you have to do it quick. That woman's going to kick us out in a minute or two."

I could see a flash of anger in his watery old eyes as he motioned with his head toward the woman behind the counter. He'd heard her, though he hadn't been able to see her, and he knew she'd tried to blow me off and had treated me like dirt. I think he was trying to tell me that if he'd been his normal self, he'd've lit a fire under her, and I didn't doubt that he could've.

He patted my hair with his good hand, smiling with half his face, and motioned for me to turn the form in.

I knew he was happy, and I was, too. Though more determined than anything else.

I straightened up and faced the woman again. "Here it is," I said, sliding the form toward her. "All done, and in plenty of time." The clock said eight minutes till five.

She stared at me.

"There it is," I said, nodding at the form.

She kept staring.

"Lady," I said, beginning to wonder if she was having a seizure or something, "we've filled it out. Now we want the license."

She reached slowly for the form, then, with a backward glance at me, went to the typewriter and began to type the information onto the official license. At one point, she stopped dead and said, "Is this information correct?"

"Of course it is," I said.

"He don't look that old to me," she mumbled.

"I know he doesn't. It surprised me, too."

As she came back to the counter with the license, she said, "You both have to sign at the bottom, all three copies, no carbons. Then swear that all this information is true, and if it's not, be held for perjury."

I snatched the license from her, fuming that she'd think we'd lie about our own selves. I signed the bride's name, then squatted down again by Mr. Howard's chair. Holding the form against the arm of his chair so he'd have something to write on, I showed him where and how many times to sign his name. Standing again, I slid the license back to the woman, who started that staring again.

"There it is," I told her. "Signed, sealed, and delivered. At least, our part of it."

"I don't know what you take me for," she said, as her face began to get red, "but I am not a fool. Do you think you can stoop down on the floor and fill out the form and then sign for both of you while that big ox is standing over there in plain sight, and me not know it? I don't know what's wrong with him, he can't sign his own name, but this thing's not legal."

She reached for the form, crumpling it as her hand came down on it. Quick as a snake, I braced my hands on the counter and flung myself across it, my legs dangling in the air. I snatched the form away from her and slid back down on my side.

Smoothing the papers as best I could with trembling hands, I hissed, "You do what you have to do with this thing and you do it now. I'm not marrying that big ox over there, although how anybody that's carrying around as much blubber as you are can call anybody else big, I don't know. The man I'm marrying is down here in a wheelchair," and I stabbed my finger down toward him, "and his name is Mr. Howard Connard, Senior—hello, does that ring any bells?—not that it's any business of yours who I marry. Now, move that fat ass of yours and finish this up!"

The woman at the typewriter had stopped typing and was rising from her chair. The one crossing the room clasped her papers to her bosom and stood there with her mouth open.

The one in front of me had paled considerably. "Mr. Howard Connard, Senior?" she said. "I thought he was dead."

"Well, he's not. He's right here," I said, "in good health and sane mind, with the exception of a weakness in his side. And by tomorrow, I am going to be *Mrs*. Howard Connard, Senior, and if I ever have reason to come back into this office, which I don't ever plan to again, I expect to have better service than I've gotten today."

"Yes, ma'am," she said, swallowing hard and pulling a Bible out from under the counter. "If y'all have no objection to swearing on the Bible, put your left hands on it, and answer 'I do,' if you do."

"Left hands?"

"Yes, ma'am, and raise your right ones."

"Raise your right hand, honey," I said to Mr. Howard as I reached down and lifted his half-dead left one up over the edge of the counter onto the Bible and covered it with mine to hold it there.

The fat woman read from the license: "We hereby make application to the Register of Deeds for a marriage license and solemnly swear that all statements contained in the above application are true. We further make oath that there is no legal impediment to such marriage. Say, 'I do.'"

"I do," I said.

"Ahdo," Mr. Howard said from below the counter, sounding

like a sneeze or somebody from Georgia. She didn't question it, though.

The woman tore off our copy of the license to take to our preacher and, in a fast, practiced jumble of words, asked if we wanted an additional document with a gold seal suitable for framing for three dollars extra. I certainly did, thinking I'd put it on the mantel in Mr. Howard's living room, along with the knickknacks left over from the first Mrs. Connard, Senior.

"I hope y'all will be very happy. That'll be forty-three dollars, total."

"Forty-three?" I didn't remember paying that much for a license before.

"Yes, ma'am, twenty of that goes to the North Carolina Domestic Violence Fund. The rest for processing."

"Well, I don't plan to be needing that fund, but if we have to pay it, I guess we will."

I scrambled through my purse and found a couple of twenties and some ones, noting that all that was left was two tens and some change. But if Mr. Howard's name could bring about the kind of change in attitude I'd just witnessed—not once after learning who I was marrying had that woman looked at the clock, which now said six minutes after five—I figured it for the best forty-three dollars I'd ever spent.

Chapter 24

Before we left the Register of Deeds office, the woman handed me a Newly-Wed Sample Pack, a plastic bag filled with some of the necessities for starting married life. As soon as Skip had pushed Mr. Howard out into the hall and we were on our way out of the courthouse, I tore into it. I hadn't had any showers for the bride and we hadn't sent out any wedding invitations, so this looked to be the only gift we were going to get.

"Look, Mr. Howard," I said, pulling out a roll of paper towels. "Isn't this nice? And here's some deodorant and a bottle of Scope. And, look, a box of Bounce and a whole book of coupons that'll come in real handy. That was nice of her, wasn't it? And after being so put out with us for coming in late."

"She was nice there at the end," Skip said, as I held the door for him to push Mr. Howard's chair out of the building. "Uh, Etta Mae, I couldn't help but notice, but are you gettin' married again?"

"Yes, I am."

"To *him*?" Skip whispered as he pointed at the back of Mr. Howard's head.

"That's right. You wanta make something of it?"

"No-o-o," Skip said, shaking his head and frowning as he thought about it. "I just kinda hoped I was still in the runnin'."

"Oh, for goodness' sake," I said, rolling my eyes.

We'd reached the car and I opened the door as Skip helped

Mr. Howard out of the chair and into the passenger's seat. He folded the wheelchair and put it in the trunk, while I made sure Mr. Howard was comfortable.

"I know it's hot, honey," I said to him, "but we'll cool off as soon as I get the car started. Skip, crawl in the back, and let's go."

"Do I have to get on the floorboard again?"

"I guess not," I said, straightening my seat after he slid behind it. "At least not till we get closer to Delmont. But don't you mess up my clean clothes back there. Move them over so you'll have some room."

As we headed back toward Delmont, I kept an eye on the rearview mirror, watching for a blue-and-white van. I was beginning to think that the Pucketts had given up and gone back to Gastonia. Or maybe Skip had just imagined they were after him. So far, the only evidence I'd had that they were even in Delmont was my trashed trailer and Junior's sore head. And there could've been another explanation for both, though I didn't know what it could've been.

"You doin' all right, honey?" I asked Mr. Howard.

He smiled and nodded, but he looked tired and a little peaked. The heat, I expect, was getting to him. And the excitement, too, of course.

"Just lean your head back," I told him, wishing I had a newer car with body-conforming seats, "and rest awhile. We're almost home, and I think we better put off the ceremony till tomorrow. You need your supper and you ought to get to bed early." I hated not tying the knot while I had the chance, especially since Junior might be home by morning, but I had to take care of Mr. Howard. I didn't think he could stand much more excitement or physical exertion. I mean, just getting in and out of the car put a strain on him.

"All right, Skip, get down on the floor. We're coming into Delmont."

"Aw-w-w," he whined as I felt him knee the back of my seat. "I just don't fit down here, Etta Mae."

"Well, put up with it. We're almost there." But what was I going to do with him when we got to Mr. Howard's house? I hadn't thought that far ahead, being so taken up with seeing about Granny and getting the license and looking after Mr. Howard and taking that fat woman down a peg or two.

"Skip," I called over my shoulder, "have you thought about what you're going to do when we get back?"

"Whatever you think, Etta Mae."

I swear, I had my hands full with him. I wondered if every other divorced woman had to take care of their exes for the rest of their lives. At least Bernie hadn't shown up, for which I was thankful.

"Look," I said, "as far as I can tell, you've played out the two places where I thought you'd be safe. It's a settled fact you can't go back to Lurline's. For all we know, they're still watching her house, figuring you're in there. If, that is, you really did get out without them seeing you. And you can't go back to my trailer, because they know where that is. Don't you know anybody else you could stay with?"

"All my kin's gone, Etta Mae, you know that. When the mill shut down, they all had to move. They're mostly in Burlington at the mills there. Besides, I don't see why not."

"Why not what?"

"I can't go back to your trailer."

"Because, Skip," I said, gritting my teeth, "they've *been* there. They know it. They know where it is, and they probably know you don't have too many other options."

"Well, shoot fire," he said, "I'd think that'd just make it even better. I mean, why would they come back if they already been there and seen I wadn't there?"

I thought about it, and he might've been right. Surprise, surprise. The thing was, though, I didn't want him in my trailer. Somebody would have to sleep on the couch, and I didn't want it to be Skip. Which meant it'd have to be me. It was the night before my wedding day, and I had plans to make and things to do, and I didn't want company.

I thought about it some more. All my life, I'd been the one to give up my place in a bed for anybody who came along. I can't tell you how many times I'd slept on couches, roll-away cots, and pallets on the floor.

But that was all over, now that I was a grown woman with a place of my own with the final say-so on who came and who stayed and who slept in my bed.

I sighed as I stopped for one of the two traffic lights in Delmont. Glancing over at Mr. Howard, I saw he'd fallen asleep. I took a Kleenex from my purse and mopped a line of drool from the corner of his mouth. On his bad side, so he couldn't help it.

"Okay, Skip. I guess you're right. You can stay with me, but I warn you, I've got to be up and out early tomorrow morning, so you'll be on your own after that."

"Thanks, Etta Mae. Maybe I can get to Atlanta tomorrow. I'll be all right then. But I'm coming back and giving you half, don't you worry about that."

"I don't want your money, Skip, I've already told you. Although, if you want me to, I'll take half and put it in the bank for you. That way, you won't be tempted to spend it. Here we are," I said, turning into Mr. Howard's driveway. "We'll get Mr. Howard settled, then we'll go on to my place."

I drove up the curving drive, coming into the graveled parking area on the side of the house. The first thing I saw was a little green Mercedes sports car, and my heart sank through the floorboard.

"You stay right where you are, Skip," I said. "Don't get up and don't show your face. You stay right there."

"Why? What is it?"

"Mr. Howard has company. But don't worry, it's not your friends. Unless they hit the jackpot, too. Emmett'll help me get Mr. Howard in the house, so you just keep your head down and don't add to my problems."

"Okay, I will. I mean, I won't, but I wish you'd tell me what's going on."

"Just take my word for it. I'm going to have my hands full in about two minutes, and the best thing for you and me both is for you to stay out of it. Regardless of what you hear."

I pulled up close to the house so Mr. Howard wouldn't have so far to go, hoping Valerie McLean Connard wouldn't come out to help. I doubted she would, but if she did, she'd see Skip huddled on the floorboard and questions would naturally come to her mind. Skip was hard enough to explain under normal circumstances.

Under the present circumstances, when I was going to have a lot more to explain, it didn't bear thinking about.

"Miss Valerie here," Emmett whispered when I opened the kitchen door. He cocked his head toward the front of the house, letting me know where she was.

"I figured, from the car. Has she asked about Mr. Howard?"

"No'm, not a word. She eat her salat, tole me to clean the toaster, which I been doin', and went to the drawin' room to read her magazine. She take a glass of wine with her, so maybe she be loosnin' up."

"I wouldn't count on it."

"No'm, I'm not." Then lowering his voice even more, he asked, "You an' Mr. Howard get married?"

"No, Emmett, not yet," I whispered back, but seeing the way his face fell, I added, "He was too tired after we got the license, so I'm planning for tomorrow morning. Real early, before he gets too worn out."

"I don' know, Miss Etta," he said, shaking his head. "I was sure hopin' it'd be done today, before Mr. Junior and Miss Valerie catch wind of it."

"I know. Me, too. I told Junior, you know, but he may not remember it, what with being concussed and all. But putting it off just couldn't be helped. As tired as Mr. Howard is, I didn't want to put any more strain on him. Will you help me get him in the house?"

"Yessum, let me dry my hands off."

He followed me out to the car, where Mr. Howard was just coming awake. Emmett opened the door and, as he did, saw Skip stuffed down in the back. He jumped back about a foot, saying, "Whoa! What that man doin' down in the flo'board?"

It was too much to explain, so I just said, "I didn't want Valerie to see him if she came out here. She might get mad if she thought Mr. Howard was riding around with a stranger."

It didn't sound too good to me, but Emmett, frowning, nodded. He helped Mr. Howard out of the car and onto his feet. "Jes' lean on me, tha's right. I gonna get you to bed and bring yo' supper on a tray. Step real easy now."

As the two old men moved toward the house, Mr. Howard looked back at me, trying to call my name.

"I'm here," I said. "I'll help you get settled, then I have to go. I want you to get a good rest, 'cause I'll be back early tomorrow and we'll do what we didn't have time to do today. Don't you worry. I've got the license in my bag and we're going to use it tomorrow."

I hurried across the hall in front of them to turn down Mr. Howard's bed, hoping Valerie wouldn't hear us. Emmett had put fresh sheets on the bed while we'd been gone, and I thought again of how easy life could be with the help of extra pairs of hands. If you could afford to pay for them.

"I'll help him get his pajamas on, Emmett, while you fix his supper. If you don't mind. Something light is probably all he needs."

"Yessum, I thought jes' soup and some chopped-up peaches," Emmett said, eyeing the pajamas laid out on the bed.

I knew he was thinking it wasn't right for me to undress Mr. Howard. Emmett was the modest type. So I said, "Emmett, I'm a nurse and used to helping people in all sorts of ways. I could leave it all for you to do, but I think he needs to get settled in as quick as we can do it. And besides, by this time tomorrow, we'll be man and wife, and you won't think a thing about it then."

"Don' know 'bout that," he mumbled as he left the room. "Maybe I will and maybe I won't."

As I was putting Mr. Howard's feet into his pajama bottoms, there was a tap on the door and, as it opened, Valerie called, "Daddy Connard? How are . . ." Then she saw me. "*What* are you doing?"

"Getting him ready for bed," I said, snatching up the bottoms to cover Mr. Howard's scrawny parts as he let out a croak of embarrassment.

"This is too much," she said. "First, I catch you in my husband's room, and now here you are in my father-in-law's room. Every time I turn around, there you are. I want to know what right you have to go and come in this house like you own it?"

I wanted to tell her, oh, I wanted so bad to throw it in her

face, that this house was all but mine and that from now on she'd
have to ask my permission to go and come in it. But I didn't.

I reined in my tongue and my temper and swallowed the
words I wanted to say. Instead, I said, "I'm sorry, Miss Valerie, I
thought you knew I work for Mr. Howard. We've just come back
from a drive and he's very tired."

"Emmett can help him. Where is he?"

"Getting his supper. Lie down, Mr. Howard, and I'll elevate
your bed so you can manage a tray. Sh-h-h," I said to him, notic-
ing how red his face was getting as he tried to speak to Valerie.
I noticed, too, that she was paying no attention to him, treating
him like a piece of furniture. I spread the sheet over him and
patted his shoulder. "It's all right now. Don't you worry about a
thing."

Valerie came farther into the room, stopped right in front of
me, and put her hands on her skinny hips. "We don't need your
help anymore. Although *help* is not the right word, is it? Interference is more like it, but no longer. I'm giving you notice as of this
minute. Daddy Connard will be leaving as soon as my husband
is able to travel, so you can just get out and don't come back."

She waved a hand toward the door, dismissing me like I was
hired help. Which I was, but not really. Mr. Howard tried to rise
up in the bed, gurgling and croaking, trying to make himself
understood. He was like me—when I get mad, I can't get the
words out. And he was in worse shape than me to begin with.

I bit my lip, feeling my face redden as she dressed me down.
I wanted to get in her face with a few words of my own. No, what
I really wanted to do was smack her cross-eyed. But it wasn't the
time or place, not if I ever hoped for a happy family life. I had to
stay, or rather get, on her good side. All we needed was to know
each other better, and I didn't want to say anything that would
make her mad. Madder.

"Yes, ma'am," I said, acting as humble as I could. "Have a good night, Mr. Howard."

He reached for me as I turned to leave, tears of frustration and anger leaking out of the corners of his eyes. I took his hand, giving it a squeeze to let him know that I'd be back. One way or another, although I didn't know which.

Chapter 25

I went through the kitchen, my face burning from the hateful words Valerie had thrown at me. It was all I could do to speak to Emmett on my way out the door. I got to the car and slid in, so undone I didn't know what to do.

"Can I get up now?" Skip asked as I closed the car door and slumped in the seat.

My eyes filled up and my chest ached as I sat there thinking of all I'd been through, not only that day but, seemed like, all my life. There hadn't been any need for Valerie to speak to me that way. All I wanted was what was best for Mr. Howard, which was what he wanted, too. The Junior Connards hadn't paid any attention to what he wanted. All they'd been concerned about was what was easiest for them. Which was to have Mr. Howard put away where they wouldn't be worried with him or about him or about anybody getting close to him.

And the way she'd treated me! Like I was trash. With not even common courtesy. I'd taken her husband a gift of a Whitman's Sampler, and I'd taken care of her father-in-law. And instead of thanking me for doing what she should've been doing, she'd treated me like dirt under her feet.

"Etta Mae?" Skip moaned. "I'm hurtin' down here."

"Okay, Skip," I said, turning on the ignition. "We're going now. And, no, don't get up yet. I haven't seen anybody following us or looking for you, but you'd better play it safe and stay down."

"Where we going?"

"All I know to do is go to my trailer and hope you're right that they won't look there again."

"What about my Low Rider?"

Shoot! One more thing I'd forgotten about. But then I said, "You can't fly it to Atlanta, can you? It'll be safe where it is."

I turned onto Old Oak, looking both ways for a blue-and-white van. To tell the truth, I really didn't expect to see one by then. I was beginning to think that Skip had no reason to be afraid. His so-called friends were probably in Gastonia doing a lube job or putting a patch on somebody's tire.

For all I knew, whoever'd torn up my trailer had been after Junior and hadn't made a mistake when they'd put him in the hospital. Maybe his wife had raked somebody over the coals the way she'd done me, which was reason enough to lay into him. Maybe Valerie ought to be the one hiding on the floorboard of a car.

That scared me as I thought about it. What if whoever it was meant to do her harm, too? Should I call and warn her? Would she listen to me? Not a chance in the world. She'd hang up on me. I thought about trying anyway, not wanting a soon-to-be member of my family to be hurt, regardless of how much I would've liked to've hurt her myself. On the other hand, it was *her* husband who was laid up in the hospital, so that ought to be warning enough.

Driving through town and around the square, I headed the car out Springer Road toward the trailer park.

"You hungry, Skip?" I asked, mentally counting the money I had left.

"'Bout to starve. Let's stop and get something."

"Okay," I said. "I'm going to pull into the Porky Park Drive-Thru and get something to go. You stay real still, and maybe the girl at the window won't notice you down there."

"I'll take two chopped barbecue sandwiches, an order of Tater Tots, and one of onion rings. Can we stop somewhere else for a six-pack or two?"

"No. I'll get Cokes here, then no more stops."

I gave our order at one window, then, following the car in front of us, drove on to the pickup window. When the bags were handed to me, the hot, rich smell of hickory-smoked barbecue filled the car. Skip groaned as the smell reached him.

Dusk was settling in by that time, and as I pulled back onto Springer Road, I turned on the headlights. Glancing in the rearview mirror at the same time, I nearly ran off the road.

"Skip! There's a blue-and-white van two cars behind us! It's hard to see, but it sure looks like what you described."

"Oh, Lordy, what're we gonna do?"

That's what I was asking myself, until I saw one of those portable signs on wheels up ahead by the side of the road. "Hold on," I said, "there's an Auto-Wash-It up here on the right."

I turned in and got in line behind two other cars. I held out two one-dollar bills through the window to the man in the little shack before leaning across the seat to roll up the windows. That gave me a chance to see what the van was doing, as I twisted and turned to reach the back windows, too.

"What's goin' on, Etta Mae?" Skip asked. "Why're you rolling up the windows? It's hot down here."

"We're at the car wash, and we'll be going through in a minute. Now, listen, Skip, as soon as the water pours down so they can't see anything, get up and climb in the front seat. Then when the brush starts over the car, you get out and stay in the car wash till I drive away.

"Wait, wait a minute," I said, craning to see in the side mirror. "Oh, wow, I thought they were going to pull in behind us, but looks like they've parked on the street. They're waiting for us to come out.

"Here we go. Get ready." I put the car in drive, turned off the radio to get the aerial down, and pulled into the car wash onto the metal tracks. Gallons of soapy water poured over the car, front and back. We couldn't see out, so I figured nobody could see in.

"Get on up here, Skip, and be ready to hop out."

He put a leg over the front passenger seat and squirmed on over, half sitting on the bags of barbecue. I snatched them up before he flattened them.

"I'm gonna take a sandwich with me," he said, pulling out one wrapped in greasy waxed paper. "I could eat a horse, I'm so hungry. How long you want me to stay in this car wash, and where you want me to go when I get out?"

"I don't know, Skip," I said. "Let me think. Wait as long as you can, 'cause I'm hoping they'll follow me. Soon as you think we're well on the way, you sneak out and come on to my trailer. Stay off the main streets, and walk, don't try to hitch a ride. It's only a mile or two, so it won't take you long. And don't come barreling in. Hide somewhere and watch my trailer till you're sure nobody's around."

"Sure wish I had my Low Rider."

"Get over it," I said, as the flood of water pounded on the roof. "Here comes the brush! Get out, Skip, get out now!"

He flung open the door, barbecue sandwich in one hand, while a spray of water flew into the car. He slammed the door just as the huge rolling brush hit the windshield, and I couldn't see what happened to him. Right after the brush, another wave of water gushed over the car, rinsing it off, and I started laughing at the thought of Skip's soaked sandwich. By the time the car went through the drier, I was laughing and crying at the same time. Nervous and scared.

I turned right at the street and headed toward the trailer park. It was almost full dark by that time, but, sure enough, there was the van edging into the light traffic, a few cars behind me. I was relieved to see it, because I was leading them away from Skip.

On the other hand, I was leading them toward me.

Chapter 26

My first thought was to head back to Mr. Howard's where there'd be people around. My second thought was that I couldn't stay there all night, even if Valerie'd let me in for a little while. Which she wouldn't.

Then a third thought struck me. The van wasn't following Skip at all. They must have picked up my car after we got back to Delmont, because there'd been no sign of them in Abbotsville or anywhere around the courthouse. No way they could've seen Skip in the car, since they'd never been close enough to us. The more I thought about it, the more it seemed likely that they hadn't known where Skip had been all afternoon, so they hadn't even followed him from Lurline's to Mr. Howard's. What they were doing was tailing me, figuring I knew where he was and would lead them to him.

I didn't feel a bit better with that thought.

I almost turned around right then and there. The safest place for me was the sheriff's office. *Oh, yeah,* I thought, *and what if Clyde Maybry's on duty?* Lot of good that'd do me.

The only thing I could do was what I'd started out to do—just go home, get ready for my wedding, and hope they'd get tired of waiting for Skip to show. And hope he'd have sense enough to stay away as long as they were there.

I was so tired when I parked beside my trailer that I could hardly climb out of the car. No sleep the night before and a long, busy day afterward. During that time I'd gone from the jail-house to the courthouse and from being an assault suspect to a bride-to-be. All of that would make anybody tired. But my laun-dry had to be brought in and put away, and something done with all the barbecue, deep-fried onions, Tater Tots, and Cokes smell-ing up my car and waiting to be eaten.

It took two trips to get everything into the trailer, each trip giving me a chance to look around for the van. I hadn't seen it when I'd turned into the trailer park, so I had hopes that they'd given up on me. After all, they knew where I lived, having visited the night before, so they could find me anytime they wanted to.

After putting my clean clothes away, I sat on the bed, holding my giraffe for comfort, and wondering if I should pack a suitcase for my wedding. Mr. Howard and I hadn't planned a honeymoon. He just wasn't up to a long road trip. I would've loved to've gone to Disney World, which was my dream vacation. To go to the Magic Kingdom and take that futuristic Space Mountain ride would thrill me to death. I'd tried to get Bernie to take me there on that honeymoon, but he'd won a trip to Gatlinburg for selling so many cars. I'd enjoyed it pretty well, what with all the handcrafts, sou-venirs, and cute little Smoky Mountain bears made in Taiwan they had for sale, even though they didn't have anything to compare with Space Mountain. Skip and I had gone to Myrtle Beach on that honeymoon, where we'd both gotten sunburned so bad we couldn't bear to touch each other. I could still smell the Noxzema if I put my mind to it. Bobby Lee, although we'd never been mar-ried and never would be, had taken me to the Quality Inn over by the airport that first time. After that, it hadn't much mattered where we went or where we were. It was a honeymoon every time we got together.

I jumped up from the bed, kicked my shoes off, and went barefooted to the kitchen. Too much to think about in the here and now to dwell on the past, which I didn't intend to let myself do any more than I could help.

I looked at the door to my trailer, seeing the broken lock, the snapped chain, and sighed. If anybody's interested, it's not a good idea to live in a trailer park with no way to keep the trash out. The best I could do was hook a chair under the doorknob. That wouldn't keep a child out, but it would make enough noise to wake me if somebody tried to get in. And Jennie would be keeping an eye on me. *Just let me get through this night*, I thought, *then I'll be Mrs. Howard Connard, Senior, and nobody'll mess with me again.*

Arranging everything on the wobbly table by my recliner so I wouldn't have to get up again, I sat down to eat. If you've ever tried a barbecue sandwich that's been sat on, let me tell you it's not the most appetizing-looking thing you might choose to eat. But, looks aside, it sure was good.

The Tater Tots looked more like mashed potatoes, so I by-passed them. And the Coke was half water by that time, but it was wet and cold. It'd been a long time since my McDonald's lunch, so I sat in the recliner enjoying the spicy taste of hickory-smoked pork and trying to get my tired mind to figure out how I was going to get Mr. Howard and me to the preacher the next morning without Valerie knowing about it.

The chair under the door started sliding across the floor, me sitting there too amazed to move or chew as I watched it with a mouthful of barbecue. The door opened as easy as if there'd been nothing there to scotch it, and two men walked in. I knew who they were since all the Pucketts looked pretty much alike, but I didn't know at first which one was Roy and which was Harley. Both of them had dark hair, but one, the heavier-set one, had short hair with a rattail hanging down the back of his neck. That had to be Harley, or so the red-embroidered name said on his striped mechanic's overalls, grease-stained and stiff. The other one, Roy according to the sewn-on name under the Texaco star on his gray shirt, wore matching gray pants.

His uniform, I guessed, put him a cut above his brother in the employment category. He probably worked the cash register at the gas station, which goes to show how trusting some people can be.

"What the hell are you doing, just walking into my house?" I demanded, swallowing my mouthful. I was afraid of them. Anybody with any sense would be. But I knew the type. If you cringed and cried and begged, they'd figure they could do whatever came to mind to do. And enjoy it the more they could scare you. On the other hand, they wouldn't put up with much lip from anybody they could shut down with a fist to the mouth.

"Feisty, ain't she?" Harley said.

"Shut up, Harley," Roy told him, with a jab of his elbow. "We don't aim to bother you. We just want to know where Skip's at."

"I don't know where he is." I tucked my skirt around my thighs, thinking for the first time that long skirts had their benefits and wishing I had one on right then.

"Don't give us none of that," Harley said. "We know he was here, so where's he at now?"

"I tell you, I don't know. He *was* here. Last night, but then he spent the night with a friend of his across town. I don't know who," I quickly added, not wanting them to go after Lurline. "He said somebody he went to high school with, I don't know who."

"You believe her, Roy?"

"I don't know if I do or if I don't." Roy stood quiet and still, his eyes looking around the room. He gave me the creeps.

"All I know," I said, "is that he's not here, so you might as well leave right now." I got up out of the recliner and stood behind it, hoping it was time to show a little backbone.

"Who's gonna make us?" Harley said, smiling now, and I knew I'd made a wrong move by standing up. "I think she knows where he's at, Roy."

Roy stared at me, searching my mind it seemed like, while he studied what to do. Finally he nodded. "She knows."

"I don't! I tell you I don't. You better get out of here. My neighbor is listening out for me and, and, you just better leave."

"She can show us where he is, Roy," Harley said, stepping closer.

Roy moved his hand, like he was giving a signal to a dog. "Bring her."

Harley was quicker than he looked. He grabbed my arm and dragged me across the arm of the chair as I threw the watered-down Coke in his face.

"Get away from me! Don't you touch me! Turn me loose!" I kicked him in the shin, wishing I still had my shoes on.

He shook me till my head flopped back and forth on my neck.

"Get her on in the van," Roy said, looking out the door to see if anybody was hearing me.

"Wait! Wait," I said, holding on to the recliner while Harley pulled. "You don't know who I am. I'm Mrs. Howard Connard, Senior." Almost, but I didn't say that. "You better not mess with a Connard in Delmont, don't you know that?"

"Oh, I'm scared to death, ain't you, Roy? What do I care about ole man Connard?" Harley snatched at me so hard that I lost my grip on the back of the recliner, smacking my leg against the footrest.

"So you're a Connard, huh?" He pulled me close enough to smell the motor oil and Brut cologne fighting with each other. "Well, the Connards ain't done nothin' for us but close the mill and watch us starve. I don't give a flyin' flip for none of 'em, and ole man Connard's the worst of 'em."

It shocked me to the bone to hear such a thing about Mr.

Howard. Everybody respected him. Whether they liked him or not, they gave him respect, which was what I wanted some of.

"Get her on out," Roy said, as he stepped out on my cement patio. The thought of Mr. Howard hadn't even slowed him down.

Harley pulled me out the door, nearly breaking my hand as I tried to hold on to the frame. I was crying by that time, scared and without a weapon, now that I'd shot Mr. Howard's name at them and it'd been a blank for all the good it'd done.

There was nothing else to protect me, and I could see myself in the back of their van, being driven all over town till I either told them where Skip was—which I really didn't know—or until they got tired and stopped to dump me off somewhere. And no telling what they'd do before they dumped me. For all I knew, they'd take me to Gastonia and make me a white slave. The Pucketts had been known to do worse, and had served time for it, too.

I took a deep breath and screamed my lungs out. Harley clamped a smelly hand over my mouth, but I finally got a knee jammed into his private parts. Not hard enough to do any real damage, but enough to make him take his hand off my mouth and clutch himself.

"Dad blame the dad-blamed sorry luck," he moaned, gasping for breath.

Then he pulled his arm back to hit me.

"Don't you do it," I said low and hard, with my teeth gritted together. "You hit me and Bobby Lee Moser'll wipe the floor with you."

Roy reached over and pulled Harley's arm down. "Bobby Lee Moser? He still a deputy 'round here?"

"You bet your ass he is," I said, "and you're already in trouble for even touching me. He'll kill you."

"Turn her loose and let's go."

"The bitch kneed me, Roy."

"Moser'll do worse than that. Now turn her loose and let's get out of here."

Harley dropped me hard, making my head flop against the side of the trailer. I just sat there, my legs spraddled out and my head ringing. Roy and Harley turned to leave, trotting toward the shadows of the trees and bushes beyond my trailer.

I wasn't knocked out. I could see and hear what was going on. I just couldn't make myself get up and do anything. But I heard a crash of limbs and bushes beyond my line of sight that sounded like a herd of elephants breaking through. Roy juked to one side, while Harley crouched down, ready for what was coming at him.

Skip flew through the air toward Harley, yelling, "Hang on, Etta Mae, I'm a-comin'!" He landed hard on Harley and they went down together, rolling on the ground.

Chapter 27

Shaking my head to clear the ringing in it, I got to my hands and knees. Skip and Harley were flailing away at each other as first one then the other rolled on top. A swirl of dust covered them so I couldn't see who was getting the worst of it. From the sounds of their grunts and curses, I figured they were pretty well matched. Skip was taller and probably heavier, but Harley was meaner.

I heard a van door slide open somewhere in the dark, and hoped that meant Roy was booking it. Between the two of us, Skip and I could handle Harley, if I could just get to my feet. I started crawling toward the trailer door, focusing on the telephone to call for help, but stopped when I heard Roy running back from the van.

"Turn him over, Harl," Roy yelled. When I looked around, I saw Roy standing over the two grunting men with what looked like a spray can raised over his head. I heard the little marble in it rattle as he swung it back and forth, trying to get a bead on Skip.

"No!" I yelled. "Don't hit him!" I reached the two steps to my trailer and pulled myself up on wobbly legs.

I heard a thump as the spray can came down on flesh. Harley let out a yell. "*Ow!* Goldang it, Roy, that was me!"

"Turn him over, then."

The next sound was different, as it clanged across Skip's head. He slumped on Harley, and the fight was over. Harley pushed him off and struggled to his feet as Skip lay sprawled out on the ground. All I could think was, if the spray can was full, they'd likely killed him.

"Search him," Roy said.

They both bent over Skip's body, pulling papers, wallet, comb, Swiss Army knife, and a bunch of other things from his pockets.

"Stop lookin' at everything," Roy told Harley. "Just take it all. We'll go through it later."

They stuffed everything in their own pockets while I watched them pick over Skip like buzzards at a roadkill. Poor ole Skip, I thought, there goes the lottery ticket that had been his first stroke of good luck since high school. I could've cried for him. Instead, I slid to the edge of the patio, listing like I'd had one too many, and lifted my pot of geraniums.

Just then, Jennie's outside light came on and Jennie's husband walked out yelling, "What's goin' on over there?"

Roy and Harley worked faster, pulling Skip's boots off and running their hands in them. Roy had Skip's shirt unbuttoned, searching for anything taped to his chest or back.

"Etta Mae!" Mack called, as he walked to the edge of the light. "You all right over there?"

"Call the sheriff," I yelled, running toward Harley, who was the nearest to me.

I raised the geranium pot and crashed it down on his head. The pot shattered, potting soil, roots, leaves, and flowers crumbling around his shoulders. He shook himself and stood to face me.

"Let it go," Roy said, standing and pulling at Harley. "We got everything. Come on, let's get goin' before Moser gets here."

Harley snarled and gave me a push that plopped me down on the ground. Then he stepped over Skip, and he and Roy disappeared into the dark, running through the bushes to their van.

As I heard the van motor start, I turned to poor old Skip, lying there dead to the world. Putting my hand to his neck, I felt a slow but strong pulse under my fingers.

"He dead?" Mack leaned over us, shining a flashlight on Skip's scratched and dirt-covered face.

Jennie, breathing hard, ran up behind him. "I called 9-1-1," she said. "They'll be here in a minute. You all right, Etta Mae?"

"I guess so. I can still move, which is more than Skip can do." I turned his head slightly to the side and saw a bleeding gash right behind his temple. "Skip? Skip, honey, wake up."

His mouth fell open as a deep snore came from the back of his throat. Not a good sign. In the distance, we heard the EMS sirens and the *whump-whump* blare of cop cars. I laid my head on my knees, thinking that two million dollars was not worth losing your health over. Not even one million dollars.

"That makes two, Etta Mae," Clyde Maybry said. He stood over me as I sat in a chair inside my trailer. His big gut strained his uniform, as well as his breathing. I could hear each breath wheezing in and out as he talked. "Seems like it's kinda danger-ous for anybody to come see you, don't it? Word gets around, you're not gonna be having so many visitors."

"Clyde," I said, carefully feeling the lump on the back of my head from hitting the side of the trailer, "if y'all would do more patrolling out here, you wouldn't have things getting out of hand so bad."

He gave me a hard look. Then, breathing heavily, he licked his mouth. "Sheriff's gonna be lookin' into this real careful. We've transported two head wounds to the hospital from your trailer, and he's gonna want some answers. We may have to clean out this trailer park 'fore we're through, and if I was you, I'd get myself straightened up."

I jumped up, flaring with anger. Grasping Jennie's arm to steady myself from the dizziness, I said, "Clyde Maybry, I didn't have anything to do with what happened here. Either last night or this night. I can't help it if there're two Pucketts running around the county knocking people over the head and leaving them for dead, while you stand around accusing me of, of I-don't-know-what."

"Etta Mae," Jennie said, putting an arm around my shoulders. "Come on, honey, sit down. You ought not be jumping up like this. Let me take you to the hospital and get that knot on your head looked at."

"In a minute, Jennie. Deputy Maybry here doesn't think I need to go to the hospital. He's already checked it himself and decided I need to answer his questions more than I need medical treatment. How's that gonna look in *The Delmont Weekly Press?* Huh, Clyde, huh?"

"Go put her in my car," Clyde said to Jennie. "I'll take her to the emergency room."

"The hell you will," I said, and sat back down as another wave of dizziness hit me. "I wouldn't get in a car with you again if I had to walk to the hospital. Now go do your job, Clyde, and pick up Roy and Harley Puckett. They're who you ought to be after, not me."

"Calm down, Etta Mae. I got to investigate the scene."

"Investigate the scene, my foot. You've got a victim and an eyewitness. What else you need before you go after them? A Seeing Eye dog?"

He stared at me with pretty much the same look Harley had given me. "You got a smart mouth on you, Etta Mae, and you oughta keep it closed. You're mixed up in two crimes here, and you're right before gettin' yourself charged with 'em."

I sprang up again and got right in his face, mad enough to

clear my head. "Let me remind you of something, you fat tub of lard. Remember what you did right after I broke up with Bobby Lee the first time? Remember how you used to come by here in your patrol car, tapping on my door after midnight? Remember how you begged to get in? Remember that? And remember how I promised not to tell Billie Jo if you'd just leave me alone? Well, let me tell you I *am* going to tell Billie Jo. I'm going to tell her what you do when you're supposed to be patrolling. And I'm going to tell her mother and your preacher and the sheriff and whoever else will listen. You come in here, throwing your weight around, because I wouldn't let you in my bed. Well, let me tell you, you're not *ever* getting in it. I don't take in married men and I don't take in cheating men. Or fat, ugly men, either!"

Clyde's face had gone slack when I mentioned his wife and mother-in-law. He swallowed hard and said, "We can talk about this later. After I make my report and everything." Then, turning to Jennie, he said, "I'd appreciate it if you'd drive her to the hospital."

Chapter 28

They'd put Skip in a room down the hall from Junior Connard's, so if I'd wanted to, all I had to do was walk from one to the other to get a firsthand view of the Pucketts' handiwork. I didn't want to, though. I sat in Skip's dark room, listening to him snore.

A doctor in the emergency room had looked at the bump on my head, checked my vision and blood pressure, and told me to take it easy for a while. I felt all right, except when I leaned my head back against the chair. It would be sore for a few days, but I could live with it. Skip, on the other hand, was being kept overnight for observation, and since I'd not been able to talk to his doctor, I didn't know how bad hurt he was. So I sat by his bed, or rather slept in a chair by his bed, and worried about him. It was the least I could do.

The hospital was still and quiet, except for the occasional rattle of carts on the waxed floor out in the hall. I dozed off and on in the chair, waking now and then when a nurse came in every hour or so to check Skip's vital signs.

I'd spent the previous night in the sheriff's office, and this night in the hospital, and the only thought getting me through it all was that the next night would be spent in Mr. Howard's bed. I'd read in *Bride* magazine that a bride-to-be should get a lot of rest before her wedding day, long nights of sleep and nutritious meals and all that, so she'd be fresh and lovely for the big day. So much for that recommendation as far as I was concerned.

I was fully awake by seven o'clock, what with the clatter of breakfast trays and the change of shifts out in the hall. I washed my
face in the sink in Skip's room and rinsed out my mouth, trying
not to look in the mirror over the basin. I was a wreck, with only
what was in my handbag to make repairs with. My pretty dress,
the one I'd hoped to be married in, was dirty, torn under the arm,
and, even though I always used a feminine-type deodorant,
pretty much sweat-stained. Wrinkled by now, too, in spite of its
rayon content.

Skip groaned and mumbled as I was getting ready to leave. I
went over to his bed and smoothed his hair back, looking closely
at his swollen eye and split lip.

"How're you feeling?" I whispered.

"Etta Mae, is that you? What happened?"

"Roy Puckett brained you with a spray can—a full one, I
think—and you're in the hospital."

"I am? I thought it was Harley."

"Roy came up behind you, else you'd've beat the tar out of
Harley."

He grinned, then put his hand up to feel his head. "How bad
did I mess him up?"

"Oh, real bad. He wasn't walking too good, and Roy had to
drag him to the van."

"I wadn't gonna let 'em hurt you, Etta Mae," he said, with that
satisfied smile on his face. I don't know why beating somebody
into the ground gives so much pleasure to some people. Of course,
some people need to be beat into the ground, so if you can do it,
I guess it's worth being proud of. Even if you put yourself in the
hospital doing it. I didn't want to point that out to Skip, though.
When somebody's recuperating, their spirits need to be kept up.

"Etta Mae?"

"What?"

"You gettin' married today?"

"Come hell or high water."

Skip sat up in bed and swung his legs over the side. "I'm going with you. Where's my clothes?"

"You can't leave here! Lay back down. I swear, Skip, you know better."

"Shoot, hon, I'm all right. See?" He slid off the bed and stood up without a quiver or a sway.

"But you might have a concussion. You better get back in that bed. I'm gonna tell the nurse on you."

"I'm goin' with you, so just hush up about it. Roy didn't even break the skin, just dinged me a little."

"Dinged you, my foot," I said. "He put your lights out."

"Naw, I been hit worse than that by a two-hunnerd-pound defensive lineman. Where's my britches?"

I pointed to the closet and tried to fix my face with what I had, while he went into the bathroom to put on his clothes. I didn't know what to do with him, afraid he'd keel over on me if he went with me, but not sure how I could keep him here if he wanted to go.

"I could use a shave," he said, coming out of the bathroom, drying his face. "Bath, too, I reckon."

"We both could," I said, meaning a bath. "I've been thinking, Skip. You really want to go with me to my wedding?"

"Yeah, I got to get my bike, an' you're gonna need some help with that ole man, gettin' him in and out. And you'll need a witness, won't you?"

"I thought the preacher could scare somebody up, maybe his secretary or something. But why? Why do you want to be a part of this? Lurline thinks I've lost my mind."

"But it's what you want, Etta Mae. And if it makes you happy to have that old man, why, then, I want you to have him."

"That's just so sweet, Skip," I said, having to wipe my eyes, thank goodness, before I'd put on my mascara. "Here you are, right after losing your two-million-dollar ticket to that Puckett riffraff, and all you're doing is thinking about me. I swear, Skip, I don't think I could do it, if I was you."

"I ain't worried about that two-million-dollar ticket. All it did was bring trouble down on me, make me lose my friends, and get you mixed up in it. Easy come, easy go, I always say."

He was right. That's what he'd always said, and it was the way he lived. Still, he was a bigger person than I'd given him credit for.

I wet the end of a towel and rubbed at the dirt on my dress, most of it from the times I'd been thrown to the ground. There wasn't much I could do about the rip under my arm, except not raise my hand. I hated having to get married in such a sorry state, but by this time, it was catch-as-catch-can. I couldn't risk going home, since we were on such a tight schedule that would, I hoped, keep us out of Valerie's way. Besides, I'd wanted to be married in the dress I had on, so that's what I'd be doing, regardless of how it looked.

"Okay, then. Here's what we have to do," I said, and told him that Valerie was the big stumbling block, and that I planned to pick up Mr. Howard when she left the house to come to the hospital to see Junior. "So we don't want to run into her on our way out."

"I got it," he said, although there was always some doubt as to what Skip ever got.

Chapter 29

After checking the hall for any sign of Valerie, like smoke or brimstone, and sneaking down three flights of stairs to the basement level, we came out into the hospital parking lot.

"I think my car's over this way," I said, heading for the visitors' lot. "Jennie drove me here last night, and Mack followed in my car so I'd have it this morning. There it is." I pointed toward it, sitting between a BMW and a new Toyota.

"Sorta stands out, don't it?" Skip said.

"I wouldn't knock it if I was driving something that won't keep the rain out."

He grinned and got in the passenger seat, while I scrambled through my bag for the keys. "Here they are." I cranked the car and pulled out. "First thing," I said, "I'm going to cruise this lot and see if Valerie's here yet. Look for a little green Mercedes sports car. That'll be her."

I drove up and down the rows of parked cars, though at that time of morning there weren't that many visitors. It was easy to see that her car wasn't there.

"You have any money, Skip?"

"Yeah, I got a few dollars."

"Then let's go to Hardee's and get a sausage biscuit and some coffee. We'll come back when we're finished and maybe she'll be here by then."

That's what we did, and, sure enough, we saw her little green car as soon as we pulled back into the visitors' lot.

My heart started pounding then, I was getting so excited. Nothing was going to stop me now. My hands trembled on the wheel as the moment I'd been counting on came closer and closer. It was the strangest feeling, because sausage and coffee and bread dough started sloshing around in my stomach, and I thought I was going to be sick. A lot of people get scared as they get close to the top of the ladder of success. I'd read that somewhere, and I guessed that's what was happening to me. A few second thoughts are to be expected, now and then, when you're just about to get ahead.

Skip was right on my heels when I went into the kitchen at Mr. Howard's house. He'd smiled to himself all the way over there, looking out the window and patting his hand on his knee in time to Alan Jackson on the radio.

"I'm gonna get me one of them one of these days," he'd said.

"One of what?"

"Ford trucks."

I shook my head, having nothing to say about the way his mind worked. I couldn't understand him, which was nothing new, but I think I'd be a little down in the mouth if I'd had my ticket stolen off me. One good thing, though, we didn't have to worry about being followed by the Pucketts anymore. They'd gotten what they wanted when they picked Skip clean, and as Skip noted, he was just happy to be off the floorboard.

Losing his lottery ticket didn't seem to bother him at all, being just as eager to help me realize my dream as he'd been about his own. There's something to be said for taking every day as it comes, and having no ambition to better yourself. That way, as Skip said, you never had to worry about being disappointed.

"Emmett," I said, as soon as I got in the door at Mr. Howard's house. "Today's the day. Is he up and dressed?"

"He been up. Tell me he feel like a young man again. You really gonna do it, Miss Etta?"

"I am. I surely am, if Mr. Howard's still willing. And sounds like he is. Oh, Emmett, you remember Skip Taggert, don't you? He was on the floorboard yesterday, but today, his troubles're over. He's going to help me with Mr. Howard."

"How do," Emmett said, shaking Skip's hand. "I 'member you from the time you burned up that football field. Lordamercy, you sho' could run."

Skip grinned, reliving his days of glory. Maybe I would've, too, if I'd had any.

"How long before Valerie gets back, you reckon?" I asked Emmett.

"Won't be long. She talk to the doctor 'fore she left, and she say she bringin' Mr. Junior home this mornin'."

"Oh, Lord. Then we better get a move on. Skip, help me get Mr. Howard out to the car."

"I'll just pick him up and carry him. Then I'll put the wheelchair in the trunk. Won't that be easier?"

"Quicker, too," I said, hurrying back to Mr. Howard's room. "Let me speak to him a minute."

He was sitting there already in his wheelchair, nodding off, with his thin white hair flopping down over his forehead.

"Mr. Howard, honey," I said, squatting down by his side. "You getting a little rest before you bite the bullet again?"

He jerked his head up and gave me one of his sweet lopsided smiles, garbling about how happy he was to see me.

"Here, let me fix your hair." I took a brush and a travel-sized can of hair spray out of my bag and put him to rights. "There. You're as handsome as a groom ought to be. Skip's here, you remember Skip from yesterday? He's going to get you in the car, and when we get back, you'll be a married man. Think you can stand it?" I grinned at him.

He nodded, his eyes sparkling, and, quick as a flash, his good hand reached for my breast. "No, you don't," I said, grabbing his hand. "You sure are sprightly this morning. And," I leaned over and whispered in his ear, "dirty-minded."

That just tickled him to death, because he liked to think he could do more than he really could. I always pretended that his groping around got me all hot and bothered, which made him feel like a whole man again, instead of just a half. That was the least I could do in exchange for wrapping me up in his name and his reputation.

I did get a sinking feeling about that time, though, thinking of how that name and reputation hadn't stopped Roy and Harley Puckett the night before.

"Y'all ready, Etta Mae?" Skip said at the door. "We better go if you are."

"Skip's going with us," I told Mr. Howard. "He'll make it easier to get this over with before Valerie gets back."

Skip scooped up Mr. Howard and headed for the car. I folded the wheelchair and carried it down the hall toward the kitchen.

"Wish us luck, Emmett," I said. "When we get back, there's going to be a new Mrs. Connard, Senior. And she'll outrank Mrs. Connard, Junior."

"All the luck in the world, Miss Etta," Emmett said, smiling. "I be happy for you and Mr. Howard and for me, too. I too ole to be scroungin' aroun' for no new place to live, givin' up my pension an' all. You ain't goin' back on yo' word, are you?"

"Not for all the tea in China," I said. "Emmett, I'm counting on you. It's going to be up to me and you—I mean, you and I—to see that Mr. Howard has a long and happy old age. Now, if Junior and Valerie get back before we do, don't say a word about where we are, 'cause I don't want them to take it out on you. Just wait till we get back and, with a marriage certificate in my hand, I'll take on both of them."

"I hope the Lord bless you, Miss Etta, for takin' care of both us ole men. I have a wedding lunch ready when you get back."

Skip settled Mr. Howard into the front seat of the car, then came back for the wheelchair, saying he'd stick it in the trunk. "Hurry up, Etta Mae. If we don't get goin', Mr. Connard's gonna have a stroke."

"Don't say that!"

I followed him out to the car and waited while Skip got in the backseat, his knees sticking up practically in his face. We left, but I didn't feel sure we were going to make it until we got out on the highway, still checking the rearview mirror for a blue-and-white Ford Windstar and sweeping the cars coming toward us for a little green Mercedes.

The Universal Harvest Church was about three miles off the Abbotsville Highway on North Ridge Road. It was a medium-sized brick building sitting in a grove of trees in a farming community. There was a white steeple laying out in the field beside it. They'd had a steeple fund going for several years and had finally gotten together enough to buy one, but not enough to pay for a crane to put it on top of the church.

"I'll tell you," I said to Mr. Howard and Skip, "if the Reverend Mr. Haliday's not here, I'm going to kick myself. I should've called him and told him we were on our way. Even though I told him yesterday it might be this morning."

"There's a car parked over there by that side door," Skip said. "Reckon it's his?"

"Oh, thank goodness," I said, turning into the graveled parking area and pulling up beside the old black Cadillac. "I bet it is, it looks like a preacher's car. I'll run in and let him know we're here and ready to go. Skip, watch out for Mr. Howard while I'm gone, okay?"

"Take your time, Etta Mae," Skip said. "I'm in no hurry."

I rolled my eyes, and went to find the preacher.

Chapter 30

"You need *two* witnesses," the Reverend Haliday said. He stood in front of the pine podium from which he preached the Gospel every Sunday morning and every Wednesday night, wearing navy blue polyester Sansabelt trousers and a short-sleeved white shirt, open at the collar, that was thin enough to show the sleeveless undershirt underneath. He was a stout man, broader through the chest than anywhere else. He'd served in the Marines before being called to serve the Lord, and he still had the Marine Corps buzz cut to prove it. He was much admired by his hardscrabble congregation, because he would work with the best of them, pitching in at apple- or bean-picking time, saying he could pick souls for the Lord at the same time.

I sank down on the front pew, just done in with one more snag in getting this wedding over with. I *knew* we needed two witnesses. Of all people who should've known, it was me. I'd been through it twice before, but each time we'd either had friends with us or there'd been somebody at the magistrate's office to stand up for us.

"Well, since we brought one with us," I said, nodding at Skip, "I guess I thought there'd be somebody here who could help us out."

The Reverend Haliday shook his head. "We're just a country church," he said. "We have a volunteer come into the office a couple of days a week, but today's not one of 'em." He felt sorry for us, I could tell, as he stood there with his Bible in his hand ready to do the job, if we'd done ours.

The reverend hadn't turned a hair when I'd straightened him out about who the groom was. Like the woman at the Register of Deeds office, he'd at first thought Skip was the lucky man and Mr. Howard my father. That was one of the things I liked about the reverend, the times I'd attended his services. He took everything as it came, like whatever it was had been ordained. Nothing ever got away with him.

"Maybe you could come back about five o'clock," he said, trying to be helpful. "People'll be coming in then for prayer meetin', and any of them'd be glad to stand up for you."

Five o'clock, I thought, too late. Mr. Howard would be worn out by then, and Valerie and probably Junior, too, would be at his house to close the door in my face. If all three of them weren't on the way to Raleigh by then.

I just shook my head, pretty close to tears by that time with the frustration of it all.

"Isn't there somebody you could call to come on out?" the reverend asked. "I just hate to see your plans torn all to pieces like this."

"No worse than me, Reverend," I said. I looked at Mr. Howard, sitting there in his wheelchair looking spry and alert. Mornings were the best time for him. Skip stood by the pew I was sitting in, taking it all in.

"Why don't you call Lurline?" he said.

"She wouldn't do it." I shook my head again, looking down at my lap at the smear of dirt on my pretty dress that hadn't come out, in spite of my sponging with a wet towel. "She did everything she could to break us up. Besides," I said, my heart thudding with a sudden remembrance, "I forgot to tell her I wouldn't be in to work this morning. She'll be so mad, she'd never help us."

"Aw, I bet she would," Skip said. "Won't hurt to try, anyway. I'll call her, if there's a phone around here."

"Okay," I said, shrugging. "Might as well try, but I don't have much hope. Call her at the office, that's where she'll be."

Skip followed the reverend out of the sanctuary, leaving Mr. Howard and me alone. I looked around the quiet room with its cushionless pine pews and plain choir loft. An upright piano sat to one side, with neatly stacked hymnals on top. A wasp buzzed in a corner of the ceiling. It was nothing like the First Methodist Church in town, with its carpeted aisles and maroon pew cushions and carved altar rail. But it was a sanctified church, and I craved the blessings we'd get here on this marriage because I figured we'd need them.

Given the fact that nobody else was handing them out.

"I guess I didn't think this out too good," I said to Mr. Howard. "I'm real sorry to drag you around like this and then have everything fall through."

He shook his head, and said something that I was too tired and too disappointed to try to figure out. He reached for my hand with his good one, giving it a squeeze to help my way-down feelings. I knew he was counting on me, since he was in no shape to help make any arrangements.

When you don't have your health, you're pretty well handicapped in all areas of life.

"Well, one good thing," I said, trying to buck myself up. "I'm no quitter. If we don't get it done today, I'll think of something else. Our license is good for sixty days, and if Junior moves you away, well, I'll just turn Raleigh inside out till I find you. So I don't want you to lose heart. I'm going to be Mrs. Howard Connard, Senior, if it kills me."

We sat there holding hands in the quiet church, waiting to see if Lurline would put aside her plans for my life and find it in her heart to come to our rescue.

"She's comin'," Skip called, a big grin on his face, as he and the reverend came back into the sanctuary.

My heart leaped up. "She is?" I couldn't believe it. "What'd she say?"

"She didn't much want to at first. Said it turned her stomach—uh-oh, sorry," he said with a glance at Mr. Howard, who didn't seem to mind. "But she said okay, after I told her that I had other plans that didn't have another marriage in them. I don't mean to hurt your feelings, Etta Mae, but I been thinkin' about what you said, an' you're right that we had our chance an' it didn't work out. So I want you to marry whoever you want to. That's what I told her, and she said she'd do it, but she wouldn't like it."

"I don't care whether she likes it or not, if she'll just come on. When will she be here?"

"She's on her way. Ten, maybe fifteen minutes."

I sagged against the pew in relief. Maybe it'd all work out, after all.

"Y'all just make yourselves at home while you wait," the reverend said, as he took a hymnal from the top of the piano. "I'll just use this time to select the hymns for prayer meeting tonight, so I'll be right here when you're ready."

After the longest fifteen minutes of my life had passed, a car door slammed and we all looked up to see Lurline come in the main door of the church, swishing her prissy self down the aisle. She wore one of her white nylon uniforms and white cork-soled wedgies. Slinging her large crocheted bag over her shoulder, she folded her sunglasses and stuck them in it.

"I don't like this one little bit," she announced as she got to the altar, "but what're friends for but to help when they're needed?"

"Oh, Lurline," I said, jumping up to hug her. "I just thank you so much. I'll never forget it."

"See that you don't," she snapped. She ran her critcal eyes over Skip and me, taking note of our stained and dirty clothes, Skip's unshaven face, and my lack of cosmetic enhancements. "You two look like something the cat drug in," she said. Then, turning to the reverend, she went on, "Let's get this show on the road. I have a business to run."

"Yes, ma'am," he said, straightening up like most people did when Lurline gave orders. "Now, let's bring the wedding party all up here together, right around me."

"Lurline," I whispered as we moved toward the altar rail, "I guess I won't be in to work today."

"Do tell," she said, giving me a cold eye.

Mr. Howard said something, holding out his good hand to Skip. "He wants to stand up, bless his heart," I said. "Skip, would you mind helping him? He can lean on me. Here, put his bad side next to me."

We got that done, and I was gratified that Mr. Howard wanted to show that he had some manly strength left by standing by my side for the ceremony.

"Do we have a ring?" the reverend asked.

I sagged, almost bringing both Mr. Howard and myself to our knees. One more thing I'd forgotten.

"It's not necessary," the reverend quickly said. "I just asked to know what part of the ceremony to leave out."

I didn't want any part left out. I wanted the whole works, but you don't always get what you want when you have to do every-thing yourself.

"Ring," Mr. Howard said, although it sounded like "whrin." He stuffed his good hand in his suit coat pocket and pulled out a ring with enough diamonds on it to bug my eyes out.

"Man alive!" Skip said, staring at it.

"Now that's a ring," the reverend said, admiring it as Mr. Howard handed it to him.

"Why," Lurline said, sharp and critical like she always was about anything that wasn't her idea, "it's a *dinner* ring."

"I don't care what it is," I declared, knowing in my heart that Mr. Howard had probably raided the first Mrs. Howard Connard, Senior's jewelry box. And why not? I thought. He was in no con-dition to go buy something especially for me, and I didn't mind a secondhand one at all. And *she* certainly couldn't use it. Be-sides, it was the thought that counted.

"It's beautiful, you ole sweet thing, you," I said, kissing him on the cheek, and trying to figure out why I could be so happy to finally be getting my wish to marry him, while some deep, mournful dread was welling up so bad in my insides that I thought it was clouding up to rain all over the world.

The reverend cleared his throat. "Dearly beloved," he said, and in no time at all I was the second Mrs. Howard Connard, Senior, in spite of the way my insides felt.

Chapter 31

As soon as the ceremony was over and Lurline had signed the marriage certificate, she slung her bag on her shoulder, unwilling to stay a minute longer. With her mouth all screwed up, she said that she hoped we'd be very happy.

"Lurline," I said, pulling her aside, "thank you for doing this, even though I know you don't approve of it. But please be happy for me. So much has happened so fast that I hardly know what I'm doing. Why, would you believe that Mrs. Julia Springer offered me a job managing the Hillandale Trailer Park when I thought she was going to kick me out? And now I don't even need it. Oh, Lurline," I said, putting my arms around her and fighting off the tears, "be happy for me."

"Oh, for goodness' sakes, Etta Mae," she said, straightening herself up. "Of course I wish you all the happiness in the world, not that I think this is the way to get it. But to each his own, I always say."

I watched her walk down the aisle and out the door of the church, leaving me with my new husband and my former husband, who'd been my new one's best man. Of all the people I knew, Lurline was the one who most loved to say "I told you so," so she'd be waiting for her chance with me.

I didn't care. The deed was done, even though it'd taken the starch out of Mr. Howard. He was so washed out that he went to sleep as soon as Skip got him back in the car. Which was fine with me. He needed to keep his strength up for our wedding night.

Skip crawled into the backseat, and I headed the car back to Mr. Howard's, where I intended to put him to bed and put Skip on his motorcycle and send him on his way.

None of us had much to say as we went through town, and I spent the time admiring my ring, wedding or dinner, it didn't matter to me. It was a knockout, but somehow it didn't give me the comfort I'd thought it would. In fact, I kept having to blink my eyes to keep that black, lonesome feeling I'd had in the church from spilling down my face and across my dress until it filled up the whole car.

I turned off Old Oak into Mr. Howard's driveway and came face-to-face with a patrol car from the sheriff's department on its way out.

"What now?" I asked, then thought I'd purely die when Bobby Lee got out and walked over to my window.

He leaned down and propped his arms on my window. I looked straight ahead, not wanting to meet his eyes, even if they were behind dark shades. I held on to the steering wheel as tight as I could so nobody would see my hands trembling.

"You want me to back up?" I asked.

"That's all right, I can get around you," he said. "We just brought Junior's car back. Found it about half a mile from the trailer park." I could feel him breathing and hear the creak of leather on his duty belt as he looked over at Mr. Howard in the front seat and Skip in the back.

"Hey, Bobby Lee," Skip said.

"Hey, Skip."

I felt Bobby Lee's gaze return to me, and all I wanted to do was put my head against his chest and beg him to just get me away from there. But I didn't, because I had what I'd wanted for so long. You have to appreciate what you have because what you get might be worse.

"Been for a drive?" he asked.

"Yes. Just, you know, riding around a little," I said. "Skip's in town for a little while, and he's been helping with Mr. Howard. He's been staying at Lurline's." I wanted to be sure that Bobby Lee knew that Skip was not with me. Not that it mattered, considering.

"Catching up on old times," Skip chimed in. I could've wrung his neck since that could've been taken two different ways. "Yeah, we've had a busy coupla days. I got here just in time to really help Etta Mae out. Tell him what you did today, Etta Mae."

I ground my teeth together. "He's not interested, Skip."

"I bet he is," Skip said, not getting any kind of hint that I didn't want to talk about it. "I bet everybody's gonna be interested. Why, Etta Mae, this whole town's gonna sit up and take notice." And he jabbed me on the shoulder, tickled over the amazing union he witnessed.

"What'd you do today, darlin'?" Bobby Lee said, real soft and low. "I'm always interested in what you do."

I would've picked a better time and place to tell him, though to tell the truth, I'd've just as soon not had to tell him at all. In making my plans for this happy day, I'd tried not to even think about Bobby Lee.

Skip jabbed me again. "Tell him, Etta Mae."

I closed my eyes, took a tighter grip on the steering wheel, and said, real fast, "I just got married to Mr. Howard Connard, Senior."

Nobody said anything for a minute. I took a quick glance in the rearview mirror at Skip, who was grinning from ear to ear, and a sidewise one at Mr. Howard, who was nodding off again.

Bobby Lee said, "Huh," sounding like somebody had knocked the breath out of him.

Then he stood up straight, looking across the roof of the car with his hands gripping my window. I wanted to reach over and cover them with my own and tell him that it was all right, that somebody who could put up with him better than I could would come along, that we were both better off without all the electricity that popped and crackled around us, that a decent, respectable marriage couldn't be made on a Quality Inn motel bed.

I didn't do any of that. I just squinched my mouth together and set my mind to being Mrs. Howard Connard, Senior.

"Well," Bobby Lee said, stepping back from the window, "just stay where you are, and I'll pull the squad car around you."

He walked off without a backward look, got in his car, and drove around us. I saw Wendell in the front seat with him, talking, but Bobby Lee looked straight ahead, his mouth set as hard as I'd ever seen it.

"That wadn't like Bobby Lee," Skip said, "walking off and not even sayin' congratulations, or anything. Don't he like Mr. Connard?"

"I don't know what he likes," I said, putting the car in gear and driving on up to my new home with an ache somewhere in the middle of my chest.

It got even worse when I saw Valerie's little green Mercedes and Junior's brushed gold Seville parked side by side in front of the garage.

Chapter 32

"What's the matter, Etta Mae?" Skip asked, after I parked the car, turned off the motor, and just sat there.

"Nothing, just thinking."

"Well, it's gettin' hot back here. You want me to take Mr. Howard in? He's about wiped out."

I looked over at my third husband, who didn't look as peppy as the other two had right after the ceremonies. He was asleep again, his head leaning against the window and his mouth open. I felt bad for putting him through so much, but he'd wanted it as much as I had.

Worse, even. The whole thing had been his idea from start to finish. Marrying him had never entered my mind until he brought it up. And kept bringing it up, until I'd begun thinking, *Well, why not?* So it hadn't been something I'd concocted on my own. It had never even occurred to me that Mr. Howard Connard would be within my reach. Too far above me, I guess.

I knew nobody would believe me.

And that brought me back to what I had to face when we went into the house, and I began to get back some of my determination to see it through, regardless. Things were going to get rough, but, let's face it, nothing I'd done to, for, or with Mr. Howard was anywhere near what Junior and Valerie had planned for him. It was up to me to stand up for what he wanted and to take care of him. That was the bargain.

I began to think of what that would mean for me. No more trailer living, no more unair–conditioned car, no more working for Lurline, no more put-downs by receptionists, clerks, and sales-people, and I began to feel better. I was the second Mrs. Howard Connard, Senior, and there wasn't a damn thing anybody could do to undo it.

"Etta Mae?" Skip said.

"What?"

"He needs to get to bed, and I need to get outta this car."

"Okay. Here's what we're going to do. If you don't mind taking Mr. Howard in, we'll get him settled first thing. Then you get your bike and go on to my trailer. I don't reckon the Pucketts'll be after you now. They've got what they want and I hope you'll let 'em have it and not tangle with them again. Something good'll come along for you, Skip, so just let that lottery ticket go and make the best of things. That's what I always try to do."

There was silence from the backseat for so long that I turned around and looked at him. He was studying the roof of the car with a smile on his face.

"Skip?"

"What? Oh, sorry, I was just thinkin' over what you said, and you're right. I got to let that go and get on with something else."

"Good. I don't want you messing with Roy and Harley again. They wouldn't think twice about doing you some real damage, and I don't want to be worrying about you.

"Now Skip, listen a minute. When we go in the house, Mr. Howard's son and his wife're going to be there, and they're going to raise some ever-living hell when they hear what we've done. I want you to just ignore it all and let me handle it. I'm the one who has to live with them—well, I mean get along with them in the future—so it has to be handled right."

"What're they gonna do?"

"No telling what they'll do or what they'll call me. But you just let 'em get it out of their system, and don't try to take up for me or anything. Just go on back to my trailer, and I'll see you there in a little while."

"You're not gonna live with Mr. Howard?"

"Come on, Skip, of course I am, but I have to pack some clothes and get some personal things to move over here. I'll do that and come back here later today. But what I'm trying to tell you is that you can stay in my trailer as long as you want to. The lock's busted, but it's safe enough for you."

"That's real nice of you, Etta Mae. I 'preciate it, since I couldn't get much rest over at Lurline's. She was always makin' plans for me, tellin' me what I ought to do and all."

I laughed. "Now you know how I feel. But her heart's in the right place, when all's said and done. Now, come on. Let's get Mr. Howard inside."

"I'll get him," he said, crawling out behind me. "You just hold the kitchen door for me, and I'll come back for the wheelchair."

As I followed Skip with Mr. Howard in his arms into the kitchen, Emmett stood watching us. He didn't look real happy.

"You get it done, Miss Etta?"

"It's done, Emmett, all legal and sanctified. Are they here?"

"Yessum, they in the drawin' room. Mr. Junior, he don't like to move too much. Give him a headache, he say. Miss Valerie, she already mad. She say where Mr. Howard? An' I say he gone fo' a ride. An' she say with who? An' I say I not rightly sho' who with. An' she cut loose, 'cause she say she *know* who with, an' it be you. An' she don't like it, say she gonna call the po-lice, till Mr. Junior, he say don't be too hasty with them kinda calls. They jus' sittin' in there now, an' I don't know what they sayin' by this time."

"Well, don't worry about it, Emmett," I said, trying to buck myself up, along with him. "We'll get Mr. Howard to bed, then I'll go in and talk to them."

Then, remembering, he said, "I made some nice sammiches and some crab salat and a few other things for yo' weddin' lunch, Miss Etta. Mr. Howard, he don't eat that kinda stuff no more, but I can fix you a nice plate."

"Thanks, Emmett, but I don't think I could eat anything right now with what's facing me in the living, I mean drawing, room. Maybe later. Maybe, even, with Junior and Valerie. Wouldn't that be nice?"

Emmett frowned and shook his head, like he'd heard dreaming before and this was some of it.

Skip chimed in, "I could eat something."

"I get it ready fo' you right now," Emmett said. "You come on back in here when Mr. Howard get settled, an' I feed you good. Least somebody enjoy a weddin' lunch."

"I'll enjoy it later, Emmett," I said, touched that he'd gone to the trouble. "I promise I will. I've got to face the music sooner or later, and sooner is better."

He mumbled something as I went into the back hall behind Skip and Mr. Howard, something about being glad he could stay in the kitchen.

Mr. Howard held on to my hand as we got him arranged in the hospital bed in his room, wanting me to stay with him. I had to whisper and croon to him a little, telling him I needed to get some of my things moved, telling him I'd be back and that he needed his rest before our wedding night. I told him that nothing could separate us now, that once I'd moved in, he'd see so much of me he'd want to run me off. He was smiling when I left.

I stood in the back hall awhile, getting myself together, listening as Skip brought the wheelchair into the kitchen and leaned it against the counter. I heard him tell Emmett what he wanted on his plate, and then his heavy footsteps to the kitchen table. I'd as soon Skip had gone on and left, not wanting an audience for the knock-down-drag-out that I knew was coming. The way Skip had flung himself into the fray the night before when he thought Roy and Harley were hurting me made me wonder what he'd do if Valerie blew her top. Which was exactly what I figured she was going to do.

The worst thing about it was that I looked so bad. I was still wearing my Kathie Lee Gifford polka-dotted dress that I'd put on the morning of the day before. Except now it was smeared with dirt that I hadn't been able to get out, and the rip in the underarm seam kept getting wider every time I moved. Catching a glimpse of myself in the gold-framed mirror in the hall, I almost lost heart. I was a wreck. My foundation, eye shadow, blush, and lip gloss were long gone, and my hair was windblown and sweaty. I was in no shape to take on those two, especially Valerie, who, being a TV personality, knew all about shading and blending, smooth coverage, and lip plumping.

Maybe I ought to go home first, I thought, just slip out the back and get a shower, change clothes, and make myself up. That would at least put me equal with Valerie in the personal hygiene department. Well, almost equal.

But I was afraid to leave. Afraid to stay, too, if the truth be known. If I left without telling them that Mr. Howard was my responsibility now, they might move him out while I was gone.

I wouldn't put it past them. They could pick him up and put him in Junior's big car and take him to some fancy rest home in Raleigh while I was at home in the shower. Emmett would try to tell them, but maybe he wouldn't, being so afraid of them turning him out. But even if he did, they had no reason to believe him.

I could see myself running all over Raleigh, in and out of nursing homes down there, looking for my husband. It'd take Mr.

Sitton and a crew of lawyers to get him back, and I didn't have the money for it.

No, the thing to do was face them now. Just walk in there, produce the marriage certificate, stake my claim, and lay down the law. Regardless of how frazzled I looked or how ripe I smelled.

Elizabeth Taylor probably hadn't figured on her Passion having to last two days running without a reapplication, but I was putting it to the test.

Chapter 33

I took a deep breath, reminding myself that I was somebody now, with the name to prove it, and walked down the hall toward the living, I mean drawing, room. The Oriental carpet kept my heels from clacking on the floor, so Junior and Valerie didn't have a clue that I was coming.

I guess it was something of a surprise when I appeared in the door.

Junior raised his eyebrows, like he couldn't quite place me, but Valerie shot up from her chair like she'd been goosed. Although I didn't know who'd want to do it.

"Are you here *again!*" she screeched, her face all twisted and strained, which never helps with delaying the aging process.

Before I could say a word, she screamed, "I want you out of here *now*. Right this minute!"

Act like a lady, I told myself, and looking her straight in the eye, I said, "Sit down and shut up."

It surprised her so, that she did it. Kind of took her breath away, too. Junior still had that addled look on his face, which may or may not've been permanent.

At that moment in time, I didn't care. All I wanted was to let them know who I now was and that they were no longer needed. Except on holidays when families are supposed to get together.

"For your information," I said to Valerie, "I'm here again for good. And I'm just letting you know that Mr. Howard and I got married this morning. I'm real sorry I didn't get a chance to invite you to the wedding, but what with one thing and another, well, I didn't much think you'd want to be there. Anyway, that's all I have to say, except I want you to know that I will take care of him and you don't need to worry about moving him out of his home or anything like that. And that's all I wanted to say."

Valerie looked like somebody had slapped her. She turned white as a sheet, and her mouth worked hard to get something out that wouldn't come. Junior's mouth just dropped open.

"Married?" he said. "You've *married* him?" He put a hand up to the small bandage on his head, like what was underneath was beginning to bother him.

"Here's the proof," I said, walking over to his chair and showing him the certificate. "It's all legal. You don't have to worry about that. I wanted it done right."

"Let me see that thing," Valerie snapped, reaching for it.

I snatched it away from her and said, "You can read it from here. I paid three dollars extra for this gold seal, suitable-for-framing type of a certificate, and I don't want it to get crinkled."

"I don't believe this," she said, squinching up her eyes as she read it.

"Believe it," I said. "As you can see, I'm the one responsible for Mr. Howard now, so you both can go on back to Raleigh knowing he's in good hands."

Valerie rolled her eyes so far back in her head, I wasn't sure they'd ever get back to normal. Then she snapped, "What're you going to do about this, Junior?"

"Not sure I can do anything about it," he said. "It all looks legitimate to me. I didn't think the old geezer had it in him."

"Well, stop thinking and *do* something!" Valerie snapped.

"I don't know what you want me to do," he told her. "As far as I can see, there's not much *to* do."

"This just makes me sick," she said, flopping back against her chair. "You make me sick, and this, this little gold-digging country hick makes me want to puke."

"*Country hick!*" I yelled. "Who are you to call me a country hick? I'll have you know I'm a high school graduate and I have my certified nurse's assistant degree, and I'm not somebody who just fell off a turnip truck! I own my own home and my own car and I have a good job, you slick TV bitch!"

I stopped and tried to maintain. This was not going so good, mainly because I was letting things get out of hand. Valerie was only acting like I'd expected. It was up to me to keep a ladylike tone.

"I'm sorry I said that," I said, trembling from the effort to lie with poise and grace. "I hope, after you've thought about it, you'll see that I can relieve you of your concern about Mr. Howard, and that you'll see your way to accepting me as part of your family.

"Now, I have to go and get my things together for the move. That'll give you time to say goodbye to Mr. Howard, and I hope you'll at least pretend to be happy for us, so you won't be upsetting him."

I turned and started out of the room, more than ready to get out of there.

"Just one minute," Valerie said, like she was the queen of something. "I'm calling Ernest Sitton to come over here, and we'll just see how legal all this is."

That put my heart in my throat, but I didn't let her know it. "Fine," I said. "I'll be back in a couple of hours, and we can all have Emmett's wedding lunch together."

"Emmett," I said, still trembling from the face-off, as I pushed through the swinging door to the kitchen. "Will your wedding lunch save for a while?"

"Yessum, I guess. But it won't save too long with all that mi'naise in everything. Them sammiches might need a little extra wrappin' to keep 'em from gettin' too hard to bite into."

"If you don't mind, let's put it all up and maybe somebody'll feel like eating it for supper. I really do thank you, Emmett, for making something so nice on our special day, and I'm sorry it seems to be going all to hell."

And with that, I turned away, trying to fight the tears that stung my eyes.

"Sorry, Emmett," I said, getting a grip on myself. "It just looks like nobody's happy for me. Us, I mean. I didn't expect anybody'd be dancing in the streets, but I didn't think everybody'd be against us."

"Mr. Junior an' Miss Valerie give you a hard time?"

I laughed as best I could. "You could say that. She ought to be riding a broom instead of that fancy little car out there."

"Don't let her worry you," Emmett said. "That jus' the way she be. I never seen that woman happy for anybody, but I don't talk about nobody, so don't take what I say wrong. But I think that woman why Mr. Junior stay on them golf courses so much."

"You may be right. It's a settled fact that I was worried about the wrong one all this time. I thought it'd be Junior who'd give me a hard time, but I'm thinking now that he'd come around if she'd get off her high horse."

"Mr. Junior all right. He a real nice man when Miss Valerie not around. But don't tell him I say that. Nor her, neither."

"Don't worry about me repeating anything, especially to those two. I just wish they'd go on back to Raleigh and let us get back to normal." I wiped my face with my hand, trying not to smear what little mascara I had left.

Then, remembering my other responsibility, I said, "Looks like Skip's gone. He get off all right?"

"Yessum, he say he roll that motorbike down to the street and crank her there, so he won't 'sturb Mr. Howard. Seem like to me that some other folks ought to do the same." Emmett rolled his eyes toward the drawing room. "When you reckon they take off from here?"

"No telling. But I do know things aren't going to get any better until they do, especially when I get back here with all my clothes and things. And that's where I'm going now. Emmett, I don't really know how to go about this, but I need to move in over here. Is there a closet I can use, and maybe a drawer or two? I don't want to mess up the way you have things fixed, so if you'll just find me a little space to put my things up, I'll try to get settled in."

Emmett stood there, shaking his head from one side to the other. "Miss Etta," he said, "that ain't no way to do. You Miz Howard Connard, Senior, now an' you jus' tell me what you want an' I fix it for you."

I stared at him, as I began to realize that Emmett was doing exactly what I'd wanted from this marriage, and he was the very first one to do it. He was giving me the respect that was supposed to come with my new name, and the realization of it lifted my head and straightened my shoulders.

But I still didn't know just what I was supposed to do with it, or how to act when it came. I smiled.

"Wherever you think best, Emmett," I said. "Let's just hope that by the time I get back, those two in yonder will be gone."

"Maybe they will and maybe they won't. Either way, you *the* Miz Connard now an' you s'posed to be here, so you jus' bring yo' clothes and move right on in. Like you s'posed to be here. Which look like to me, you are."

"That's right! I *am* supposed to be here. It's what Mr. Howard wants, and last time I looked, this was *his* house and *his* right to say who lives here and who doesn't."

I stopped and leaned against the counter, a sad thought coming to mind. "If he could talk so anybody could understand what he's saying, there wouldn't be this problem. He'd straighten it all out in a minute."

"You right about that," Emmett said. "Mr. Howard sho' know how to tell peoples what to do an' how to do an' he don't take no back talk from nobody. 'Spec'lly from Miss Valerie, she watched herself 'round Mr. Howard when he the way he used to be. She jus' get all bossy since he can't say nothin' she understand now."

"Well, I guess you and me'll have to stand up for him, Emmett. We'll have to let her know what's what."

"Yessum," Emmett said, turning toward a cabinet and taking out a box of Reynolds Wrap to cover the food. "Maybe that be yo' job, Miss Etta. I don't b'lieve I better let her know any what's what. I got to get these sammiches wrapped up 'fore they not fit to eat."

"I understand, Emmett. I know you can't say anything to her, but I sure do appreciate you backing me up and helping me and Mr. Howard. I know I'll have to take her on by myself. I just have to remember that I'm standing up for Mr. Howard and doing his talking for him."

Emmett's shoulders started shaking, and as he turned back to me, I saw him laughing. "No'm, Miss Etta, ain't no way you do his talkin' for him, least the way he used to do it. You didn't know him when he ruled the roost 'round here, an' lemme tell you, he a pistol."

Well, at least I could picture it, and it gave me the first real pleasure I'd had all day, the thought of Mr. Howard putting Valerie in her place.

"I'll just have to do the best I can," I said, laughing with him. "But I better get out of here and get my things together. I'll be back later this afternoon, after Mr. Howard wakes up from his nap."

I opened the door and started out.

"Miss Etta? I mean, Miz Connard, ma'am?" Emmett came around the counter and held the door for me. "Ole Emmett happy for you. I know Mr. Howard think the world of you, an' I jus' wish you lots of years of good luck."

I swear, the day had been up and down, up and down. I had gone from feeling happy to feeling sad to feeling so mad I could've pinched somebody's head off. But there was Emmett, calling me by my new name and wishing me what nobody else had done or would do. Except maybe Skip.

I could've cried my eyes out. But I bit my lip, trying to hold it back, nodded my head, which was all I could manage, and went on to my car.

Chapter 34

Before going back to my trailer, I drove out Mill Run Road and turned off on the dirt road that led to Granny's house. Red dust boiled up around and behind my car, and I had to roll up my windows and practically suffocate in the heat to keep from getting covered in it.

I sailed right on past Boyce and Betty Sue's house, feeling no need to visit with them. As far as I was concerned, they could take a flying leap, the way they treated Granny. Not that I'd let Granny know I felt that way—it'd just give her more reason to stay mad at them.

I pulled up beside Granny's house, parking under the oak that was covered with enough wisteria vine to make a shade for the front porch as well as the Camaro. I shook my head at the parched yard, brown and straggly from lack of water, and thought to myself that it wouldn't hurt Boyce to come over and keep it nice for her. But Granny's pots and cans of flowers on the porch were blooming all over the place. Granny couldn't live without her flowers, and they got watered when nothing else did.

Bless her heart, I thought, as I climbed the rickety steps to the porch, and decided to buy her some decent pots when we went to Walmart's on Saturday. Every other flowering plant that lined the porch and sat on tables was planted in a Maxwell House coffee can.

"Granny?" I called, opening the screen door and sticking my head in. "Granny? It's me, Etta Mae."

"Come in here, young 'un," she called back. "I been thinking about you all morning. Come give me a big ole hug."

She came running out of the kitchen, wiping flour from her hands on her apron. Wisps of white hair flew wildly about her wrinkled face, a mustard-colored smear was on her cheek, and her Reeboks left a trail of Red Band flour with every step she took. When Granny cooked, she went at it like Sherman through Georgia.

"Watch where you step, sugar," she said, holding out her arms, just beaming to see me. "Betty Sue's been here again with that yapping little poodle of hers. Leaves dog doo all over the place. It's a Tootsie Roll here, and a Tootsie Roll there, 'cept I can't see good enough to find 'em. So watch where you put your feet."

Laughing, I hugged her, smelling old hair, bacon grease, and the Opium bath powder I'd given her last Christmas. She hadn't known what to make of the name, but she'd liked the smell it gave off. She'd said, "Well, I'll use it, but I won't tell anybody what it is."

"What're you up to, Granny?"

"Gonna make me some fried pies. Got up this morning with a taste for 'em. Peach, I'm thinkin'. But what's going on with you, coming to see me two days in a row? Let's take a chair out on the porch. It's too hot to be inside with the stove running and dog doo-doo everywhere. I declare, it's past time for some cool weather. But we'll pay for it, mark my words, when winter gets here." Granny lived by the *Farmers' Almanac*, so she knew what she was talking about.

We went back on the porch, moving toward the shade of the tree and hoping for a breeze. She took a rocking chair and I sat in the swing next to her.

"Well, Granny," I said. "I came to tell you what I did this morning. Remember that old man I had in the car yesterday? The one you warned me about? Well, you're looking at the second Mrs. Howard Connard, Senior, sitting right here on your front porch."

She put her hand to her mouth, and her eyes began to sparkle. Even the dull one with the cataract. "Child! Why didn't you tell me? I oughta known it, though, there was something about that ole man that made me want to watch out for him. Well, the ole coot's got better'n he deserves, gettin' my sweet grandbaby. Oh, honey, I'm so happy for you. I hope you don't never have to work again. Land, I tell you, and you've heard me say it a million times, but a woman's lot is a hard one even with a good man, without having to put up with one that won't work, or that drinks or gambles it away when he does work. Love gets frittered away right along with the money that jumps outta his pockets, and I'm glad there's gonna be somebody to take care of you now."

I laughed, brushing away a honeybee that'd gotten a whiff of my hair spray. "I don't know, Granny. Looks like I'm going to be doing most of the taking care of, considering the state my new husband's in."

"Don't you worry about that. A man who can't get outta bed but can still pay the bills is worth any of 'em healthy as a horse that can't." She reached over and patted my knee. "I'm happy for you, honey. You just enjoy that fine house and all them fancy cars and whatever else he's got, and don't let what anybody else says bother you."

"Well, that's just it, Granny. His son and his wife have been so mean to me, especially her. I try not to lose my temper, but it's hard."

"Why, you just lose your temper if you want to, honey. All the Bible says is don't let the sun go down on your wrath. It don't say nothing about when it's shining. Sometimes you have to let folks know you're not gonna take whatever they want to throw at you. You just cut loose if you need to. Put your foot down, and remember who you are, a Wiggins and now a Connard."

I laughed. "And a Taggert and a Whitlow. It's about time I quit collecting husbands and their names."

"Don't fret over that, either," she said, pushing off her rocker with one foot. "Before you know it, you'll be too old to care whether there's a husband around or not, so enjoy yourself while you can."

"I want you to enjoy yourself, too. And just as soon as I can, I'm going to do something about this house. Have it air-conditioned, for one thing, and painted, too. And get you a clothes drier, so you won't have to be hanging clothes out on the line in all kinds of weather. That old TV needs to be upgraded to a size you can see. And whenever you want that cataract operation, you just let me know. I'll pay for it all. Mr. Howard will, I mean. You just tell me what you need, Granny, and I'll see that you get it."

"Law, honey, I don't need a thing. I got everything in the world anybody could want or need. You just enjoy that ole man, if he's able, and if he's not, well, just enjoy what he's got. But," she said, reaching over and patting me again, "you take care of him, too. An' I know you will. You got a good heart, Etta Mae, and always have had. Why, I remember when you were just a little thing. Mean as a snake if anybody crossed you, but always sweet as you could be if you were treated right."

"I guess I'm still mean as a snake every once in a while." What I'd done to Bobby Lee's windshield came to mind, but I put it out just as fast as it'd come in. "Well, Granny, I'd better be going. Got to move to my new house today. I just wanted to stop by and tell you I'm a married woman again, and to tell you that I'll be able to help you out a little more now."

"You just take care of yourself, that's all I want. Now, before you go, come on back to the kitchen and let me cook for you. I haven't cooked for you in I don't know how long."

"I can't, Granny, I've got to get on back. But I'll bring Mr. Howard out one of these days and we'll eat supper with you."

"You do that, honey. We'll get us a mess of beans from the garden, and I'll fry up one of them hens been scratching the yard all up."

"Mr. Howard can't eat fried. Could you stew it instead?"

"Why, honey, I do the best stewed chicken in two counties. And I'll put some dumplings in with it, and anybody can eat that. Etta Mae, my garden made the best Big Boy tomatoes this year, but Betty Sue came and got all my ripe ones this morning. I'll make her save some for you next time you come."

She stood up as I did, and I put my arms around her, feeling how little she was. And getting shorter, seemed like, every time I came. I smoothed her hair back and said, "Take care of yourself, and call me at Mr. Howard's if you need anything."

I gave her another hug and slipped my last five-dollar bill into her apron pocket.

Chapter 35

When I pulled in beside my trailer, I didn't see Skip's Low Rider anywhere. It was a relief in a way. I needed time for myself while I packed for the big move. On the other hand, it was always good to know where he happened to be at any given minute, since wherever he was you could usually count on trouble being there, too. I swear, for anybody as basically sweet as Skip was, he could get into more trouble than anybody I knew. And not even know it, half the time.

I went inside and jacked up the AC, wishing I didn't have to face the mess that Harley and Roy had made of my things. But I did, and it was just as I'd left it with no sign that Skip had been there.

I headed for the shower, shedding clothes as I went. Looking at the rip under the arm of my Kathie Lee dress, I was relieved to see it was along the seam, and easily mended. But I didn't have time for that.

After standing under cool water for fifteen minutes and getting my hair clean again, I felt a hundred percent better. I really wanted to wear my Dream Angels bra, but without the bikini panties to match, I decided against it and pulled on a set of sheer embroidered bra and panties in a basic nude color. I would've loved to've put on some capri pants or a pair of shorts, but figured with Junior and Valerie still around, I'd better go a little more formal.

And, oh Lord, Mr. Ernest Sitton, who was going to show up

over there sometime or another, had to be faced, too. So it had to be a dress of some kind. I dried my hair and put it up in big rollers, trying to decide what to wear. Not that I had much choice when it came to dresses, since I didn't have that many, having to wear mostly nurse's uniforms for my job, you know.

By the time I'd done my face and combed my hair, packing all my beauty aids as I went, I'd decided that clothes were clothes, whether or not they had designer labels. So I put on a white V-neck sleeveless T-shirt and an extra-short khaki skirt and a pair of flat sandals.

If Valerie wanted a fight, I'd be dressed for it.

Practically everything in my kitchen had been ruined and thrown out, but I was about to cave in by that time. I fixed some cheese toast and opened a Diet Coke, which would have to do me until I ate my first real meal as the new Mrs. Connard.

Just as I finished eating, the telephone rang and I reached for it, thinking it'd be Skip.

"Etta Mae?" Lurline said. "Are you home?"

"Hey, Lurline. Yes, I guess I am, but not for long. I was going to call you and thank you again for standing up for us today. That was real sweet of you."

"Don't mention it," she said. "I can't say I was exactly thrilled to do it, but you were bound and determined to marry that old man, regardless of my opinion. Now that it's done, though, I just have to accept it and make the best of it."

I wanted to tell her that it wasn't up to her to accept it or not, much less have to make the best of anything I did. But there was no need to make anybody else mad at me, so I told her I was glad she felt that way because I would always count her as my friend.

"I know you will, Etta Mae. I don't expect anything less from you, but you're going to have to watch yourself. It'll be awful easy to get used to the high life and think you're too good for your friends. I don't want that to happen to you, and I hope you'll appreciate it when I take you down a peg or two if I see it happening."

"I will, Lurline," I said, closing my eyes at the thought of it. "You don't need to worry about me changing or anything."

"Well, you never know. Remember that Scoggins girl who hooked herself a doctor? She couldn't see where she was going, her nose was stuck up so high. Actually, he was just a foot doctor, so she didn't have much to get so high and mighty about."

"I'm not going to get that way, Lurline."

"I know you're not, because I'm going to tell you if you do. But that wasn't why I called. Have you seen Skip?"

"Not since we got back from the church. I told him to come over here and stay as long as he wanted to. But he's not here, and I don't see any of his things."

"Well, that's just it. I came home early, which is another thing I want to talk to you about, and all his stuff is gone."

"Really? You think he's left town?"

"I don't know what to think. He was raised better than to go off without a see-you-later or a kiss-my-foot. But if he's not with you, I guess that's what he's done. Well"—she heaved a heavy sigh and went on—"he'll show up sooner or later, I expect. Anyway, the other reason I called is I wanted to give you a bachelorette party, but since nothing would do but you had to jump the gun and get married so quick, it'll have to be a lingerie shower instead. Either kind is supposed to be given before the wedding, but you didn't give anybody the chance, did you? Anyway, since you're not a bachelorette anymore, that's out. But we can at least get a lingerie shower in before the wedding night, so you'll have something nice to wear. We'll have to scramble to get it done, so looks like tonight has to be it."

"Tonight?" I didn't know what to say. I was touched that she wanted to do that for me, but I still had Valerie and Junior and Mr. Sitton, to say nothing of Mr. Howard, on my mind. And on my hands. "That's so sweet, Lurline. I'd love to have a lingerie shower, but tonight, well, tonight's going to be kinda busy."

"Oh, don't give me that, Etta Mae. That old man's going to need a cattle prod to get him started, much less to keep him going."

"Lurline!" I yelled. "Don't talk like that. Besides, what I meant was his son and daughter-in-law are still there, and I'm trying to get some of my things moved, and, well, I'd enjoy it more if we could do it another night."

Dead silence on the line, while Lurline let me know her feelings were hurt.

"Well," I said, feeling obligated to please her, as usual, "maybe we can work it out. It'd be all right, I guess, if you wouldn't mind doing it over at Mr. Howard's. You know I wouldn't feel right about going out with the girls on my wedding night. That wouldn't look too good."

"Why, that's just the ticket," she said, suddenly cheerful again, now that she'd gotten her way. "You know I wouldn't insist on tonight if it wasn't going to be a lingerie shower, which just has to be before the wedding night. I did want to have it at my house, but this way, we'll all get to see inside that house, which I've always wanted to do. Now, there'll just be a few of us—oh, and you can invite Junior's wife, too. The more the merrier. I'll call everybody else and tell them we'll meet, when? About seven, I think. I can't wait to see inside the Connard house. You reckon that colored man of his could fix us some snacks? You know how it is,

Etta Mae, this is such a last-minute thing, I'm not going to have time to make a dip or do a dump cake or anything else."

The woman had more nerve than anybody I'd ever heard of. "That'll be fine. Emmett fixed a wedding lunch that nobody but Skip ate, so we'll just put that out and let everybody help themselves. But, Lurline, there's just one thing, and I hope you won't take this wrong, but I wish you wouldn't call Emmett that."

Dead silence again. Then she said, "See, Etta Mae, that's the kind of thing I'm talking about. Already you're changing and thinking you're better than other people."

"Wait one minute, Lurline. Don't point your finger at me. All I'm doing is telling you that Emmett's feelings will be hurt if he hears you say that and he's been good to me and I don't want one of my friends making him feel bad."

"Well, to-do-de-doo. Don't you think I know better than to say it to his face, but I ought to be able to say whatever I want when I want to. To my *friends*, that is."

I leaned my head against the kitchen cabinet, wondering why I ever tried to argue with her. "Okay, Lurline, let's change the subject. If you hear from Skip, tell him again that he's welcome to stay in my trailer as long as he wants to. In fact, I'd like having him here. He could look after things for me, and maybe even change a few lightbulbs."

She was in good spirits by the time we hung up, and she ought to've been. She'd run over me with her inconvenient plans, made me mad and made me feel guilty, and on top of it all, made me do the apologizing.

As I hung up the phone and walked out of the kitchen area, I saw a piece of paper pinned to the back of Bernie's recliner. *What now,* I thought, as I unpinned and unfolded it, and tried to read a scrawl written in pencil.

Dear Etta Mae, I'm doing what you said you would do if you won a lot of money. Don't worry about me I will be OK. I am glad you are happy and hope you always are. Love from your loving ex, Skip.

PS, the Pucketts didn't get it. I had it hid all the time, you'll never guess where. In your new husband's wheelchair (check it out) when we went to get the license and I got it out today when we had the wedding. Ha, ha on Harley and Roy.

It took me a minute to remember what I'd said I'd do if I'd won the lottery. When I did, I started smiling and wondered if Skip was finally getting some smarts. He'd taken my advice and slipped out of town without telling anybody he still had a winning ticket. And that devil had hidden it where nobody'd think to look, and just in time to keep Harley and Roy from getting their hands on it.

That was the best thing I'd heard all day. Except for when Emmett called me Mrs. Connard.

Chapter 36

I packed my old Samsonite suitcase with some everyday clothes and filled two tote bags with my hot rollers, hair dryer, shampoo, conditioner, color extender, and various other beauty aids, and some personal items I won't mention. Then I put my favorite stuffed animals in a couple of Winn-Dixie grocery sacks, and wrapped my Barbies individually and laid them in a Seagram's 7 cardboard box. Draping my hanging clothes over my arm, I started loading the car.

It was a little sad to be leaving my trailer, as well as my total privacy. Already my single-wide was beginning to look empty, even though I wasn't moving any furniture. I wondered if I ought to have a yard sale and get rid of it. It'd all be snapped up in a minute, if I did. But storing it might be the best. Just in case I needed it again. On second thought, that was no way to start wedded life, making plans for when I wouldn't be again. I hated leaving my new couch, and wondered if I could make room for it at Mr. Howard's somewhere.

Well, maybe not. As is usually the case, you have to give up something in order to get something else.

After a last walk-through to be sure I wasn't leaving anything vital to everyday use, I looked around the living area. The lock on the door still wasn't fixed, and I had the happy thought of asking Emmett to come out and put in a new one. It was going to be nice to have someone to call on for little household repairs like that.

Then I had another, even happier thought, one that cheered me up considerably. Depending on the amount of household and personal money Mr. Howard decided to give me, I might be able to keep up the rent on my trailer space and just let it sit there.

Rent, I thought. Not twenty-four hours ago I'd made a deal with Julia Springer to manage the park, so I wasn't going to have any rent to pay. I sat down on the unblooded end of my couch and thought it through. I would purely enjoy telling that woman that I didn't need her charity anymore, but the more I thought about it, the more I could see the benefits of sticking with the deal. I could manage the park in my spare time and keep my trailer available, too. In fact, as the wife of a wealthy man, I was going to have more spare time than I'd ever had in my life. It wouldn't hurt to keep my hand in a little business of my own, and one thing was for sure, if anybody knew how a trailer park ought to be run, it was me, having had so much experience with mismanaged ones.

Besides, I wouldn't mind having a second home. Lots of well-to-do people have them. You know, for visitors and times you want to be by yourself. Why, Junior and Valerie might even appreciate having their privacy when they came to visit. They might like a cozy trailer as a change from Junior's old room or the impersonal ambiance of the airport Quality Inn.

I felt better with the possibility of not having to sell the trailer or my furniture. It's not every day that you have something all your own with not a cent owing on it, and I hated to have to give up that sense of security. Another satisfying thought struck me: with my new status, Julia Springer would have to treat me as a business partner instead of as the beneficiary of her Christian, but unpredictable, goodwill. I closed the door behind me, feeling considerably better about any number of things.

As I backed out of the parking space with a smile on my face,

Jennie leaned out her door, yelling congratulations and saying that she'd see me tonight. Lurline had been burning up the phone lines already, proving again that she was hell on wheels when she decided to do something. Before the hour was out, the news of my wedding would be all over town, and probably with Lurline's own special version of it. I wondered what Hazel Marie would think. I knew what the other one would, and it made me laugh.

Driving out of the trailer park, I headed toward town and my new home. I knew I was going to feel more like a visitor than a homeowner, even after I moved in. But I'm the type to make the best of whatever I have to put up with, so I figured it wouldn't take me long to feel at home.

Dang it, the way some people drive! I hit the brakes and swerved to the right, getting out of the way of a van that had passed and cut in too close in front of me.

"Oh, hellfire!" A hot flash of adrenaline concentrated my attention. It was a blue-and-white van with a little Confederate flag flapping from the aerial.

The Pucketts! There they were, slowing down and speeding up. I looked around at the other traffic, which wasn't much, but nobody was taking notice. I gripped the steering wheel with both hands and tried to think of what to do. Harley and Roy probably wouldn't run me off the road in broad daylight, but as crazy as they were I didn't want to chance it. It was a settled fact that they'd be mad as hornets at not getting Skip's lottery ticket, and what could I do about that? I couldn't tell them where Skip was regardless of what they did to me—you can't get blood from a turnip. But they could sure get blood from me, and that's what worried me.

The van sped up a little, and I eased out to try to pass it. Then it slowed down, and I had to slam on my brakes again. Looking around, I'd've given anything to see a cop car on my tail, even Clyde would've been a welcome sight. But all I saw were cars with drivers intent on their own business, paying no attention to anybody else's for a change.

A strip mall with a Shell station was coming up on the right, and I thought of zipping in there and hightailing it to a phone. Before I could do it, though, the van surprised me by turning in at the station first. I breathed easier, hoping it wasn't the Pucketts after all. Or that they'd run out of gas.

I glanced in the rearview mirror as I passed the station and couldn't even breathe for a minute, much less easier. The van was doing a quick 360 and pulling back out into the road. It came roaring up behind me until all I could see in my rearview was that flat-nosed grille.

I sped up, but it stayed right with me, tailgating so close that I was afraid they were going to bump me. *Cause a wreck!* That's what they'd do. Then stop and say they'd take me to the hospital. They'd get me out of there before anybody called for help.

I gripped the steering wheel and floorboarded it, zooming past the city limits and hoping for the first time in my life that I'd get pulled for speeding. I passed a pickup, blowing my horn, and zipped in close in front of him. The van followed me, riding side by side with the pickup until the driver got scared off and slowed so the van could slip in behind me again. The pickup driver gave us all the finger, and I couldn't blame him.

By the time I reached Main Street, I had to slow down or hit a pedestrian or two. The van slowed, too, but didn't back off. I was able to think a little better by then, and the first thing I thought of was that I didn't want to lead the Pucketts to Mr. Howard's house.

The sheriff's office! That's where I'd go.

No, I wouldn't. By the time I got there, went in, and reported

236 Ann B. Ross

it, they'd be gone, and what could be done then? I'd have to leave, and the Pucketts would pick me up again. Cops wouldn't do anything unless they saw with their own eyes what Bobby Lee called an infraction of the law.

As I went down Main Street, I saw one empty parking space on the opposite side of the street, right in front of Eckerd's Drug Store. Which meant it was also in front of Mr. Sitton's office upstairs. Sometimes an answer pops up right in front of your eyes. That's where I'd go and just wait the Pucketts out. Maybe even get Mr. Sitton to slap a restraining order on them. Then the sheriff would have to make them leave me alone.

What with Main Street traffic, such as it was, I had slowed down considerably, but I didn't turn on my left-turn blinker or give any indication whatsoever of my intentions. Just jerked the wheel and made a half U-turn in front of an oncoming SUV that was signaling for the same parking space I was aiming for, getting a horn blast and another finger for my trouble. But I got the space first, ramming the front tires into the curb as I came to a stop. I grabbed my purse by its gold chain and ran across the sidewalk to the door to Mr. Sitton's office.

Once inside, before going up the stairs, I looked out the glass in the door and was able to see the van make a right on Rosemont. Going around the block, probably, and probably cussing their heads off. Whew.

I turned and climbed the stairs, trying to slow my heart rate. When I got to Mr. Sitton's door, I stopped and straightened my skirt and mopped my sweaty face with a Kleenex.

Then, straightening my shoulders, I barreled in to face Mr. Sitton's secretary, determined not to take anything off her.

Walking right up to her desk, where she was peering at a computer like she didn't know how to use it, I said, "I need to see Mr. Sitton. Is he in?"

"He's in," she said, without turning her head, "but he's busy. Besides, he doesn't see clients in the afternoon."

"He'll see this one. Tell him I'm here, please."

She drew herself up straight, breathing a deep one through her nose. Then she slowly turned to look at me for the first time since I'd been there. When she recognized me, I could see her face tighten and her thin mouth get all puckered up. She gave me one of those blank stares, like it was beneath her to even notice me.

Fuming, I said, "Tell him Etta Mae is here. I'm a fully paid-up client, and I have something important to talk to him about."

"Don't come in here making demands, young lady. I've already told you he doesn't see clients in the afternoon. It's the only time he has to catch up on records and paperwork. Not that I have to explain anything to you."

"Which door is his?" I asked, turning to scan the three inner doors. "I'll tell him myself, if you're too lazy to do it."

She half rose out of her chair at that, not accustomed, I guessed, to being talked back to.

"Don't you dare disturb him. You better leave or I'm calling the sheriff."

I turned back to her and gave her a pretty long stare myself. Even did a little looking down my nose, too.

"Do you know to whom it is you happen to be speaking?" I said, but before I could tell her she reared back and let me have it.

"I don't care *whom* I happen to be speaking to," she said, twitching her head on each word. "Just take yourself out of this office. You're not seeing Mr. Sitton today." Then she jerked her head back around to the computer, like she was through with me. But under her breath, she muttered, "High-and-mighty little *twit*."

Leaning across her desk and getting right in her face, I said, "You don't want to get into a name-calling contest with me, believe me you don't. I've got some names you've never even heard of, but you'll know they fit when you hear them. Now listen to me, you frizzy-headed ole bat, I am Mrs. Howard Connard, Senior, and I want to see Mr. Sitton. Now."

She sat real still, gazing past her computer. Then she slowly turned to me, her eyes wide with surprise, and said, "I don't believe it. Not Mr. . . . you can't . . ."

"Yes, I can. May I see Mr. Sitton now?"

"I'll tell him you're here," she said, as meek as that type person can be when they're put in their place.

Getting up from her chair, she came around the desk and tapped on one of the doors. She kept her eyes trained on me like she was afraid I'd jump her. She wasn't in any danger by then, though she had been a couple of minutes before.

"He'll see you now, Mrs. Connard," she said, holding the door for me, and I reaped the first reward of my newly wedded state as I sailed in past her.

Chapter 37

"So Howard's married again. Remarkable, I must say." Mr. Ernest Sitton sat behind his desk, both hands resting on it, but the fingers of his right one tapped a pile of papers, one finger at a time, over and over.

He'd taken the marital news of his old friend and income-producing client without turning a hair. That surprised me. I thought, next to Junior, he'd be the one most likely to rant and rave over it. But no, he'd just nodded his head and said, "I guess you have proof of this marriage?"

"Right here," I'd told him, digging in my bag for the marriage certificate, which I intended to keep on my person until all likelihood of being questioned about it was long past and gone.

He'd studied it for a while, then said, "I'm a little taken aback that Howard didn't invite me to attend. He's seldom taken such a big step without my advice." Meaning, I guessed, that his advice would've been Don't Do It. But you never know, so I gave him the benefit of the doubt.

"Well, we'd planned to have a big wedding, with engraved announcements and a reception for all our friends. But Junior was hell-bent to put him in a Raleigh nursing home, which is where Mr. Howard would be right this minute if I hadn't stepped in. So we didn't have time for anything but a quickie." He blinked, and I quickly added, "Wedding, quickie wedding."

He handed the certificate back to me, and said in an offhand way, "Big difference in ages, wouldn't you say?"

I agreed, because you can't deny facts, then I said, "I don't mind, and neither does he." Meaning, in a nice way, that if we didn't, nobody else should.

He'd nodded and went to tapping his fingers again.

Then he said, "Howard's been my friend for thirty years, so you'll forgive me if I ask a few personal questions."

I nodded back and said, "Depends on how personal." Figuring he wanted to know about those intimate details that everybody speculated about, especially when two unlikely people tie the knot. You know, the pictures that come into your mind when you try to imagine how they manage.

He gave a quick smile, almost too quick to see, and said, "You certainly don't have to answer if you don't want to."

"I know. The first advice you ever gave me was to keep my mouth shut."

"Hm-m-m. Yes. So I did. Well, Mrs. Connard," he started, and I smiled, almost secure now with my new name since a lawyer had just recognized out loud that it really belonged to me. "So, tell me. Just what do you expect to gain from this association?"

"Association? It's a marriage to me," I said. "And I don't know what you mean by what I expect to gain from it."

"Oh, come now. Just give me an idea of what you want to get out of it."

"Oh, I get it," I said, thinking that this was one person who might understand what I wanted from Mr. Howard. And what I was willing to give in return. Pleased that he was so interested in my deepest desires, I got up from my chair and walked to the window overlooking Main Street. I hoped he'd be interested enough to listen for as long as it took to outlast the Pucketts, because I saw their van parked in a loading zone down the street.

"You knew my daddy," I said, turning toward him but staying close to the window. At his nod, I went on, "And I expect you knew, and maybe still know, some more of my Wiggins kin. That being the case, maybe you'll understand when I tell you that all I've ever wanted was to better myself. I thought I was paving the way to that when I took my CNA course, which I graduated from with honors, I'm proud to say." I took another quick look out the window, and saw Harley get out of the van and walk toward a Pepsi machine on the sidewalk. Sighting confirmed. It was the Pucketts' van, just as I'd suspected. I hoped they'd burn up in the heat and perish of thirst while they waited for me. Turning back to Mr. Sitton, I went on. "But it didn't take long for me to learn that it was going to take more education than I could afford to get what I wanted.

"You're an educated man, Mr. Sitton, so you know what I'm talking about. Think where you'd be and what you'd be doing if you hadn't gotten all the schooling I see the diplomas for hanging on these walls. Detailing cars, for one thing, or bagging groceries at Ingles or Winn-Dixie, for another. Or selling shoes at the Pick'n'Pay. You have to have an education these days to better yourself in any way. Or, like in my case, if you can't afford one, marry somebody who's already reached a better place."

Glancing out the window again, I saw Harley hand a cold one to Roy. Then he slid back into the van and left the door open with one foot propped on it.

"So," I said, "that's what I hope to gain from marrying Mr. Howard. And I'm willing to take care of him for the rest of his days in order to get it. Not only willing, but happy to do it. It's a good exchange."

"Well," Mr. Sitton said. "Well. A very practical take on the marital bond, I must say, and I applaud your candor. No beating around the bush with you, is there? I appreciate the fact that you didn't try to convince me of your undying love for a man who can barely speak or walk. I wouldn't have believed you if you had, so I'm glad you didn't."

I grabbed another quick look out the window and saw no change, trying to decide if Mr. Sitton's words had an edge of sarcasm to them. It's hard to tell with lawyers, don't you think? But I played him straight.

"No, I wouldn't do that, Mr. Sitton, because I don't love Mr. Howard," I said, daring to face him directly with as direct an answer as I could give. "At least, not with the kind of love I've already had a bait of and that's never done anything for me but tear my heart out. In fact, if I'd loved Mr. Howard with that kind of love, I wouldn't have married him. I'd've run as fast as I could in the other direction. So, no, what I feel for him is much better in the long run.

"But I expect what you're really asking is if I married him for his money. And I'll say yes, because that's part of who he is. But it was for his name, more than for his money. Just as an example of what I mean, would you be giving me all this time if Etta Mae Wiggins had come to see you? No, you wouldn't. But you had the time for Etta Mae Connard, and so did that so-called secretary of yours. Now, if you want to talk about what Mr. Howard feels for me, I'll just tell you straight out. He's got the hots for me that just won't quit, and, believe it or not, with what I have to offer he may be getting the best of the deal. Regardless of what you might think about my ulterior motives."

"Well," he said, squirming a little in his chair. "Well, that's straightforward enough. And, uh, upon reflection, I might be inclined to agree with you on who's getting the best of the deal in this, ah, association." His pale face reddened all the way across his scalp. I could see the pink skin under the white strands on the top of his head. Men are all alike.

I looked out the window again, then did a double take. The van was pulling out into traffic. And there was a deputy, who'd made them leave the loading zone. Licking my lips to hide it, I had to smile.

And I also had to get out of Mr. Sitton's office and get myself over to Mr. Howard's while the getting was good. Poor ole thing, over there resting up for his wedding night. I needed to be there when he woke to be sure he was feeling up to it.

"So," I said, relieved that the coast was now clear, "I guess none of this was a surprise to you, since Junior's probably already called, screaming bloody murder. He said he was going to ask you to come out there and talk to all of us. Set me straight, as Valerie said."

"As a matter of fact," he said, reaching for a pile of pink slips, relieved, I thought, to turn to business matters, "I do have a note here to return a call to him. I haven't gotten to it yet but, yes, I expect you're right. He'll be upset by this turn of events. But it won't make any difference to his situation. Vis-à-vis his father's estate, that is."

"Well, vis-à-vis Junior and me, I'm glad to hear it. I wouldn't want to get between father and son, so I hope you can reassure him on that point. And Valerie, too, if you don't mind, because she's having a flat-out fit over this."

He smiled in a distant kind of way, and said, "I'll do my best on that score."

"Well, I better be going. Mr. Howard's going to be awake pretty soon and he'll wonder where I am."

As I headed for the door, he got up from his chair and walked across the room with me. Holding out his hand, he said, "Perhaps I'll see you later in the day, if that's what Junior wants." He shook my hand, and went on, "I'm sure everything'll work out fine, Mrs. Connard. Please accept my congratulations."

I was grinning so hard I could hardly answer. But I squeezed his hand to let him know how much I appreciated his good wishes. I started out the door, then turned back to him. "Say that one more time, if you don't mind."

He raised his eyebrows, then quickly understood. "My very best wishes," he said, with one of those flickering smiles. "Mrs. Connard."

He closed the door behind me as I crossed the outer office with a light step and an even lighter heart. And a smile on my face. Without looking at ole tight-ass glaring at me from behind her desk, I flipped her off and bounced on out of there.

Chapter 38

When I got to the bottom of the stairs, I took my time leaving the vestibule. Looking up and down the street and checking the passing traffic and parking spaces, I searched for any sign of the Pucketts.

Then I dashed across the sidewalk to my car and quickly backed out, still watching all the mirrors. My one big fear was that they'd follow me to Mr. Howard's, and I couldn't have that. It was up to me now to look after him, and the thought of Harley and Roy barging in and scaring him into another stroke raised the hair on the back of my neck.

The big problem that kept rolling around in my mind was how I could get rid of the Pucketts on a permanent basis. I couldn't go around for the rest of my life watching rearview mirrors and peering out windows before I stepped outside. I thought about just facing them off and telling them in no uncertain terms that Skip was gone and I didn't know where he was or when he was coming back.

Would that work? It sure hadn't the night before. I couldn't figure what I could do to rid myself of them. They were the most determined pair I'd ever seen, which shouldn't have surprised me since all the Pucketts were known to be stubborn as mules, never turning loose of anything once they latched on. Why, I remembered hearing that one of them tracked a man who'd stolen a bluetick hound, which wasn't worth the money it took to feed, for months and months. Followed him to Florida and back to Easley, then over into Madison County until he got that dog back. Then sold the dog to somebody else.

I drove around several blocks, turning and twisting as I looked for the van, hoping I'd lost it for good. Then it came to me that if I kept doing that, I could run up on the Pucketts when they might otherwise not ever have found me. So I straightened up and headed straight for Old Oak Avenue, watching all the time.

I didn't feel safe until I turned into the driveway and the first of Mrs. Connard's trees and bushes hid me from the street. When I got to the house, the first things I saw were the cars I'd been hoping were on their way to Raleigh. But no, Valerie and Junior were still there, expecting, no doubt, that Mr. Sitton was going to rescue them from my presence in their family.

Good luck on that little deal, I thought, smiling at the thought of the end run I'd made by getting to Mr. Sitton first.

I took an armload of clothes from the backseat and went into the kitchen where Emmett was. He must've stayed there to keep out of Valerie's way.

"Hey, Emmett," I said, as low as I could without outright whispering. "I guess I'm moving in."

"Put them clothes down, Miss Etta, I'll get 'em all in for you. An' I cleaned out the closet in the room next to Mr. Howard's. It a sittin' room now, but they's a big closet in there, an' I'll put everything there till you make whatever 'rangements you want to."

"Thank you, Emmett, I was wondering where you'd want me to put all this." I cocked my head toward the front of the house. "They still here?"

"Yessum, an' they ain't happy."

"Too bad," I said. "They're not going to be any happier when they talk to Mr. Sitton." I smiled, wanting to share my happy feeling. "He *congratulated* me, Emmett, and I tell you the truth,

I felt more married when he did that than I did when the preacher pronounced us. I can't wait to tell Mr. Howard. How's he doing, anyway?"

"He still kinda tired. Jus' kinda wiped out, seem like. Been sleeping off an' on all afternoon."

"Did he eat any lunch?"

"Yessum, a little. But he don't ever eat much, so that don't worry me. I'm a little worrit, though, 'bout all this sleepin' he been doin'.'"

My heart gave a quick jump, wondering if I should call his doctor. "You don't think he's failing, do you?"

"No'm, I don't guess. Jus' us'lly he perk up by this time of day, then give out again right about suppertime."

"He's had a busy day," I said, thinking of the early morning wedding which wasn't part of his usual routine. "Not physically, though, because I've taken him on drives that lasted longer than we were gone this morning, and they didn't faze him. So, if he's so tired, it must just be the excitement of it all, us getting married, Junior getting hurt, and Valerie getting on her high horse. Emmett, I'm going to depend on you, since you've been with him longer than anybody else. What do you think? Should I call the doctor?"

"No'm, I don't reckon so. I think what the matter is, is he jus' sleepin' till Miss Valerie go home. He tryin' to keep her outta sight an' outta mind."

I smiled. "He's pretty smart, so I bet that's it. But, Emmett, let's keep an eye on him, and if you don't like how he's doing, tell me. Or just go ahead and call the doctor. You've been taking care of him so long that I trust what you think of his condition."

"Yessum, I will. I know you got yo' hands full with them two in yonder. I hear Miss Valerie rantin' an' ravin' 'cause Mr. Sitton ain't here yet. You might oughta tell 'em you already seen him."

"I want to visit with Mr. Howard first. Seems like I haven't seen him all day, I've been so busy. I'll just tiptoe to his room and spend a few minutes with him, and hope they don't hear me till I'm ready to face them." I looked toward the dining room door, dreading what lay behind it.

"Oh, Emmett," I said, before leaving, "one more thing, and I really hate to ask this, but I couldn't get out of it. Some girlfriends of mine want to give me a shower tonight, and they wouldn't be put off to a more convenient time. Would it be all right if they came over here? I suggested it, because I didn't want to leave Mr. Howard on the first day of our wedded life. But I don't want it to be any trouble to you, so we could just put out a few of the things you fixed for lunch, and maybe they won't stay long."

"Why, Miss Etta," Emmett said, "you don't have to ax me can you have yo' friends come over. You jus' tell me, an' I fix it up for you. I be happy to see this ole house have a party again. An' we got plenty to serve them ladies. I'll set the dining room table and have it all nice for you, don't you worry 'bout a thing."

What a relief. I'd been afraid he wouldn't like me inviting people in and taking over the house like I owned it. I didn't need nor want Emmett thinking I was taking advantage of him or of Mr. Howard's things, and then sulling up on me. My new name didn't give me a license to lose the friends I already had.

I sneaked out of the kitchen and across the back of the center hall, then into the small one that led to Mr. Howard's room. I listened outside the door to be sure he was alone.

Hearing nothing but the murmur of Valerie's voice from the drawing room, I opened the bedroom door and slipped inside. Mr. Howard was lying in his hospital bed, the head of it slightly elevated, which was the way he liked it. He seemed to be sleeping, his eyes not quite closed and his mouth not at all. A soft snore fluttered his lips with each breath, and I thought of Bernie, who'd run me out of bed more than once with the nerve-shattering noise he made. I could live with this, and sleep with it, too.

I walked over to the bed and took Mr. Howard's good hand, my heart sinking as I felt how thin and frail it was. Then I remembered how happy I was making him and was glad that I could brighten his life. I mean, when somebody has to live with a handicap or an infirmity like he had, it does you good to be able to give them a little enjoyment now and again.

"Mr. Howard," I whispered, "don't wake up if you don't want to, but I just wanted to tell you what's been going on. I know you must be wondering, all closed up in here, not knowing who's doing what. You just keep in mind that I'm always working for us and doing the things you can't do, and that I'm always thinking about you."

He batted his eyelids, looking straight up at the ceiling like he was trying to figure out where he was. I took a Kleenex and wiped his mouth. "It's me," I said. "How're you feeling?"

He finally focused on me, giving me that little half smile, which was the best he could do, and tightened his hand on mine.

As he tried to speak, I shushed him, telling him to save his strength for later on. Then I told him how Mr. Sitton had taken the news, and he nodded, pleased to hear it. His eyelids kept closing down on him, although each time they opened he looked at me with all the love I knew was in his old heart.

Then I told him about the party that'd be later in the evening, telling him we'd keep it quiet and not disturb him, but that if he didn't think we ought to have it in his house, to just tell me and I'd call it off.

"You," he said, straining to get the words out. "You," he tried again, pointing at me. "You-er 'ouse. Now."

My heart melted. I leaned over and kissed his face. Then to tickle him, I said, "I would invite you to the party, but I'm afraid you'd be embarrassed. It's going to be"—and I leaned close and whispered—"a *lingerie* shower. What do you think of that?"

His eyes flew open, sparkling with the thought of what usually turned men on, regardless of how feeble they were.

"Knowing those girls," I went on, "they'll give me something nice from Belk's or Dillard's. Or maybe even from Victoria's Secret! How about that?"

He liked it. I could tell. So I kept on telling him how Emmett was going to set the table for us, and who I thought would come, then how I was moving my clothes in, meaning I was going to stay and be with him all the time. Then I mentioned Valerie and Junior, and how I thought they would come to terms with our situation and go on back to Raleigh, and how happy the two of us were going to be.

By that time, he'd dropped off again, his eyelids and mouth fluttering as he breathed. I put his hand back under the sheet and patted it, telling him I had to go talk to Valerie and Junior, but that I wasn't going anywhere else.

"I'll be here for you from now on," I whispered. "And things will be done the way you want them to be."

I didn't think he heard me, but the books say that a part of the mind never sleeps. So I hoped some of what I'd said got through, because I meant it.

As I turned to leave, he suddenly stirred in bed and grasped the metal handrail with his good hand, grunting and striving to pull himself up.

"Ehra Mae, way . . ." he called.

I came back to his bedside, concerned because his face was even more strained than his words. He grabbed my hand again, as he turned loose of the rail and flopped back in bed. The lines in his face deepened as he tried to say what was on his mind.

"Geh Ernes'," he croaked, jerking at my hand like it was an urgent matter.

"Ernest? You mean, Mr. Sitton?"

He nodded his head hard, squeezing my hand even harder. "Geh 'im. Need . . . nee' take." He stopped and looked at me with the frustration of a once-mighty man who'd lost all his powers. "Nee'," he strained to say. "Take care."

"Oh," I said, catching his meaning. "Don't you worry, I'll take care of myself and you, too."

He shook his head on the pillow, back and forth, back and forth, while tears of frustration leaked out of one eye. "I. You. Ernes'." He took a deep breath, looking straight at me, hoping, I guessed, that I would read his meaning in his eyes. "I . . . wan' take . . . care *you*. Need see . . . Ernes'."

I leaned my head on the metal handrail, tears flooding my eyes, just melting away inside.

"You're the sweetest man in the world," I whispered. "Now don't worry, Mr. Ernest Sitton will be here in a while and I'll tell him you want to see him."

He fell back in relief, nodding his head and loosening my hand. I pulled the sheet up again and smoothed it down. Then, whispering that I'd be in the drawing room, I left.

As I pulled the door closed, I heard the soft snoring begin again.

Chapter 39

As I came out into the center hall, the front doorbell rang and I stood there wondering if it was my place to answer it. I didn't hear any sounds of movement from the drawing room, so Valerie certainly wasn't going to do it.

Then I heard the swinging door from the kitchen swish open and shut, and Emmett came through the dining room, headed for the door. I stepped back, not knowing who had come calling and thinking I ought to maybe wait in the kitchen, in case it was somebody for Junior or Valerie.

I needn't have worried. It was Mr. Sitton, and he was my bud now. I walked down the hall and shook his hand.

When I turned around to motion him into the drawing room, Valerie was standing with her hands on her bony hips, glaring at me. If looks could kill, I'd be in my grave.

"Come have a seat, Mr. Sitton," I said, just like I was used to having guests in a house instead of a single-wide. "They're waiting for you, I think. Hello, Valerie."

"Mrs. Connard, to you," she hissed as I passed her.

"Oh, well, then," I said back at her, "that makes two of us, doesn't it?" And proceeded to take a chair by the hearth. Though there wasn't a fire in it, as hot as it was.

Junior was sitting across from me in a matching wingback. He gave me a small smile, though he still had a slightly addled look to him. That could've been from an ongoing headache, though, from his concussion. Headaches like that usually lingered for a while, and what with having to listen to Valerie bitching all day, I didn't doubt that he was suffering. To say nothing of worrying about where I fit in.

Mr. Sitton sat on one end of the couch, sinking into the down cushions that Emmett had to fluff up after anybody touched them. I prefer foam rubber myself, so your cushions will keep their shape.

Valerie jerked a side chair away from the wall and plunked it down next to Mr. Sitton. She smoothed down the backside of her dress as she took her seat. When she kept staring at me, with her mouth all primmed up, I realized I'd taken her chair. I hadn't meant to do that. I mean, it wasn't on purpose, so I started to get up and let her have it. I didn't care where I sat, but about that time, Mr. Sitton took out some legal-looking papers from a folder in his briefcase and I sat down, not wanting to interrupt a lawyer's train of thought.

"I understand you're all concerned about how Howard's new marital state will affect his estate and the beneficiaries thereof," he began.

"We certainly are," Valerie said. "But what I want to know first is this. How valid is this so-called marriage? Daddy Connard is obviously not of sound mind, so it seems to me that anything he enters into of a legal nature under his present circumstances could be annulled or declared invalid." She stopped, seeing Mr. Sitton's surprised stare and Junior over there covering his eyes with one hand. "Or something," she finished.

"Valerie," Junior said, very quietly.

"I assure you," Mr. Sitton said, "that I am in close contact with Howard, seeing him weekly at the least. I have been made aware of his strong feelings for this young woman, and even though the marriage itself came about more quickly than I'd been led to believe, I knew that was his intention. Now, as to his mental acuity and decision-making ability, I have had no indication of any impairment of his judgment at all. So, there are no grounds to petition for an annulment or a declaration of invalidity. Much less of mental incompetence." He shuffled some papers, and said, "Now, let us move on.

"Junior, I believe you've be apprised of certain provisions concerning the distribution of your father's estate, so there's little need to reiterate them."

Valerie jerked her head toward her husband and said, "What? What provisions?"

"I've told you, Valerie," Junior said. "He's referring to the trust Daddy set up for me, and which we already benefit from."

"Well, I *know* about that," she said, "but what about the provisions for the rest of the estate?"

"I don't know anything about that. It's Daddy's money, and he hasn't seen fit to tell me what arrangements he's made. All I know is what he's already done for us."

"So?" she demanded of Mr. Sitton. "What happens to the rest of it? Surely, what he's put in trust for us is not all there is."

"I am not at liberty to reveal the terms of Howard's will, as you should know." Mr. Sitton turned sideways, facing away from her and addressing himself in Junior's direction. "The rest of your father's estate is also in trust, set up to benefit certain persons and charities in which he has long had an interest. At the present, he is himself the lifetime income beneficiary and is also a trustee, along with myself. He added my name after suffering his first stroke to forestall any question as to the impairment of his faculties. But, I assure you, your father is not unable to think and act wisely."

There was silence in the room, as they absorbed this information, and as I tried to understand what he was talking about.

"So who are the certain persons and charities that are now in line for what should remain in the family?" Valerie asked, frowning and gripping the sides of her chair. "And how much are we talking about?"

"That information is beyond the scope of this discussion," Mr. Sitton informed her. "The question before us and the subject of this discussion, as I understand it, is the status of the new Mrs. Connard."

I perked up at this, especially since it made Valerie screw up her face like she was about to spit.

"The way it stands at the present," Mr. Sitton said, adjusting his glasses as he glanced at one of the papers, "Mrs. Connard, *this* Mrs. Connard," he said, peering at me over his gold rims, "has no viable interest in the estate, since everything is in trust, despite the spousal rights operative in this state. Except, of course, she will share Howard's income, which, I assure you, Mrs. Connard, will be adequate to cover all reasonable living expenses."

"You mean," Valerie said, sitting forward in her chair with the beginnings of a smile, "the will is fixed so that she'll get *nothing*?"

"According to the present arrangements," Mr. Sitton answered, "you are correct. Unless—"

But before he could finish, Valerie threw her head back and let out a real unladylike laugh. "So much for marrying a crazy old man for his money, wouldn't you say?" And she gave me one of those television-personality smiles that says one thing and means another.

"Unless," Mr. Sitton said again, doing a little glaring of his own, "in the event of Howard's demise with no change in the present arrangements, she should petition for spousal rights, as I would advise her to do and which would most likely be granted. However, Junior, nothing can affect the trust that is in effect for you."

"We *know* that," Valerie said, cutting off the smile like she was taking a commercial break. "What we're talking about here is the remainder of the estate. So, you're saying that she'd have to go to court to get any of it? And undoubtedly the present beneficiaries, whoever they are, would contest any petition she might make. Is that right?"

"Quite possibly. However, the courts look with sympathy upon a surviving spouse and tend to grant her, or him as the case may be, a livable portion. For the present, though, Mrs. Connard," he said, nodding toward me, "you won't need to worry about an income. Howard is well able to meet your daily expenses for as long as he lives."

I guess that was a relief, though I'd never given it much thought, assuming that Mr. Howard was pretty well loaded and could pay our bills. Valerie, though, was acting like she'd won the lottery. She flung her head up and watched me with a pleased glint in her eye. And a smirk on her mouth.

"Well, that's about all I can say at the present," Mr. Sitton said, "but I think I've addressed your concerns. I'd like to speak to Howard now, if it's convenient."

He stood up and shook Junior's hand, asking him how he was getting along after his accident, which reminded me that I needed to speak to Junior about that myself. Then, shaking my hand and nodding to Valerie, he left to see Mr. Howard.

I started to follow him, but Valerie said, "Just one minute, *if* you don't mind."

"Well, I do, but that probably doesn't matter."

"I hope you heard what Ernest said about suing the estate if something happens to Daddy Connard."

Don't you hate it when somebody says "if something happens" to whoever, when what they mean is "if he kicks the bucket"?

"I want you to know," Valerie went on, "that we will fight you every inch of the way if you try to get your hands on anything

Daddy Connard has. And I mean *any* thing: money, stocks, trust funds, furniture, Mother Connard's jewelry . . . *Oh, my God!* Junior! She's wearing Mother Connard's cluster ring! There must be four carats in that thing, and she's wearing it! Give it to me. Give it to me right now!"

Junior stood up, staring at my hand with his mother's ring on it. He swayed a little, but managed to say, "I think Valerie's right. You can't just come in here and make free with things that don't belong to you. So just hand it over, and we won't have to take this any further."

I opened my mouth, but before I could get a word out, Valerie said, "*You* may not want to take it any further, but for my money, she's a thief! No telling what else is missing from this house. I'm pressing charges." And she stalked toward the hall and the telephone.

"Hold on, Valerie," Junior said. "We can work this out without getting the authorities in. Let's give her a chance to confess what she's taken. Then, if she won't, we can call the sheriff."

I'd had enough. More than, in fact. I put my hands on my hips, those killer diamonds sparkling on my finger, glared at Junior, and cut loose. "You're accusing *me* of being a thief? So what does that make you? You broke into my trailer and tore up my furniture and bloodied my new couch and ruined one of my Barbies. What did you steal from me? Huh? Huh? What were you doing there? What were you looking for? Had to break the lock to get in, didn't you? Had your head beat in for your trouble, too, didn't you? Yeah, Valerie," I yelled, swinging around to her, "call the sheriff. I want him to come out here. I want to press charges against this burglar, this breaker and enterer, this, this *thief*. And maybe attempted rapist, too! Who knows what was in his mind? You want to press charges? I'll press some charges for you."

"Now, wait," Junior said, sinking back into his chair. "Wait, I can explain—"

"So can I," I said, so bummed out my head was ringing. "I can explain that Mr. Howard gave me this ring, and I can explain that I have taken nothing from this house and never will. I don't *like* what's in it. How about that? I wouldn't have a single thing in it on a silver platter. Let me tell you something, Junior Connard. I. Am. Not. A. Thief. But you are, and the police found you in my trailer with the evidence of what you did to it everywhere they looked.

"And another thing," I stormed on, just hitting my stride. "What's everybody going to think when they see you spread all over the newspapers and television for breaking into a woman's trailer? And being arrested for it?" I whirled around to Valerie, whose face had gone white at the thought. "You thought about that, Miss Late-Breaking News?"

"I . . . wait," Junior said, looking pretty strained himself. "I went there just to talk to you. To see if you were planning to marry Daddy. To, well, to try to talk you out of it. I was worried, you see. I didn't know you. And I did break the lock just, you know, to sit and wait for you to come home. I didn't mean to, but I shook the door and the screws just popped out. So I waited. I didn't touch anything, just looked around. Next thing I knew I was in the hospital. So, well, I apologize to you."

Valerie said, "Stupid, stupid, stupid."

I said, "Who's going to pay for my couch to be re-covered?"

She rolled her eyes as Junior said, "I will, and for your lock, too. But if anything else was damaged, I swear I didn't do it."

I believed him, figuring the Pucketts had jumped him because he looked like Skip from the back. But I hadn't had my full say, and I intended to get it said. "Well, and another thing. There's a pair of green mist lace bikini panties missing that's part of a matched set, and I want them back. Are they in your pocket? Or do you have them hidden away where Valerie won't find them? Sorry to tell on you, but I want them back, or I want them paid for."

"He doesn't have your bikini *panties!*" Valerie screeched, like the word itself was nasty. She glared at me with her fists doubled up and her shoulders shaking. "Tell her, Junior! Stand up for youself for a change."

"Valerie," Junior said, his voice as tired as his face looked. "Let it go, for God's sake."

"Oh," she said, flopping down on a chair and almost missing the seat.

"One last thing, Valerie, before I forget," I went on, giving her a last dig along with my sweetest smile. "Some of my friends are giving me a lingerie shower tonight. Maybe you'd like to come. You don't have to give me anything, if you don't want to."

"A shower?" she said. "You're inviting me to a *shower?*" Like that was the tackiest thing she'd ever heard. "You've got to be kidding."

"Yes," I said, honey dripping with each word, "I was."

"I think we'll be getting back to Raleigh," Junior said, holding his head with both hands. "Tonight."

"Good," I said. "The sooner the better." Then remembering my dreams of a Hallmark holiday, I said, "But we do hope you'll come back for Christmas."

Chapter 40

Mr. Sitton came out of Mr. Howard's room into the center hall on his way to the front door, wanting to be as far away, I guessed, from this picture of family happiness as he could get. As he passed the drawing room door, he stopped and raised his eyebrows at me.

Leaving Valerie and Junior in their stunned state, I hurried over to him, pleased that I was the one he wanted to see. He recognized my new position, and soon everybody else would, too.

"Howard seems a little confused tonight," he told me, his voice lowered for my ears only. "I usually can make out a few words, at least the gist of what he's talking about. But I couldn't understand him well enough tonight to proceed on any instructions he might be giving me. Has he been like this lately?"

"He's tired, Mr. Sitton," I said. "And no wonder with all the lifestyle changes he's gone through today. To say nothing of worrying about Junior, and putting up with that daughter-in-law of his. On top of the fact that even on a normal day, it gets harder and harder for him to talk clear enough to be understood as the day wears on. Mornings are the best time for him. He'll be rested then, and just as bright as a new penny."

"Well, then, that explains it," Mr. Sitton said. "I was a little worried in there with him. He just didn't seem to have enough energy to discuss any detailed legal matters. Murmured a few words, but they were too garbled for me to feel comfortable proceeding with."

I nodded, knowing how feeble Mr. Howard could sound. "Why don't I bring him to your office in the morning? You'll be amazed at how much better he'll be."

We both endured a moment of silence as the thought of Mr. Howard's wedding night and his resulting revitalization flashed in our minds. At least, I thought that was Mr. Sitton's thinking, since his face got red again.

"I mean," I said, "that mornings are the best time for him."

Mr. Sitton cleared his throat. "I could come here, if that would be easier."

"Either way. I usually like to get him out sometime during the day. Riding around, seeing people, and getting some fresh air, that's good for him. But why don't we wait and see what he wants to do?"

He nodded once and reached for the doorknob. "Good. Call me as early as you want and let me know. One way or the other, I'll meet with him in the morning and get started immediately on whatever changes he wants to make."

When he left, I stood in the hall a few minutes, not knowing exactly what to do. Valerie and Junior were still in the drawing room, talking in low voices with only one or two sharp words between them. I sure didn't want to go back in there and get into it again with them.

Emmett was busy. I heard the door from the dining room to the kitchen swinging to and fro, and figured he didn't need any disruption as he was getting ready for that blamed lingerie shower, which, by that time, I could've crammed down Lurline's throat. And in another hour or so, she and whoever she'd rounded up on such short notice would be knocking on the door.

I was tired, I realized. It's not every day that you have your dreams come true, then have to defend them to the likes of Junior and Valerie. All I wanted to do was crawl into bed somewhere. The problem was, I didn't know where that bed was.

And there was my new husband already in one, but zonked even worse than I was.

I'd go sit with him, I decided. And that's what I did, tiptoeing past the drawing room and into the back hall. With the blinds closed, Mr. Howard's room was lit by a small lamp across the room from his hospital bed. He lay there, looking more dead than alive, which was how he mostly looked until the life came back into his eyes. Then he looked like a different man.

Settling back in the easy chair by Mr. Howard's bed, I let the quietness of the room wash over me, thinking how different it was from a trailer home. I was used to the constant noise from car motors, motorcycles revving up, children playing, and neighbors yelling at each other that filtered in through the thin metal walls of my single-wide. But here in this big, strong house, I couldn't even hear Emmett in the kitchen, much less Valerie and Junior in the drawing room. All you had to do in this house was close a door and you had peace and quiet.

Except for Mr. Howard's soft snoring, which didn't come anywhere near the racket of a trailer park.

Even as the quiet of the room made me want to lean back and drift off to sleep, my mind kept going over and over the legal information that Mr. Sitton had given Junior and Valerie. I didn't understand just what my future situation would be, moneywise, but it had come through loud and clear that Mr. Howard had set up his finances at some earlier point when he hadn't foreseen a new wife on the horizon. A little oversight that had tickled Valerie no end. But that could be changed, if I'd understood Mr. Sitton right. For now, though, there was plenty coming in, enough to take care of what we needed and wanted. So I'd worry about any changing that had to be done later on when I had Mr. Howard in better shape.

Just having enough for daily needs meant being rich to me. Lurline once said that she really didn't want to be rich. She just wanted enough to buy whatever she wanted. That's the way I felt, too.

It didn't much matter that Mr. Howard had arranged for all his money to go to this and that charity, and to Junior. I intended for him to live a long and happy life with plenty of time to do some rearranging, if he had a mind to. And if he didn't, why, I'd worry about that when the time came. Besides, I'd always been a good saver, so there was no reason I couldn't put a little away for a rainy day out of whatever he was getting now, which Mr. Sitton had said was more than enough to get by on. I was used to clipping coupons and sending off for rebates and shopping the sales, so I couldn't see that I was going to have any problems with money.

I rubbed my hand across my face, trying to stay awake since it wouldn't be long before Lurline and whoever she'd invited came trooping in. As I did, I saw Mr. Howard's folded wheelchair leaning against the wall. I started smiling, remembering how Skip had used it to hide his lottery ticket.

That rascal, I hadn't expected him to be smart enough to pick such a good hiding place. He couldn't've found a better one. Who would've thought to look through an old man's wheelchair?

Then, frowning at it, as I remembered that he'd written "check it out," I eased up out of the chair and tiptoed over to the wheelchair. It was one of those lightweight folding kind, made of metal rods with leather seat and back, not one of the motorized ones since Mr. Howard wasn't exactly confined to it. He didn't need to have a motor so he could operate it himself, because he always had Emmett or me to push him wherever he wanted to go.

I picked it up, turned it around, looking to see if I could find where Skip had hidden his ticket. There were leather pockets on both sides of the seat for carrying one thing or another. I ran my hand through both and found only a little packet of Kleenex, a wadded-up used one that I threw into the trash, a stick of Juicy Fruit gum, some cellophane-wrapped peppermint candy, and Mr. Howard's wallet, which I left right where it was.

There was no other place that I could see where Skip could've hidden his ticket, so I guessed he'd just stuck it in one of the pockets. Probably the one on the left side, since Mr. Howard couldn't use his left hand to rummage around with, if Skip had even thought that through. Who knows, though? Skip had proved to be smarter than I'd given him credit for, although some people just have dumb luck, and Skip had always had his share of that.

As I refolded the wheelchair, I noticed that one of the rubber handgrips on the back of the chair was loose. I twisted it to tighten it up, but it didn't want to fit as tightly as the other one. I pulled it off to get it started again, and saw what looked like a wad of foil stuck down in it.

Using one prong of a pair of scissors from Mr. Howard's dresser to pry out the foil wad, I realized that it was a wrapper from a stick of chewing gum. When I unfolded it, I could barely make out the tiny little pencil scribbles on the white side. It was hard to read, but as I finally made out the writing, I couldn't keep myself from laughing. I had to put my hand over my mouth so I wouldn't wake Mr. Howard.

Then, as Skip's words sunk in, I felt tears well up in my eyes.

Juicy Fruit aroma from the wrapper made the words even sweeter:

> Etta Mae Wiggins Taggert Connard
> IOU $1000000 soon as I get it.
> Watch your bank account.
>
>   Love, Skip

I had to sit down. That Skip, he'd really do it, I didn't have a doubt in my mind, unless he lost it before he got to the bank. It was too much to take in, and I almost shook Mr. Howard awake to tell him about it. I didn't, though, because Skip's promises were about like Skip himself. Well meant, but not something you'd want to depend on entirely. Oh, I knew he'd do whatever he said he'd do unless his circumstances changed, and changing circumstances for Skip could mean anything from scratching the eight ball to needing an overhaul on his motorcycle.

But maybe I was misjudging him. I'd wait and see if my bank account got real healthy all of a sudden. Of course, Skip hadn't even considered taxes, since I doubted he'd ever paid any, much less made plans for April fifteenth ahead of time. That lottery ticket could put him in jail if the IRS people took out after him, which they'd been known to do to other big winners. So if he did give me any of his winnings, it'd be up to me to put some aside to pay the taxes on his share as well as mine. A million dollars wouldn't go far after that. Still, it was the thought that counted with any gift, no matter how small or how little you considered the obligations of it.

I put the Juicy Fruit wrapper in my pocket for safekeeping. It probably didn't mean a thing, but you never know, do you?

Chapter 41

I drew a chair up close to Mr. Howard's bed and, reaching through the bedrail, patted his hand. He didn't stir, so I made myself comfortable, and before I knew it, I was catching up on all the sleep I'd been missing, but not before sending a lot of good thoughts over the miles to Skip.

Wherever he was, I hoped he was safe and happy, and that I'd seen the last of him and his troubles.

When Emmett tapped on the door, I jumped up, wondering how much time I'd lost.

"Yo' guests be here in a minute, Miss Etta," he said through the closed door.

After checking on Mr. Howard and stuffing a pillow behind his back when he stirred, I made some quick repairs to my face and hair, and left the room.

Hurrying out, I thought of changing clothes for the party, but decided that if what I had on was good enough for my first wedded day, it was good enough for my first wedding shower. Even though I was somewhat worse for the wear by that time, I didn't much care. Anybody who was as determined as Lurline would have to put up with me the way I was.

Going into the kitchen from the hall, I felt even worse dressed when I saw Emmett in dark pants and a starched white jacket with a black bow tie. He looked a whole lot better than I did.

"Valerie and Junior upstairs?" I whispered.

"They gone," he said. "Packed up and got gone a little bit ago. Left Mr. Junior's car, 'cause he not feel like drivin'. He wanted to take his'n, since it bigger, but Miss Valerie, she say she not about to leave her car anywhere 'round this place, an' she say Mr. Junior, he have to suck it up and ride to Raleigh with her or stay here an' suffer humil'ation. House been real quiet ever since they pulled out."

"Well, not for long, I'm afraid," I said. "I swear, Emmett, I could do without a party tonight. Too much has gone on for me to be in a party mood."

Emmett grinned. "I know what'll get you in the party mood. I'm mixin' up my special punch for that big bowl in yonder, an' they be plenty more to come. Mr. Howard, he not able to do much partyin', but ain't no reason you can't cut loose a little with yo' lady friends. Go look at the table, an' see you like what I done."

I pushed through the swinging door, and nearly lost my breath when I saw the long dining table. Emmett had outdone himself. At least, I'd never seen anything like it.

The table was covered with a white cloth that had cutout designs all over it. Two tall candlesticks with lots of branches with candles stuck in them stood on it, one at each end, and silver trays and dishes and odd-looking silver tools of all kinds were arranged along the sides. A beautiful floral centerpiece of pink roses and other kinds of blooms I didn't know the names of brightened up the whole room. It had to've come from Sadie's Floral Shop, though, because I did recognize a few of the blue-dyed carnations she was famous for.

"Emmett," I breathed, "it's the most beautiful table I've ever seen. I've never had anything like this done for me, and I don't know what to do with it. I don't even know what all these things are, much less what they're for."

"Well, I walk you 'round an' tell you," Emmett said. And starting at one end, he pointed to a large silver tray with all kinds of pots on it. "This here yo' silver service. See, the tall one's the coffee pot and the squatty one's yo' teapot. Here's yo' sugar bowl an' yo' creamer, an' here's yo' lemon wedges an' the lemon fork, which some ladies like better'n cream."

"Oh, my, it's so pretty," I said, admiring the tiny fork with its splayed tines. "What about the tea bags, Emmett? Where do those go after you dunk 'em up and down? Just on the saucer?"

"No'm," Emmett said, cutting his eyes at me. "We don't use no tea bags. I brew it in the kitchen, like the coffee."

"Oh."

"Now, over here we have yo' cups an' saucers, an' spoons for stirrin'. An' then the crab salat's on this round tray settin' in a bed of lettuce. Then we got a congealed salat, an' over there on that side, we got yo' sammich trays. I made some fresh cucumber sammiches, an' there's some ham salat ones, an' lots of cream cheese. Cream cheese with nuts, cream cheese with pineapple, cream cheese with first one thing an' another. Then there's the fruit tray with a poppy-seed dressin' dip. An' then, you got yo' cheese straws. Lemme tell you, Miss Etta, when you have ladies come in, you got to have yo' cheese straws."

"It's like a dream," I said. "And I'll remember about the cheese straws."

"Well, us'lly I like to put out ham biscuits, too, but I didn't have enough time to do all that bakin'. But, down here at this end, you got yo' silver punch bowl an' its ladle on a silver tray, with little silver punch cups settin' around ready for fillin'. An' here's the silver pitcher for takin' 'round the room when the ladies don't want to walk back to the punch bowl. I take care of that for you, don't you worry 'bout any of it."

He moved around the table, straightening things just so, and said, "Now, I didn't put out no knives, just spoons for the bev'rages and forks for the salats. One thing, Miss Etta, you have to remember, when ladies gonna be eatin' on they knees, they don't need no extra silverware to boggle in one hand while they try to eat with the other 'un. Most times, I jus' fix up some of that finger food that don't need no silverware at all. But sometime when you want to have a set-down dinner for a lot of ladies, I'll get out all them card tables from the basement an' set 'em up in the hall an' the drawin' room. What with the dining table, we can 'ccommodate 'bout thirty-two at a set-down."

"Thirty-two." I marveled at the thought. I didn't even know thirty-two people I would want to invite. Then, "Those are the biggest candlesticks I've ever seen, Emmett. Did Mrs. Connard ever light all the candles?"

"Oh, we light 'em all the time. You s'posed to light yo' candles, even if you have 'em out just for decoratin', you just burn the wick a little an' not let the wax run down. That way they look like they used an' not fresh from the sto'. Now, Miss Etta, if you don't mind me sayin' so, them ain't candlesticks. Candlesticks only got one candle on 'em. These kind with the five branches on 'em, they called candelabrums."

I nodded my head, learning so much that I'd never known before, never having had either the single or the multiple kind. The only kind I'd had was a wine bottle with different colors of wax dripped all over it.

"It's all a picture, Emmett, like in a movie."

"You get used to it quick enough. Now, what I'd do if I was you, Miss Etta, is greet yo' guests at the do' an' bring 'em in the drawin' room. I got a tea table set up in there with a 'broidered cloth on it, an' they can put gif's on it. Then you let 'em come in here an' help they plates. They can go back in the drawin' room an' eat off they knees. While they do that, I be goin' round with a pitcher of punch refillin' they cups. Now, after they eat an' I pick up the plates, that's when you open yo' gif's. An' I'll be clearing the big table an' puttin' out the dessert, little petty fours I got the bak'ry to send us. But all that time, I keep the liquid refreshments comin'. If we time it jus' right, yo' party go without a hitch."

"Is that the way Mrs. Connard—the *first* Mrs. Connard, I mean—did it?"

"Yessum, though I don't believe she ever have no kinda shower that I remember. But she have a lot of teas, and coffees, and receptions, and the like. So we always figure out beforehand who gonna be doin' what, so it all run smooth. So, I don't want you to think I be tellin' you what to do nor runnin' yo' business, or anything."

"Oh, I don't. No, I want you to tell me. This is all so new to me, which I guess is no surprise to you, so I want your help. I want things to be the way Mr. Howard would like, so I want you to tell me."

"Yessum, I will, but if I tell you too much, you jus' call me down," Emmett said, while I shook my head at the thought. "It 'bout time for yo' ladies, so when I hear they cars drive up, I'm gonna dim the chandelier here in the dining room and light them candles. It'll be real pretty then, and look like party time in this ole house again."

"Shoot, Emmett, it already looks like party time. And here I am in this awful shirt and khaki skirt. That table's better dressed than I am. Wonder if I have time to change." Although I didn't know what I could change into that would make me even come close to the first Mrs. Connard's silver and linen table furnishings.

Chapter 42

When we heard the scratch of gravel from the first cars driving in, Emmett began lighting the candles in the candelabras, five in each, would you believe it? I ran a brush through my hair and put on some lip gloss in front of a gold-framed mirror in the hall. In spite of myself, I was getting excited. My first guests in my new home, as well as being my first night in my new home.

"Emmett," I called, "would you check on Mr. Howard now and again, in case we make too much noise and disturb him? I'll be slipping back there, too, to see about him."

"Yessum, I always check on him anyway. How many ladies you think we be havin', Miss Etta? I put out enough of that china with the gold band to serve twelve, you think that be enough?"

"Twelve? Emmett, I'd be surprised if there're two. This was all last-minute, you know, so I don't know who's coming or how many."

"Don't make no difference. We got plenty, whatever show up."

When the doorbell rang, I started toward the door, but Emmett shook his head. "It my place to open the do', Miss Etta. You jus' stand a little ways back here in the foyer, then usher 'em in the drawin' room an' let 'em get theyselves settled an' visitin' while we wait for the rest of 'em."

Foyer? I'd thought it was the hall. But I'm the quick-learning type, and *foyer* was what it would be from now on.

I could hear voices from the other side of the door, whispering and giggling with the same excitement I was feeling. I stood facing the door just like the first Mrs. Connard, Senior, had done, waiting to greet my guests in my lovely new home, even though I hardly knew my way around in it.

Six of them came in together, with Granny shoving her way in front of Lurline, Jennie my neighbor from the trailer park, Betty Sue who was Boyce's wife, and Cindy and Gladys, two of the Handy Home Helpers.

"Would you just look at this," Lurline said as she walked into the foyer, her head swiveling around to take it all in. She walked past Emmett without a glance, coming straight to me with a wrapped present in her arms. "Well, Etta Mae, you really dressed up for us, didn't you? I declare, this place is something else. Where can we sit down? I'm a working girl, you know, and I need to take a load off."

"Right in there, Lurline. Hey, Granny," I said, hugging her and getting jabbed by the corner of her present. "I'm so glad Lurline invited you. Hi, Betty Sue, Jennie. Oh, Gladys, bless your heart for coming. And, Cindy, don't you look pretty. Y'all come on into the drawing room."

"Drawing room? La-de-dah," Lurline said, almost tripping on the Oriental rug, she was so busy checking everything out.

"Sugar," Granny said, "where's your toilet? It was a long drive over here, an' I got to go."

"Right down the hall, I mean the foyer," I said, pointing. "Second door on the left."

She hurried off, her Reeboks squeaking on the polished floor between the rugs. She looked nice, though, in the navy crepe that she wore to church when she went.

As I turned to follow the others into the drawing room, the doorbell rang again, surprising me since I didn't know who else Lurline would've invited. Emmett swung the door open, and in walked Hazel Marie and Mrs. Julia Springer, bearing gifts. I liked to died.

"Oh," I said, the sight of old lady Springer on my new doorstep throwing me for a loop. In she walked, her snooty nose-in-the-air attitude making me feel I'd been caught doing something wrong. And in her friend's house, at that.

"Oh," I said again, pulling myself together. "I didn't know Lurline had invited you. I mean, you didn't have to come but, well, I'm so glad you did. Hazel Marie, you look so pretty. Come in. Come in. Mrs. Springer, here's the drawing room, but I guess you know that. Please come in. Have a seat, why don't you?" I was so flustered I didn't know what I was saying, hugging Hazel Marie and waving my hands around.

Mrs. Springer stopped in the arch of the drawing room as she surveyed the gathering of my friends in her friend's house.

"Well," she said as she gazed around the room, "it speaks well of you that you haven't changed anything, and I hope you don't plan to. Coralee Connard had excellent taste."

I could've disputed that, but I didn't want to get into it with her. The woman made me as nervous as a cat.

It didn't help any when she gave a little sniff and said, "It seems to me you'd have said yesterday that you wouldn't be needing a job." Like I'd let her down by not telling her about my soon-to-be change of lifestyle.

"Oh, no, ma'am, I mean, yes, ma'am, I do need it. I mean, I won't *need* it, but you know how it is, Mrs. Springer. Ladies in our position ought to set an example and not just sit around doing nothing."

The woman just looked down her nose and gave another sniff, but Hazel Marie grinned at me behind her back.

As we walked on into the drawing room, I was proud for Mrs. Springer to see how nice my friends looked. Lurline had claimed one of the wingbacks by the fireplace, and she was a picture in her fuchsia polyester pantsuit with gold buttons. She had a way with scarves that I never had. She had a big one with all kinds of pinks, reds, and matching fuchsias on it draped around her neck, and pinned with a rhinestone monkey on her shoulder. I didn't tell her because she'd make some remark about my clothes, but I really appreciated how she'd gotten so dressed up for the party.

Jennie had on a tent dress, which she'd told me was the only kind she'd worn since the first month of her marriage. "I've either been pregnant or trying to lose weight from the last one every day since then," she'd told me. "And these tent styles work regardless of the condition I'm in." The one she was wearing had green palm leaves all over it with a few red flowers mixed in. The material looked just like the drapes at the Quality Inn at the airport.

Betty Sue was her same quiet self, and who wouldn't be, living next door to a talker like Granny? She sat on the edge of the camelback couch, looking like she might get up and leave any minute. She had on a turquoise pantsuit with pumps she'd had dyed to match.

Gladys and Cindy worked for Lurline, as I've mentioned. Gladys had her hair pulled back in a ponytail with a big white bow on the back of her head. She wore a full skirt that she called a broomstick skirt because of all the little pleats in it and the T-shirt she'd gotten at Pigeon Forge with Dolly Parton's picture on it. Cindy was the youngest of us. She had on the kind of dress that's made for the skinny, less-than-curvy type of person. It was a sleeveless sheath that made you guess what was underneath, coming straight down from her shoulders to her ankle-strapped shoes with the two-inch soles. I don't know how she walked.

But Hazel Marie now, she'd certainly changed her way of dressing since she'd been living with Mrs. Springer. I had to admit that the plain beige silk with matching cardigan and high-heeled slides suited her better than the bright colors she used to wear. She must've had her colors done, because the dress blended right in with her skin tone and hair shade. I wouldn't even want to guess what the outfit had cost. Mrs. Springer was in one of her usual dark crepes with matching Red Cross shoes laced across the instep, every hair in place and not a wrinkle anywhere, except on her face. She was as stiff as a board, perching on the edge of the chair Emmett had pulled out for her. She kept both hands gripped on her pocketbook as she held it in her lap. Like she was afraid.to turn it loose.

I made an effort at introductions, but I wasn't too good at it. Besides, everybody knew who everybody was.

Every instruction Emmett had given me went straight out of my head, what with Julia Springer sitting there so straight and prim, as she looked around to see if I'd done any damage to her friend's house. Lord, I wished Mr. Howard was in a condition to put her mind at rest and unsquench that tight mouth. I couldn't do a thing but put up with her.

Besides, I reminded myself, if she didn't like it, she hadn't had to come. But we were business associates of sorts now, and Julia Springer was known for doing the right thing in every circumstance. Even when it killed her, as seeing me in Mr. Howard's house seemed to be doing.

"I could live in that place," Granny announced, as she came back from the guest bathroom. "Girls, you oughta go powder your nose, and take a gander at that fancy toilet."

"Sit here, Granny," I said, leading her to a chair. "You can see everything from here. You know Mrs. Springer, don't you? And Hazel Marie Puckett?"

"Everybody knows the Springers and the Pucketts," Granny said, making my stomach knot up for fear of what she'd say next. "Though I've not had the personal pleasure. What do you think of my grandbaby falling into something like this?"

Before Mrs. Springer could tell her what she thought, Lurline blared out, "Where's your husband, Etta Mae? We gonna get to meet the lucky man?"

"Oh, well, I don't think so. He said this was a party just for ladies, and he wouldn't crash it." I hurried on, not wanting to let on that a ten-minute ceremony had pooped him out for the rest of the day. "He does want to meet each and every one of you, though."

"I don't blame him for not showing," Jennie said. "What man wants to come to a lingerie shower? We'd embarrass him to death. Besides, he'll see the presents when they're on you, and he'll like that better."

"What I want to know is," Granny said, as everybody except Julia Springer laughed, "does that boy that opened the door do any cooking, too?"

"Granny! Don't call Emmett a boy," I said, hoping he hadn't heard her. "He's almost as old as you are."

"Honey, nobody's as old as I am, but don't worry, sugar, I'll watch my Ps and Qs from now on."

"Well, ladies," I said to change the subject, "I guess we can go in and get something to eat now, if you're hungry." I stood up and helped Granny out of her chair. "The dining room is right this way."

"We see it, Etta Mae," Lurline said, marching right across the hall, I mean the foyer, and up to the table. "Oh, everything's so cute. I just love these tiny little sandwiches. You didn't make them, did you, Etta Mae?"

"No, Emmett did. Betty Sue, that's the prettiest pantsuit. Did you make it yourself?"

Betty Sue blushed and smiled. She was the shiest thing. "Yes, I ran it up on my Bernina last weekend, and this is the first time I've worn it."

"She'll have dog hairs all over it before you turn around," Granny said, as she loaded a plate with Emmett's party food.

When Lurline and Cindy found the punch bowl, they hurried back to the head of the table and poured the coffee from their china cups back into the pot. I thought Mrs. Springer would drop her plate along with her mouth.

Lurline didn't even notice. "It's almost worth Etta Mae marrying that old man to have some of this punch," she said, upending her cup and filling it again. "It's mighty tasty, and I hope you got plenty. I'm gonna need it, after the day I've had, standing up at your wedding, and working overtime to make up for it. To say nothing of having to shop for your present."

Talking and oohing and aahing over the food and Sadie's floral arrangement, they loaded their plates and filled their punch cups before going back into the drawing room. I noticed that the coffee and tea were going begging, although I was glad we had both for Mrs. Springer's sake, her being Presbyterian and all. Emmett pushed through the swinging door with more punch from the kitchen to keep up with the demand, and I whispered to him, "Everybody loves that stuff."

"Yessum," he whispered back, "this a special party, so I'm goin' a little heavy on the champagne to give it more punch than it used to havin'."

As I walked back into the drawing room, I noticed Mrs. Springer sitting a little apart from the others, balancing her plate and a full punch cup. I raised my eyebrows at Hazel Marie, wondering if one of us ought to tell her what she was drinking. Hazel Marie smiled and shook her head, so I didn't say anything. If Mrs. Springer wanted to drink heavy-duty punch, far be it from me to take public notice of it.

"Where's that ole fool you married, anyway?" Granny asked, as she settled herself in a damask-covered wing chair.

"Sh-h-h, Granny, he'll hear you."

"Old as he is, his hearing's probably gone," she said, draining her cup.

"I'd go easy on that, if I was you, Granny," Betty Sue said, knowing from personal experience what a Wiggins was like with a full tank.

"You ain't me," Granny told her as she turned up the cup again for the last drop, "an' these little fancy cups don't hold enough to taste. Run in yonder and fill me up again, sugar. Besides, Betty Sue, you're the one doin' the drivin', so spend your time watching yourself and leave me alone."

I took Granny's cup and her plate for refills, hoping she'd eat enough to soak up what she was drinking. Hazel Marie followed me across the foyer and into the dining room, grinning as she headed for the punch bowl with two cups.

She nudged me with her elbow. "This one's Miss Julia's. She loves this punch."

"I didn't know she'd take a spiked drink."

"She wouldn't," she said, giggling, "if she knew it. But Mr. Sam Murdoch's been trying to get her to take a little wine now and then. They've been seeing each other, and he likes to tease her, you know, to loosen her up. I can't wait to tell him about this."

"I don't know, Hazel Marie," I whispered. "Maybe we ought to tell her. I don't want her any madder at me than she already is."

"Don't worry. I'll look after her and I'm driving. Let's just let her have a good time. Besides, she said it was the best punch she's ever tasted, and she wants Emmett's recipe for the next Women of the Church meeting." Hazel Marie doubled over, laughing at the thought of a bunch of tipsy Presbyterian women. "We'll just play dumb, and let him tell her what's in it."

We both turned when Lurline yelled across the foyer.

"Y'all come on back in here, Etta Mae. It's time you opened your presents. I want you to see what I got you. Although it's not much, not being told in time to do anything really nice."

"Oh, I'm sure whatever you got will be wonderful, Lurline," I said, as Hazel Marie and I walked back into the drawing room. "You have real good taste."

I served Granny, then sat down near the table that Emmett had draped with a cloth. It was loaded with presents wrapped in paper with parasol and ribbon and wedding bell motifs all over it.

"Open mine first," Granny said, jerking hers from beneath the pile. "You're gonna need it, if I'm any judge."

I always get self-conscious opening presents when nobody else has any to open. People sitting around waiting for your reaction, watching to see if you appreciate what they've bought like you should. I never know what to say.

As I pulled off the ribbon of Granny's present, Gladys said, "Remember, now, however many ribbons you break, that's how many babies you'll have."

"Oh, no," I cried, as the ribbon snapped apart. "Surely not."

Everybody laughed except Mrs. Springer, who looked like she'd experienced a sharp pain.

"Gra-an-ny! My goodness, look at this!" I held up a long flannel gown with lace at the neck and the bottoms of the sleeves. "I'm gonna burn up sleeping in this!"

"Not likely," she said, emptying her cup again. "Remember your granddaddy? Take it from me, with an old man you're gonna need some extry help. Coldest fe-e-et, you wouldn't believe."

"Oh, Granny, thank you so much. I know it'll come in handy this winter."

"I got it from Walmart's. Betty Sue took me this afternoon, but I didn't get any new Mason jars, 'cause I'm expectin' mine back any day now." She glared at Betty Sue, who blushed and said she'd already put up tomatoes in them.

"Do mine next!" Cindy said, handing me a package.

"Who wants some more?" Lurline sang out, carrying the silver pitcher she'd filled from the punch bowl. "Hold 'em up. I'm comin' around."

"Oh, Cindy, it's beautiful!" I pulled out a black bustier with ruffled detail and an underwire bra. "Good grief, Cindy, it's so big. What size is it? You give me more credit than I deserve. I'm only a C cup, you know." I held it up in front of me, and thought of Mr. Howard's eyes popping out of his head when he saw it on me. Mrs. Springer's back was getting stiffer and stiffer, although she was having trouble focusing her eyes. Probably couldn't believe what she was seeing.

"There's matching bikini panties in there, too," Cindy said.

"Pass it around, sugar," Granny said. "I wanta see what people're sleepin' in nowadays."

"She won't do much sleeping in that thing," Gladys said. "Wonder what Jimmy would do if I showed up in something like that some night?"

"Have a heart attack," Lurline said.

"Swaller his tongue, most likely," Granny chimed in.

A little smile twitched around Mrs. Springer's mouth. She tried to cover it as she blotted her face with a linen napkin.

"Do mine now," Jennie said, sliding a notepad and pen out of her pocket, ready to keep a record of who gave what. Somebody always did that at all the showers we went to, for the thank-you notes that hardly anybody got around to writing. "You're gonna love it."

As I opened the box and lifted up her gift, I couldn't believe it. "This is gorgeous!"

"Hold it up higher!"

"Let me see, sugar."

I stood up and held the gown in front of me. It was navy blue with white lace straps and white embroidery all over the cups of a built-in demi-bra. And it had a long, sheer flyaway skirt and a matching G-string panty.

"That'll melt that ole man's wax," Granny said.

"Just the opposite, more likely," Gladys told her, giggling.

Mrs. Springer got choked on a swallow of punch. She snorted out a laugh before she could help herself, and Hazel Marie had to thump her on the back.

"Look at this," I said, grinning so hard I could hardly talk. "It's got little white flowers on it. Thank you, Jennie, this will get a lot of use, I'll tell you that."

"Here's mine," Betty Sue said. "I hope you like it."

"I know I will," I said, beginning to slip the ribbon off her present.

"Where's that pitcher?" Granny said. "Lurline, have you emptied that thing all by yourself? Pour Mrs. Springer some, too, while you're at it. Her cup's dry as a bone."

Mrs. Springer held out her empty cup, frowning as she tried to aim it toward whoever had the pitcher.

"Don't get your drawers in an uproar, Granny," Lurline said, smiling up at the ceiling. "That colored man, oops, 'scuse me, that *gentleman* working in the kitchen just filled the punch bowl again. Cindy, why don't you take the pitcher and get us some more? I need to rest."

"Oh, Betty Sue!" I cried. "It's beautiful." I drew out a long, slinky red satin nightgown with spaghetti straps. "Oh, gosh, I hope it fits."

"It may be too long," she said. "And if it is, I'll hem it for you."

I held out my empty cup as Cindy came around with the pitcher. "Pour me some more, while you're at it." I was feeling flushed and thirsty and no longer caring if Julia Springer got herself bent out of shape. By this time, though, she was sitting over there fanning her bodice and running her fingers through her hair, so that one side was sticking straight out from her head.

"That's right," I said to Betty Sue, "if it's too long, we'll just cut it off till it fits." Then got so tickled I almost fell off my chair.

"Tee-hee," Mrs. Springer said, surprising Hazel Marie so bad that she nearly choked on a cheese straw.

I was so happy and pleased with the gifts my friends had brought that my fingers were tingling. So I had another sip of punch and unwrapped the next one.

"That one's mine," Gladys said. "I bought myself one just like it, hoping it'll stoke Jimmy's fire a little."

Everybody whooped when I pulled out a leopard-print teddy. "Gla-a-dys!" I said, my face beginning to burn. "This is too much!"

"It's not enough, if you ask me," Granny said, frowning as she looked at it. "How do you keep that back part out of your . . . ?"

"*Granny!*" I yelled. Betty Sue cracked up, leaning over to hide her red face. Crab salad fell off Mrs. Springer's fork halfway to her mouth, landing on her lap. She stared at the blob like she couldn't figure out where it'd come from. Then she scraped it up with her fork and put it on the edge of her plate, where it fell off again. She didn't notice.

"Open ours next," Hazel Marie said. "Those two right there."

I opened Hazel Marie's store-wrapped box and lifted out a beautiful white gown edged with lace and a matching peignoir, which I was afraid to try to pronounce. "Oh-h," I breathed, running my hand over the fine material. "Oh, Hazel Marie, it's gorgeous and so soft. Thank you so much."

I started the box around the circle and reached for Mrs. Springer's gift. My hands were a little shaky from all the excitement, wondering what she'd selected, considering the earlier pained look on her face at some of the other things I'd unwrapped. But she didn't seem to be paying much attention by now, as she sat over there fanning herself with a Day-by-Day devotional book she'd found on a side table.

"Oh," I said, as I held up a little blue crocheted capelike thing that came about to my waist. "What is it?"

"It's a bed jacket!" Granny yelled. Then, turning to Mrs. Springer, she said, "Where'd you find that thing? I've been looking for one for years and years. Didn't think they made 'em anymore."

Mrs. Springer looked around, her eyelids at about half-mast. Squinching up until she located Granny, she said, "I don't think they do. I have them made by . . . uh, I forget who the woman is. I'll give you her name, when I can think of it." She leaned back in her chair, still fanning.

"Let me know when you do," Granny said, then to me, "Now, sugar, that's an old-timey thing, but it's just the ticket to warm your shoulders when you're wearing some of this skimpy stuff. Just don't wear it by itself, or that old man'll croak on you."

Mrs. Springer said, "It's hot enough in here for anybody to croak." She put her head back against the chair, her knees spraddling out, and fanned her skirttail. Hazel Marie reached over and smoothed her skirt back down.

"Oh, Granny!" I said, as everybody laughed at the picture I'd make in nothing but a hand-crocheted bed jacket that would show even the little it tried to cover. Mrs. Springer sat, gazing at the ceiling as the laughter died down. Then a minute or two later, she clamped her hand over her mouth, as she tried to muffle the strangled sounds that were roiling up out of her throat.

"Oh, my," she said, her face red and her shoulders heaving, "I didn't think of that. Oh, my goodness, Sam gave me one last Christmas. Hazel Marie, do you reckon . . . ?" She began laughing so hard that Hazel Marie had to rescue her punch cup. It was empty again, so it didn't matter.

"Mine, now!" Lurline said, handing over the last package. "I guess you've figured out that we made a trip to Victoria's Secret over at the Asheville Mall. We had the most fun. I would say that you ought to get married more often, Etta Mae, but I think you already have."

I knew they'd give me a hard time sooner or later over my marital history, but we were having such a good time, I didn't care.

"Etta Mae," Jennie said, leaning over to me, "you think we ought to put out the candles before they burn down? You could use them again, you know."

"I don't think we ought to bother them," I whispered back. "Emmett will be serving dessert in a few minutes, and he'll want to keep them burning for that. But thanks for thinking of it, Jennie.

"Oh, Lurline!" I screeched, pretending to be shocked. "I can't wear this! Look at this, everybody." I stood, holding up the sheerest pink chiffon babydoll pajamas I'd ever seen. I dangled the matching sheer G-string panty in my other hand. "What if there's a fire! Can't you see me running out in the yard with the whole volunteer fire department getting an eyeful! Oh, Lurline, it's just darling, and I love it."

"I knew you would," she said.

"Thank you everybody," I said, hugging each of them in turn, until I got to Mrs. Springer, who I didn't think would appreciate it. She didn't seem to notice that I'd skipped her, though, since her eyes were so glazed over. "I've never had anything so nice before."

"Ladies," Emmett said, as he stood in the doorway, carefully keeping his eyes away from the gowns and panties that were being passed around the circle. "Dessert is now being served."

Chapter 43

~

We crowded around the dining room table, everybody reaching for the petit fours that Emmett had stacked on a tall silver thingy that had several tiers to it and a silver circle at the top to pick it up with. I made a mental note to ask Emmett what the name of it was.

"Oh, look," Cindy said, holding up one of the tiny iced cakes that she'd taken a bite out of. "This one's chocolate, and you've got white cake in yours." She studied the half that Betty Sue had just bitten into. "I just love these things, don't you? I could eat a dozen."

"They're pretty good," Lurline admitted, "but you have to eat a dozen to get what would be a decent slice of a normal cake."

I saw Granny eat one while she stood by the table, then she opened a napkin and stacked four cakes on it and wrapped them up. She slipped out to the drawing room and put them in her purse.

"I'll wash and iron that linen napkin," she whispered to me when she came back to the dining room, "and get it back to you before anybody knows it's gone."

Granny was bad about stuffing her purse with food when she went anywhere to eat. Every time I took her into town for lunch, she'd leave a restaurant with her purse loaded down with sugar packets and saltines, or half a muffin she'd not been able to eat at the time. Denny's hated to see her coming.

Emmett came out, staggering with another full punch bowl, and we all crowded around for refills. As he started back to the kitchen, I saw him cut his eyes around at us, like he wasn't sure of what he was seeing. I expect the first Mrs. Howard Connard, Senior, had never had a party like this one.

When the door swung behind Emmett, Jennie took out her notepad.

"Okay, everybody," she called. "Stop your talking and listen to this. I wrote down some of the things Etta Mae said while she was opening our presents."

"Oh, no," I said, "don't do that!"

Everybody groaned with me, laughing and poking one another with their elbows. They knew what was coming.

Ignoring my protest, Jennie said, "Let me set the scene. Now, you have to picture Etta Mae and her new husband on their wedding night. They're all alone in the bedroom, and getting ready for you-know-what, and here's what Etta Mae says. I've rearranged it a little, but not much. Here we go. The first thing she says is, 'Good grief, it's so big. What size is it?'"

Lurline got tickled so bad she sputtered punch all over the floral arrangement. Gladys bent over double, laughing until she was snorting through her nose.

"Okay, now, y'all hold it down," Jennie said. "I'm gonna read it straight through. Here goes: 'My Lord, look at this!' 'Oh gosh, I hope it fits.' 'Well, if it's too long, we'll just cut it off till it does.'"

Jennie had to stop while we all laughed.

Then she went on. "'Oh-h-h, this is too much.' 'It's just darling and I love it.' 'It's gorgeous and so soft; what is it?' 'Oh, look, it's got little white flowers on it.' 'I'm gonna burn up.' 'I've never had anything so nice before.' And finally to top it off, she says, 'This is gonna get a lot of use, I'll tell you that!'"

We were all laughing so hard we could hardly catch our

breath, although I was just the tiniest bit embarrassed. But Cindy got choked on a mouthful of cake and Lurline had to beat her on the back. Mrs. Springer leaned her hands on the table, her shoulders shaking so hard that Hazel Marie put an arm around her to hold her upright. Betty Sue blushed dark enough for her face to clash with her turquoise pantsuit, and I wondered if she'd have the nerve to repeat anything to Boyce.

Granny said, "That's the nastiest stuff I ever heard."

"Oh, get with it, Granny," Jennie told her. "You need loosening up."

"Lord, don't tell her that," I said. "She's had enough punch to keep her loose for a week."

"Speaking of which," Granny said, "pour me another cup. Lurline, come back here with that silver dipper. I swear, girl, you're hoggin' it all."

"Let's not have any hoggin'," Mrs. Springer sang out, her voice loud enough to override Granny's. "Let me have that ladle. I'll do the honors." She listed to one side, and Hazel Marie hurried over to prop her up. "I don't know when I've been so thirsey. Is that air condishioner on or what?"

Lurline swayed over to her, moving very carefully, handed the ladle to her, and waited for a refill. She had to steady Mrs. Springer's hand as the ladle passed back and forth over her cup. Lurline's glazed eyes moved from side to side with the ladle as she tried to track Mrs. Springer's aim. I knew from Lurline's loopy smile that she was having a good time, though she'd never in this world admit it.

"Whoop-de-do," she sang out, swinging her full cup around. Then she grabbed the pitcher for future refills, swung it around, and nearly lost her balance. "Whoa." She stopped and held on to the table. "Where's that fancy bathroom at? I got to pee so bad, I'm about to pop."

Cindy said, "Come on. We'll find it. I've got to go, too." She took Lurline's arm and guided her down the hall.

"Come and get it, everybody!" Mrs. Springer called, as she flipped the ladle back and forth, punch streaming down her arm. Hazel Marie reached out to rescue the ladle, but Mrs. Springer popped her hand with it. Then dipped it into the punch bowl and drank from it. Hazel Marie gasped.

A noise in the kitchen took my attention from the sight, and I eased around the first Mrs. Connard's sideboard toward the door to see what was going on. Nobody else seemed to notice, but I'd heard feet shuffling and more than Emmett's voice coming from the other room. My first thought was that Valerie and Junior had come back and were raising Cain about me taking over their daddy's house. My second thought was that, for some reason, Emmett had helped Mr. Howard out of bed and brought him to the kitchen. Which didn't make sense, but something was going on out there.

Just as I pushed the swinging door, it swung back at me. I jumped back out of the way, and Roy and Harley Puckett crashed into the dining room, the most unlikely pair that'd ever been in it, I didn't have a doubt in the world.

As the party came to a sudden halt, I sidled away from the door, trying to get to the hall and out of their sight. They were looking for me, and now that Skip had skipped, there was nothing I could tell them. Not that I would've anyway.

Jennie said, "What the hell?" and Gladys frowned at the two men, trying to place them, but figuring they didn't belong where they were. "Who is that?" she asked, but nobody answered.

Mrs. Springer straightened up, stretched out her neck, squinched her eyes at Harley and Roy, and mumbled, "Wonder why she invited them?" Then, after further examination, she said, "Why, they didn't bring any presents! That's just so tacky." And she shook the ladle at them.

Roy paid no attention to the comments. He checked out the room, and Harley grabbed a petit four and stuffed it in his mouth. "Just in time, huh, Roy?" he said. "I thought you biddies was gonna eat 'em all."

"Shut up, Harley," Roy said, giving him a backhanded pop on his arm. "We been waitin' outside long enough, an' we got bidness to take care of. Where's the Wiggins woman?"

"Right here," Granny said, popping up in front of him. "What you want with me, dumbass?"

Roy curled his lip at her, then caught sight of me. "There she is! Git her, Harley, an' hold on to her this time."

Forgetting that Harley was as quick as a snake, I turned to run. He grabbed my arm and swung me back into the room.

Betty Sue screamed and Jennie looked scared. Wondering about Emmett and what they'd done to him, I said, "Wait a minute! Wait a minute! Stop it, you're hurting my arm! Wait, I don't know where Skip is, but he's not here. He left town and that's all I know."

"What's that racket?" Lurline asked, as she and Cindy came back from the bathroom. She was still carrying the punch pitcher as she walked right up to Harley and gazed at him with bleary eyes. "Don't I know you? I don't believe you were invited. Etta Mae, if these are friends of yours, tell 'em to take a hike." She twitched her black, frizzy head of hair practically in Harley's face, then turned, swaying, toward the table.

"Let's get outta here," Roy said, pushing open the kitchen door and motioning Harley, with me in tow, through it.

"I say," Mrs. Springer bellowed, as she sidled around the table, holding on to it for balance. "Unhand that woman. I have you know thish's a party!"

They ignored her, but as Harley dragged me toward the kitchen door, he reached over and goosed Lurline. She went straight up in the air, slinging punch up on the ceiling and across the room.

"Who-o-ah! Sonova*bitch*!" She came down, twisting and turning, and, in the same motion, cracked the silver pitcher against Harley's head. He sagged, loosening his grip on my arm, and Mrs. Springer conked him with the ladle. It bounced off his head and out of her hand, flipping up in the air. She reached out and snagged it before it hit the floor. Then looked around to see who else had noticed the lucky catch.

"You see that, Hazel Marie!" she yelled, as Hazel Marie tried to get between her and Harley.

Letting Harley look out for himself, Roy reached for me and pulled me through the kitchen door.

That's when Granny went into action. Snatching up one of the candelabras, with five candles still burning, she jabbed it in Roy's face, yelling, "Leave my grandbaby alone!" She flailed away at him, as he tried to ward her off with one hand and shove me through the door with the other. "Hold still," Granny yelled. "I'm gonna tan yore hide!"

"Let him have it!" Mrs. Springer screamed, as Hazel Marie tried to hold her back. "The idea, comin' to a party without a gift. That is just not done!"

Roy held on to me with one hand, while he warded off the candelabrum with his other arm, as Granny kept poking it at him.

"Get away, Granny!" I screamed. "Don't hurt her! Stop it, don't you hurt her!" I clawed at Roy's face as he tried to brush Granny aside. She whaled the daylights out of him with the candelabrum that was almost as big as she was, slinging hot wax and burning candles all over him and me and the first Mrs. Connard's mahogany breakfront and Chippendale chairs.

"Get her off me!" Roy yelled. "Harley! Get over here an' help me!" He was cringing behind one arm, fending off Granny and her silver-plated weapon, and trying to hold on to me. I kicked and clawed at him, and between Granny and me, we pushed him into the kitchen. Mrs. Springer came rushing in behind us, yelling her head off about teaching him some manners.

Emmett stood by the counter, holding on to it with a dazed look on his face. As the four of us stumbled and fell into the room, I heard Lurline and Jennie screaming at Harley and a choked-off yell from him. The bonging sound of solid silver as it whacked against his back rang throughout two rooms.

Betty Sue came running into the kitchen, a silver sandwich tray raised over her head. With her face all screwed up and a determined look in her eyes, she crashed that tray down on Roy's head. It just about rang his bell. He crumpled at the knees, pulling me down with him.

Betty Sue stood over him, breathing hard. "I always did want to do that," she said. "To *somebody*."

Mrs. Springer got in a good one, too, just to be on the safe side, daintily leaning over and whanging the ladle against Roy's head. Granny pushed her aside and poked Roy again with the candelabrum, jabbing the branches against his face. He turned me loose and scrooched up in a corner of the kitchen, covering his head with his arms.

I scrambled to my hands and knees, my clothes twisted every whichaway, and got a whack on the bottom, as Hazel Marie came barreling through the swinging door.

Hazel Marie stooped down to help me up. "Are you all right?"

"Pull that woman's skirt down," Mrs. Springer said. "I can see her drawers. Now, I want to know what's goin' on here."

Nothing good, that was for sure, but I didn't have time to answer her. I was worried about Granny, but she still had Roy cornered and cowering.

"Look smart, boy," Granny said, waving to Emmett, as she

wedged Roy's head against the wall with the spokes of the candelabrum, black smoke from the snuffed candles curling around them both. "Lend me a knife or something over here."

"Hey, hey!" Roy yelled, trying to get himself free. The branches of the candelabrum pinned him in the corner like a forked stick trapping a snake. "Get away from me, ole woman! I'm gonna hurt you!"

"Hurt me? Hurt *me*? I'll show you some hurtin', you little pissant! You come in here, tryin' to hurt my grandbaby, I'll skin you alive! Where's that knife? Give it here, boy!"

She snatched the knife Emmett handed to her. How she held on to both the knife and the candelabrum, I didn't know, nor what she was going to do with either one.

"Granny," I said, as I scrambled over to her, "let's get 'em out of here. They've had all they can take." I was more worried about her than them, although she was holding her own and Roy, at least, was getting the worst of it.

Harley didn't sound in too good a shape, either, if the commotion from the dining room was any indication.

"Hah!" Granny said, looking at the long electric knife that Emmett had grabbed from the counter. "Plug 'er in, boy, I'm gonna fix this lowlife so he won't never touch a woman again!"

"I'll do it!" Mrs. Springer yelled. "Gimme that thing and stand back!" She grabbed the cord and plugged it into a wall socket, looking more than happy to do it. The electric knife hummed in Granny's hand as the double blades began sawing against each other. "Go to it, honey!"

"Mrs. Springer! Granny! No, don't cut him!" I yelled. I could just see them both in a jail cell for the rest of their lives. "Just hold him there, Granny, I'm calling the sheriff. Don't let him move."

"He's not movin'," Mrs. Springer said, as she took a stand

beside Granny and placed a Red Cross–shod foot on an especially tender spot of Roy's anatomy. "We'll teach him how to act around ladies. Right, Granny?"

"Damn right," Granny said.

Keeping an eye on them so they wouldn't do the kind of damage that would get them in the newspaper and a courtroom, I dialed 9-1-1.

Chapter 44

Three cop cars showed up, two of which were the entire night force for Delmont. The other one came from Abbotsville. When help was needed at the Connard place, they all turned out. They came, one after the other, up the long drive into the parking area, throwing up gravel as they jerked to a stop. Leaving car doors open and blue lights flashing across the first Mrs. Connard's garden, they ran past Emmett, guns drawn, as he held the back door open for them.

"What's going on here? What's the trouble?" Clyde Maybry panted, his breathing loud and rasping. Wendell and the Abbotsville officer bounced in behind him.

"Come on in, boys!" Lurline swayed, trying to focus her eyes. Then they rolled back in her head, and she kind of melted down into a chair. She slowly lowered her head to the kitchen table, and that was it. Zonked out of her mind.

Clyde looked around, his mouth falling open as he took in Granny standing over Roy, electric knife at the ready. He cringed when he noticed Mrs. Springer's foot placement.

"Put that gun up, boy," Granny told Clyde, "and get them cuffs out. We're right before doing some major damage here."

"You tell 'em, honey," Mrs. Springer said.

Wendell holstered his gun and, stepping gingerly around Granny, quickly handcuffed Roy. "Oh, man," Roy said to him, "I'm glad to see you. Them crazy women was about to cut me."

Granny leaned over and got right in his face. "It's called *gelding* for your information."

Gladys and Jennie were still guarding Harley where he lay sprawled on the dining room floor. They bonged him with silver trays every time he twitched. He wasn't doing a lot of it, though, since they'd already pretty much dimmed his lights.

I give Clyde credit. Not much, but some, because it didn't take long for him to organize the arrests. And this time he got it right, leaving me alone except for a lot of frowning and shaking of his head in my direction.

I did some of that, too, as I looked around at the mess in the dining room. Cakes, with icing smushed into the Oriental rug, various silver plates and trays, and leaking cups and pitchers of punch cluttered the table and the floor. To say nothing of overturned chairs and blue-dyed carnations everywhere you looked.

Before they took Roy out, safely handcuffed, I got in his face. "Roy, listen to me and listen to me good. I don't know where Skip Taggert is, or when, or if, he's ever coming back. He ran out on me years ago, and he's done it again. So, if you have tracking him down in mind, if you ever get out of this mess, don't come looking to me. I can't help you."

Clyde hoisted Roy up on his tiptoes as he headed toward the door. "I don't think you got to worry about that, Etta Mae," he said. "These boys is three-time losers. They gonna be gone a long time.

"And speaking of that," he went on, giving me a hard look, "I'd appreciate it if you'd take a long trip, too, and stay gone for a real long time. Maybe you can't help it, Etta Mae, but trouble seems to pop up wherever you are. What're you doin' here, anyway, and what kinda blowout are you havin' in Mr. Connard's house? I'm gonna want some answers from you, soon as I get these assholes on the way."

Mrs. Springer jolted upright, clearly outraged at Clyde's language. Before she could correct him, though, Granny waved the knife in Clyde's face and said, "Watch yore mouth, boy. I'll plug this thing in again."

"Disarm her," Clyde told Wendell, with a jerk of his head toward Granny. Granny was about used up by that time, so when Wendell held out his hand, she surrendered the knife without a word. Even unplugged it for him.

Betty Sue put her arm around Granny, saying, "I'll get her home and put her to bed. You think I ought to take Lurline, too, Etta Mae?"

"If you will," I said, lifting Lurline's dazed face from the table. "She's pretty much wasted. She can get her car tomorrow."

"Me and Gladys'll help you, Betty Sue," Cindy said. "If you don't mind dropping us off. We came with Lurline."

"That leaves me, and I'll be going, too." Jennie put her arm around me. "It was a great party. I don't know when I've had so much fun, and put two criminals in jail, too. Look, honey, I hate to leave this mess for you to clean up. Want me to stay a while and help you?"

"I appreciate that, Jennie, but you go on home. Emmett'll help me, or we might just leave it till tomorrow."

"I don't think so," she said, looking back into the dining room. "He's already at it." And sure enough, Emmett was on his hands and knees, blotting up punch from the rug. "Besides, this is your wedding night, remember?"

Well, it had slipped my mind for a little while, what with all the noise and excitement. Now I began to worry about Mr. Howard, if he'd heard the commotion and was lying back there wondering if his house was still standing. The whole mess just came down on me like a ton of bricks. Here I'd wanted to show him and people like Julia Springer that there was more to me than bottle-blond hair and a perky personality, and all I'd done was confirm what they'd always thought. I could've cried.

Until I saw Mrs. Springer leaning against Hazel Marie with a satisfied smile on her face. "I guess we fixed their sweet patooties, didn't we? Oh, my," she said, reaching for the back of a chair, "I'm a little dizzy."

"Hold on to me," Hazel Marie said. "We need to get you home. Etta Mae, I'm just so sorry about Harley and Roy. They're my kinfolks, you know, third cousins or something, but I wish I didn't have to claim them."

"Oh, Hazel Marie," I said, "it's not your fault. I know about family, believe me, I do."

"Ha!" Mrs. Springer said, pulling out of her slump. "Ask *me* about family and I'll give you an earful! Where's Emmett? I want that recipe."

Hazel Marie patted her on the back, saying they'd get it tomorrow, and eased her toward the front door. "Etta Mae," she said, "we'll just get our purses and go. I need to get Miss Julia in bed, but I want you to know that I wish you every happiness in your marriage."

"Oh, yes, and lovely party, my dear," Mrs. Springer said, remembering her manners, as she brushed the hair off her face. Swaying in her tracks, she tried to focus on me. "Thank you so much for having us. You must come for tea sometime soon."

When they left, I walked out on the back stoop, watching as two cop cars followed them down the drive. Clyde's was the only sheriff's car left. He was half sitting in it, with the door open, talking on his handset.

Waiting for him, I crossed my arms across my chest and shivered. Not from the weather, even though there was a definite fall chill in the air, but from the thought of how I'd ruined Mr. Howard's house, and brought a criminal element into it, too. And I'd not been in it a full twenty-four hours yet.

"Etta Mae," Clyde said as he lumbered over to me, the gravel crunching under his boots, "Wendell tells me that you've gone and married Mr. Connard. That right?"

I nodded my head.

"So I guess you live here now?"

I nodded my head again.

He just shook his. "Well, I guess if you want to tear up your own husband's house, it's no skin off my nose. But you better watch yourself, Etta Mae, he can get rid of you as quick as he took you on. He's got lawyers up the you-know-what."

"Clyde . . ."

"Wait a minute." He held a hand up. "This is just between you and me, now. I know why you married him, and I don't guess I blame you. But he won't be able to satisfy you, Etta Mae, and, well, I'm always around if you need anything."

I jerked my head up like he'd slapped me. "Clyde Maybry, I'll have you know that I am Mrs. Howard Connard, Senior, now, and you can't talk to me that way anymore."

He smiled, showing tiny teeth that didn't belong in his fat face. "Don't matter what your name is, Etta Mae. I know who you are. Just remember I'll be around."

"Get out of here," I snarled. "Take your nasty self off my husband's property and don't come back."

He shrugged, still smiling. But he left, and I stood there, feeling the cool mountain air on my skin and wondering if the Connard name had any meaning at all. It hadn't to the Pucketts, and now Clyde had acted like it was nothing to him, either. So if it didn't put me above trash like that, what was I doing with it?

I went back into the house and began helping Emmett clean

and pick up the mess we'd made. I opened my mouth to apologize for bringing the Pucketts into this fine home, and for my friends getting sloshed, and for the party turning into a free-for-all, and for the way things had turned out in general.

Before I could start, though, he said, "Miss Etta, I'm real sorry 'bout all this. They come in on me 'fore I knew it, an' knocked me windin'. Couldn't get my breath 'fore they was in here, jumpin' on you and yo' lady friends." He stood there, shaking his head. "I shoulda been on my toes better'n that."

"Oh, Emmett, you couldn't help it. Nobody could've stopped them. I'm the one who should be apologizing to you. It was me they were after—well, not me exactly. But that big ole boy I've been trying to hide in the floorboard of my car for two days. They were really after him, but they've been following me and watching Lurline's house all this time. I'm thinking they must've followed her over here, hoping she'd lead them to Skip. But he's long gone, and I hope he stays gone.

"Anyway, they're put away, and for good, I hope. I just hope my friends will be better behaved after this, and not tear up the house like they did tonight." I could feel tears of shame welling up in my eyes.

"Good thing they was here, Miss Etta," Emmett said, a soft smile beginning on his face. "Boy howdy, they sho' tore into them two, didn't they? If it just me and you here by ourselves, no telling what might happen when them two crazy men come bustin' in. That Miss Granny, she something else, an' that Miss Julia Springer, she a lady an' a half."

I brushed at my eyes and laughed with relief. "She is that. Emmett, I better go check on Mr. Howard. No telling how upset he is."

"I looked in on him while you was outside. He still sleepin'. Look like he didn't hear a thing, so he all right. Now, Miss Etta,

I got this rug clean, an' I'm gonna wrap up these few cakes left over, an' leave the rest of it till morning. I don't us'lly do that, you know, but this a special night. So I'm jus' gonna do that, an' go on to my 'partment. I'll lock the door on my way out."

He was telling me it was time for me to go to my new husband, and he was right.

As he went into the kitchen and began wrapping the leftovers in Saran Wrap, I went into the drawing room and picked up my gifts. After stacking the boxes in a pile, I turned off the lamps and gathered my silk, satin, and chiffon gowns, babydoll pajamas, bikinis, thongs, and so forth to take to the bedroom, wondering if Mr. Howard was in any shape to appreciate any of them that night.

Hearing the back door close and lock as Emmett left for his apartment over the garage, I opened the door to Mr. Howard's room. The bedside lamp was on, and Mr. Howard was sitting straight up in bed. He'd pulled himself up by the handrails. His pajama top was off, his scrawny, white-haired chest in full view.

There was a big half smile on his face, and his eyes were as bright and sparkling as I'd ever seen them.

"I've been waiting for you," I think he said, along with a few other things that nobody else would've understood.

And, yes, in case anyone is interested, he was in shape to appreciate not only my new lingerie, but a few other things as well.

Chapter 45

The room was so quiet that I could barely hear the squeak of rubber soles on the polished floor out in the hall and the whispered voices of nurses and doctors as they passed. Mr. Sitton had insisted that he talk to me in a private place, so they'd led me out of the waiting room to this small, dim office.

They were all gone now—Mr. Sitton, the doctor, the ambulance men, and the nurses—at least for a while, and I was left alone to gather my wits and decide what to do next.

"He didn't have time," Mr. Sitton had told me. "I am confident that that was what he wanted to see me about today. I know that he wanted you taken care of—he'd intimated as much on a previous occasion. As much as I'd like to reassure you on the matter, I am afraid I can't. The way things stand now, with everything in trust, my hands are tied."

"Emmett?" I asked, my hands knotting in my lap. "What about Emmett?"

Mr. Sitton studied me for a minute, then he said, "Emmett is taken care of. He'd been with Howard a long time, but you . . ." He sighed with what I thought might have been compassion or maybe just plain pity.

I'd shaken my head, still too stunned to take in all he was saying. "It doesn't matter."

"It does matter," he said. "And I intend to speak to Junior about it. He may feel an obligation, a moral duty so to speak, to see that something comes to you, even a small amount. Howard would've wanted you to have something."

I'd looked up at him, tears blurring my eyes, and said, "There's not a hope in hell of that. Especially if Valerie has any say in it. No, Mr. Sitton, I appreciate your concern, but I'll just go back to my trailer and ask for my old job back. Don't worry about me. I've been making it on my own long before this."

He'd left not long after that, saying that he'd do the best he could for me if I wanted to pursue the matter. On his way out, he'd told me that Junior and Valerie were on the their way to see to the funeral. "Howard spelled it all out in his will," he'd said. "Everything's being taken care of."

Without me, I thought as the door closed behind him. I sat in the large chair in the quiet office, looking at my hands, and wondering how long the hospital would let me stay there. I hated the thought of leaving, the thought of facing people who'd be laughing and whispering and watching me to see what kind of woman could get a man so hot and bothered that he'd stroke out on his wedding night.

I knew what they'd be saying and the jokes they'd make and the smirks they'd send my way.

Well, I thought, taking a deep breath, I'd come through worse, I guessed. At least I wasn't covered with a sheet and on my way to a funeral home.

Poor old Mr. Howard, I thought, and wiped away a tear. I'd really thought I could give him a few happy years. They would've been happy for me, too. I wouldn't have minded them at all. But now all our plans were dead and gone along with him. But then, as I thought about it, a smile twitched at the corner of my mouth, and I began to feel better.

I couldn't help it, because it suddenly came to me that I *had* made him happy. Not for years, that's true, but he'd already had a long, successful, and powerful life—a longer and better one than most people, in fact. And it'd ended with a bang.

Maybe, just maybe, if Junior had taken him to Raleigh and stuffed him away in a rest home or retirement home or nursing home or whatever, Mr. Howard would've lived another year or two. And been so miserable he'd've hated every day of it.

But this way, he'd ended his life the same way he'd lived it—in his own home, getting exactly what he wanted, when he wanted it. And what he'd wanted was me. He'd died with a smile on his face.

Even the ambulance men had mentioned it. How it looked as if he'd died happy. That's one thing I could be proud of.

I leaned my head back on the chair, with a smile on my face, too. Mr. Howard had surprised me when I'd gone into his room not four hours before and seen him sitting there with his clothes half off, wide awake and ready for love. I hadn't expected it, especially since he'd slept all through the afternoon and through the commotion of the party and the Pucketts crashing the party and the arrival of the deputies.

I'd intended to spend my wedding night dozing in a chair by his bed, and being there when he woke this morning. The intimacies of marriage could come in their own sweet time, whenever he felt up to them and as far as he was able to take them. It hadn't mattered to me, one way or the other.

But there he'd been, ready, set, and aimed for what he'd been grabbing at for months and months. So, figuring that looking might be all he could manage, I'd undressed and put on Lurline's pink chiffon babydoll pajamas with the G-string underneath. His eyes had nearly popped out of his head, and he'd practically climbed over the bedrail, half paralyzed or not.

I laughed to myself, remembering how he'd begged me to quit prancing around and come over to him. I'd lowered the bedrail on one side and climbed in. I swear, the man had strength neither he nor I had been expecting. He'd grabbed me and started kissing and rubbing his good hand all over me. Then, before I knew it, he'd rolled me over and I'd fallen out of the damn bed. We laughed, Lord, how we laughed, and I'd crawled back in, pulling the bedrail up behind me.

"Come on, you old sweet thing," I'd said, "do your worst. You can't kick me out of bed now."

So, here I was, the bereaved widow sitting in a hospital waiting room after hardly any time at all of being a wife. Well, I'd been a wife plenty of times, but I mean being the second Mrs. Howard Connard, Senior.

I stood up, put on my shoes, and gathered my tote bag. I needed to get back to Mr. Howard's house and get my things moved before Junior and Valerie showed up. The sooner I could clear out of there, the better. I didn't want to have to face them, with them wondering just what I'd done to their old daddy to transfer him from a bed to a casket.

I would move back into my trailer, thank God for a place of my own. And thank Bernie, too, for that matter. Then I'd go to the funeral. There was no way to get out of that. Maybe I'd take Granny and Lurline with me. For support, you know. I didn't have anything to wear to a funeral, especially since everybody would be watching me. Maybe I could go to Walmart's late tonight and find a black outfit. I didn't know if Kathie Lee made anything like that, she was so perky. Navy blue would do, I guessed. Anyway, going to his funeral would be the last thing I could do for Mr. Howard. I'd stand by his casket like the first Mrs. Connard would've done and like I knew he'd want me to. I'd drop a rose on his casket after the graveside service was over, and I'd accept the condolences of anybody who'd be nice enough to offer me some.

Should I order flowers for the service? Was the widow supposed to? I didn't know and didn't much care if I did what was right or not. I'd stop by Sadie's and get a rose, and let it stand for a good old man who'd thought I was the best thing that had ever happened to him.

Then I'd go home and be Etta Mae Wiggins again, just as I'd been after my other marital disappointments. The thought of Skip and his expensive promise flashed through my mind. I could've sure used a million dollars right about then, but I'd be a fool to pin my hopes on that and risk another kind of disappointment.

Time enough for rejoicing, if Skip really did come through. But for now, I just wanted to go home and crawl into a corner where nobody could find me.

I peeked out the door and, seeing the hall empty, slipped out and headed for the stairs. I didn't want to see anybody, or have anybody see me.

As I pushed open the heavy fire door at the bottom of the stairs and walked out into the parking lot, I had to squinch up my eyes from the early morning sun. I'd been sitting in that dark, quiet room for so long that I'd forgotten that the sun was up and a new day had already taken off.

Walking fast with my head down, hoping nobody would recognize and stop me, I hurried to my car. I could hardly remember parking it as I'd followed the ambulance a few hours earlier.

I didn't see him until I got to the car. He was leaning against the hood, his arms crossed, a serious look on his face. Waiting for me.

"Bobby Lee," I said, and, not being able to help it, my voice broke on the words and tears spurted out of my eyes.

"Come here, darlin'." His arms went around me, and I found the place that I'd always fitted into, up close to him.

I cried. I let it all out—crying about wanting so much and getting so little, about the clerk in the Register of Deeds office, and Mr. Sitton's secretary, about Clyde and the Pucketts and sweet, dumb Skip and about being scared and not having the rent money, and about Valerie's hateful mouth, and about Mr. Howard dying before we'd had a happy family life, and I cried because Bobby Lee had his arms around me and was whispering that I wasn't going to get away from him this time.

"What am I gonna do with you?" he said, his mouth against my hair.

"I don't know," I wailed, clinging to him like he was my last hope.

"I've been tryin' my best to hold on to you," he said, one hand holding me close and the other smoothing my hair. "This time I'm not letting you out of my sight. You up for one more husband, sweetheart?"

I stopped bawling for a minute, the meaning of his words blotting out all that'd happened in the last few days. The thought of Bobby Lee as my one true and very last husband made my heart melt inside me.

"What about your windshield?" I asked, burying my face against his uniform again, soaking it good. "And Darla Davis?"

"Oh, hell," he said, and I knew he was smiling. "You're worth a dozen damn windshields. And who's Darla Davis? You're the one I've been tryin' to catch."

"You really want to get married?" I couldn't believe how much lighter my heart was beginning to feel, even though I was still crying buckets all over him.

"I always did," he said, holding me even closer, if that was possible. "You just kept beating me to it. Every time I thought I had you, you'd turn up with another husband."

I started laughing, my shoulders shaking against him. I could feel him laughing with me, and hear the strong beat of his heart in his chest. I pressed my head against it, wanting to stay by that safety for the rest of my life.

Etta Mae Wiggins Taggert Whitlow Connard was about to be a thing of the past. Etta Mae Moser was a name I could live with.

"Bobby Lee?"

"What, sweetheart?"

"Can we go to Disney World on our honeymoon?"

"Anywhere you want," he said, his familiar hands moving over my back.

"And the Magic Kingdom, too?"

"Oh, yeah," he whispered against my hair, "and, darlin', when we get there I'm gonna take you up one side of Space Mountain and down the other. And then I'm gonna start all over again. How does that sound?"

Like the sweetest thing in the world.